To
Don and Mary MacKinnon
for
enriching my life

Thanks
to
Glenn Keator, Ph.D.
Director of Education
Strybing Arboretum Society
San Francisco, California
and the
Helen Crocker Russel Horticultural Library

Reinforced binding of hardcover edition suitable for library use.

Copyright © 1984 by Ruth Heller.
All rights reserved. Published by Grosset & Dunlap, Inc.,
a member of The Putnam & Grosset Book Group, New York.
Published simultaneously in Canada. Sandcastle Books and the Sandcastle logo
are trademarks belonging to The Putnam & Grosset Book Group.
First Sandcastle Books edition, 1992. Printed in Singapore.
Library of Congress Catalog Card Number: 84-80502
ISBN (hardcover) 0-448-18964-X E F G H I J
ISBN (Sandcastle) 0-448-41092-3 A B C D E F G H I J

PLANTS THAT NEVER EVER BLOOM

Written and Illustrated by
RUTH HELLER

GROSSET & DUNLAP, NEW YORK

A MUSHROOM
doesn't ever
bloom.

It grows
on trees
and leaves
and things...

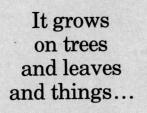

or
in the grass
in
fairy
rings.

Some grow to be...

as tall as all
of these you see,

and some
look
rather
strange
to me.

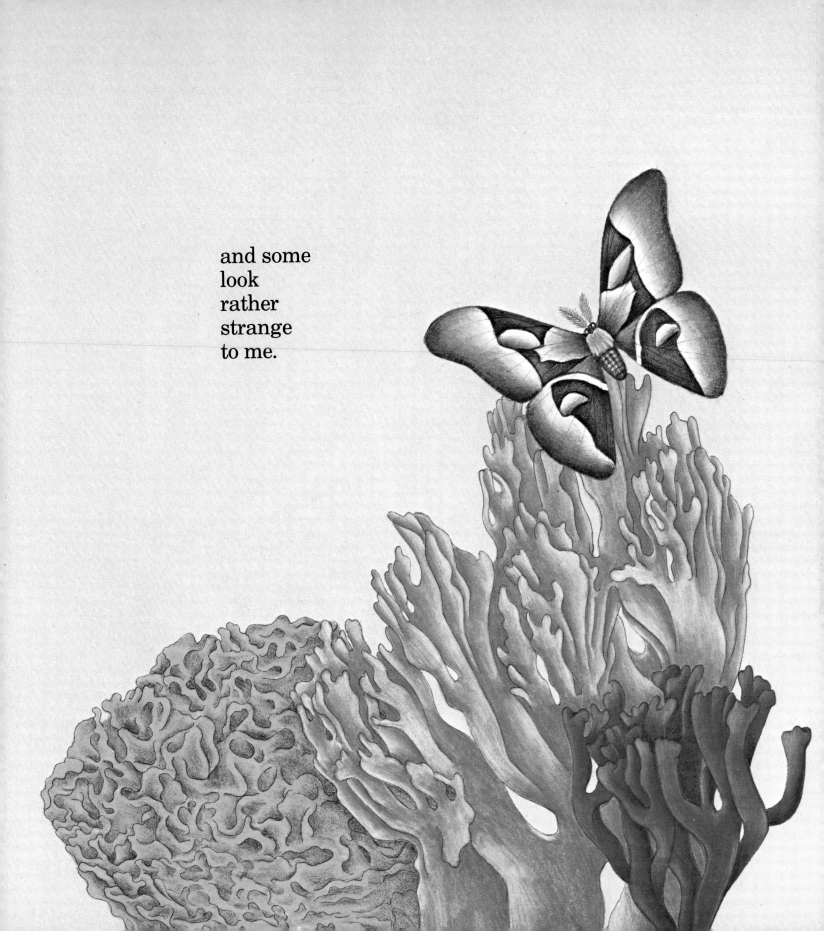

These glow at night.
We don't know why.

MUSHROOMS
all
are
called
FUNGI.

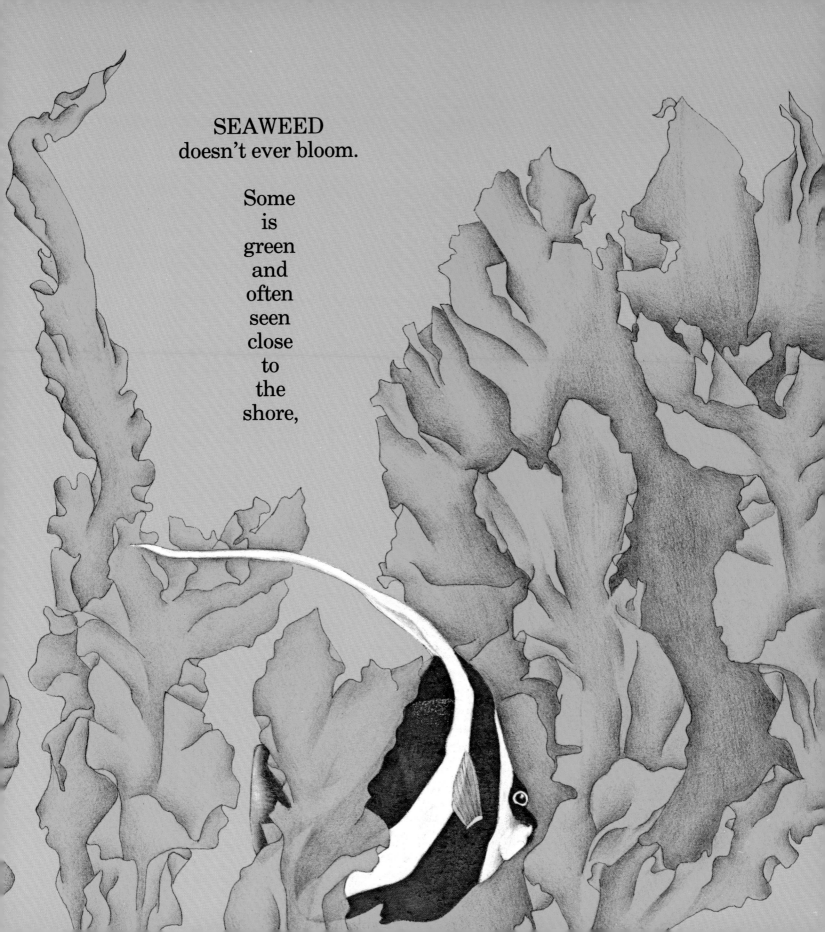

SEAWEED
doesn't ever bloom.

Some
is
green
and
often
seen
close
to
the
shore,

but
there
is
more…

deeper down
where it is
several shades of brown.

In
the
Pacific
and
Atlantic

SEAWEED
grows
to
be
gigantic.

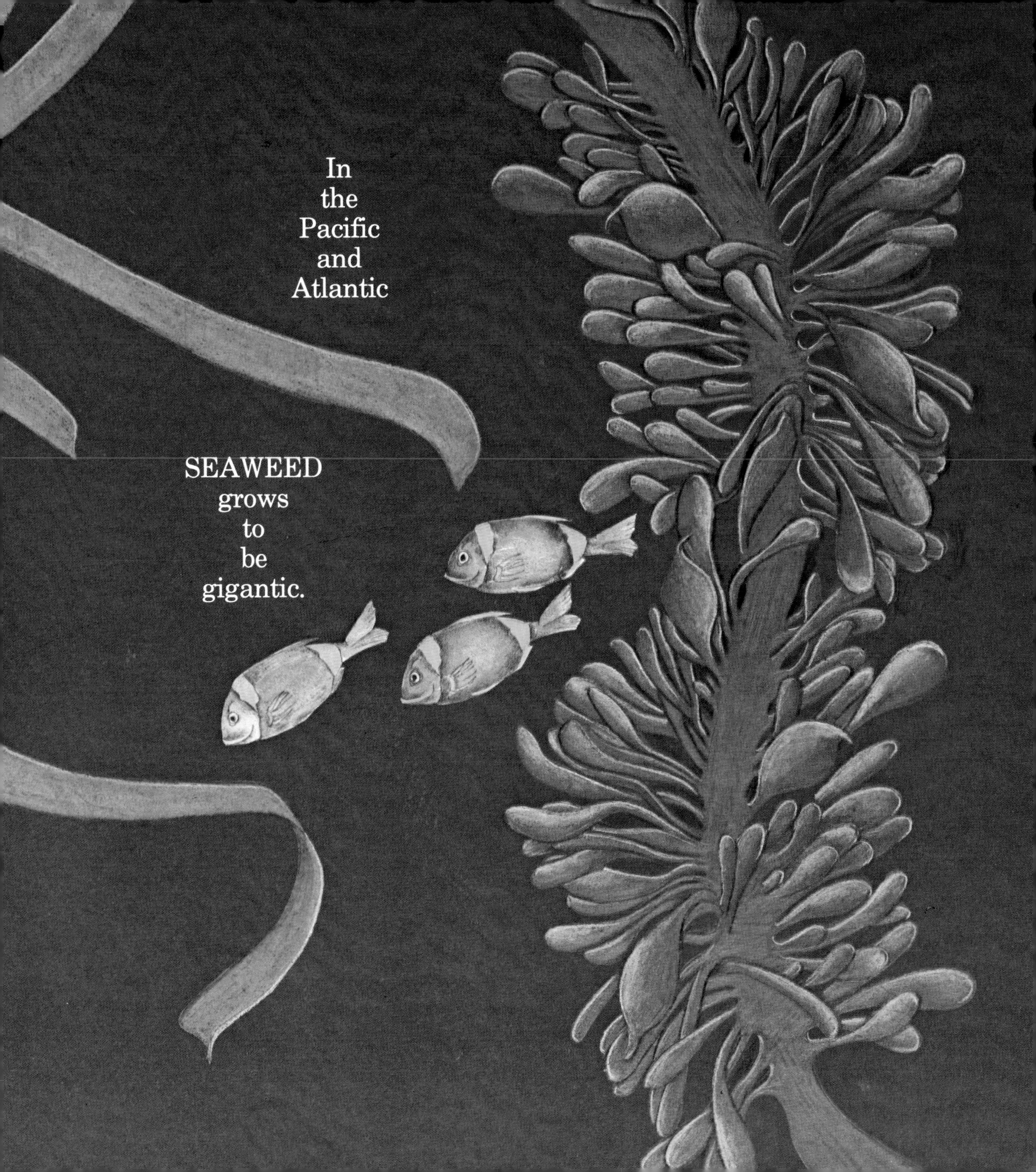

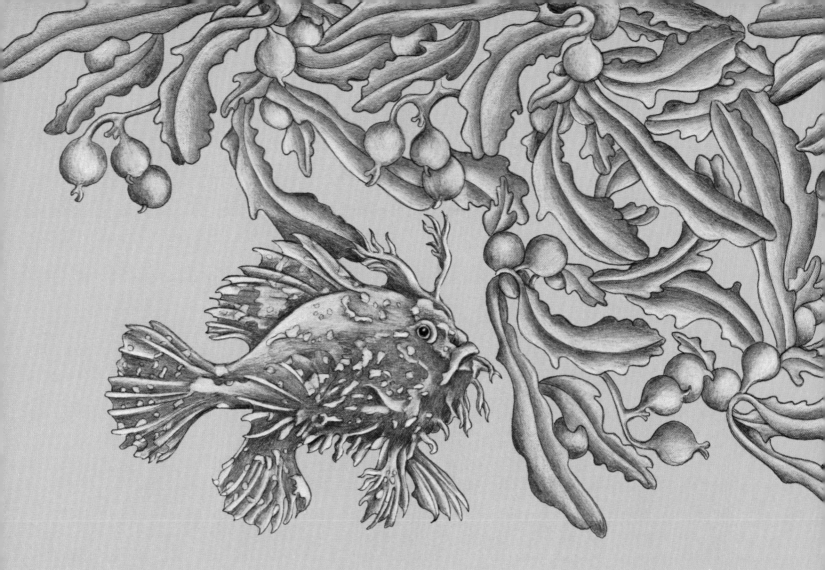

This mass has broken free
and floats in the
Sargasso Sea
where grumpy-looking fish reside…

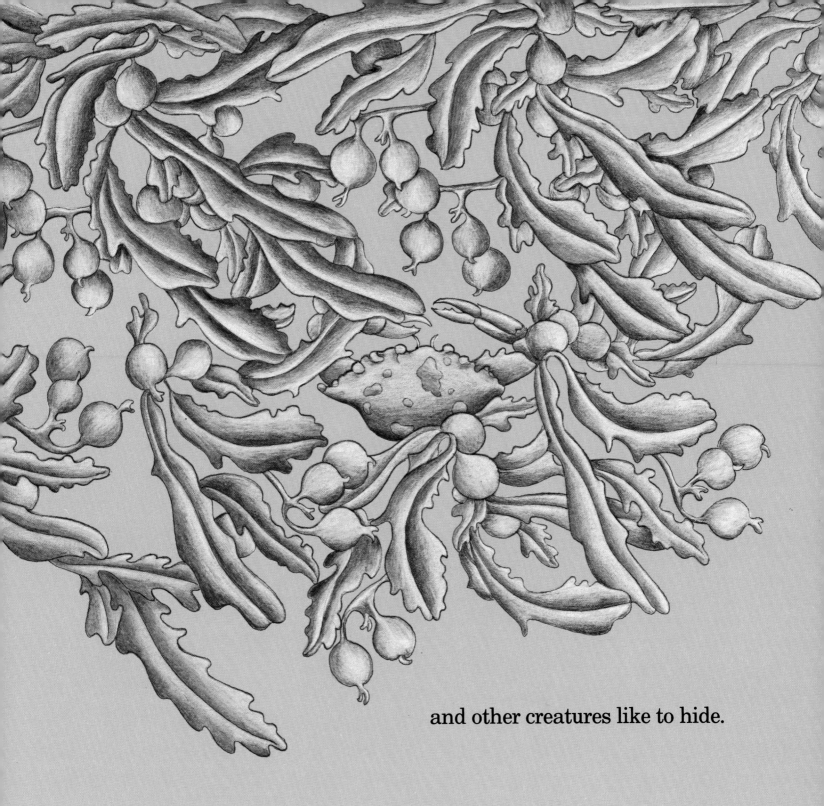

and other creatures like to hide.

Deepest on the
ocean bed
is
SEAWEED
that is
pink
and
red.

Whichever
color it may be
SEAWEED
all is called
ALGAE.

LICHEN never ever blooms.
It lives on logs
and trees
and rocks,

and
sometimes
grows
on
little
stalks.

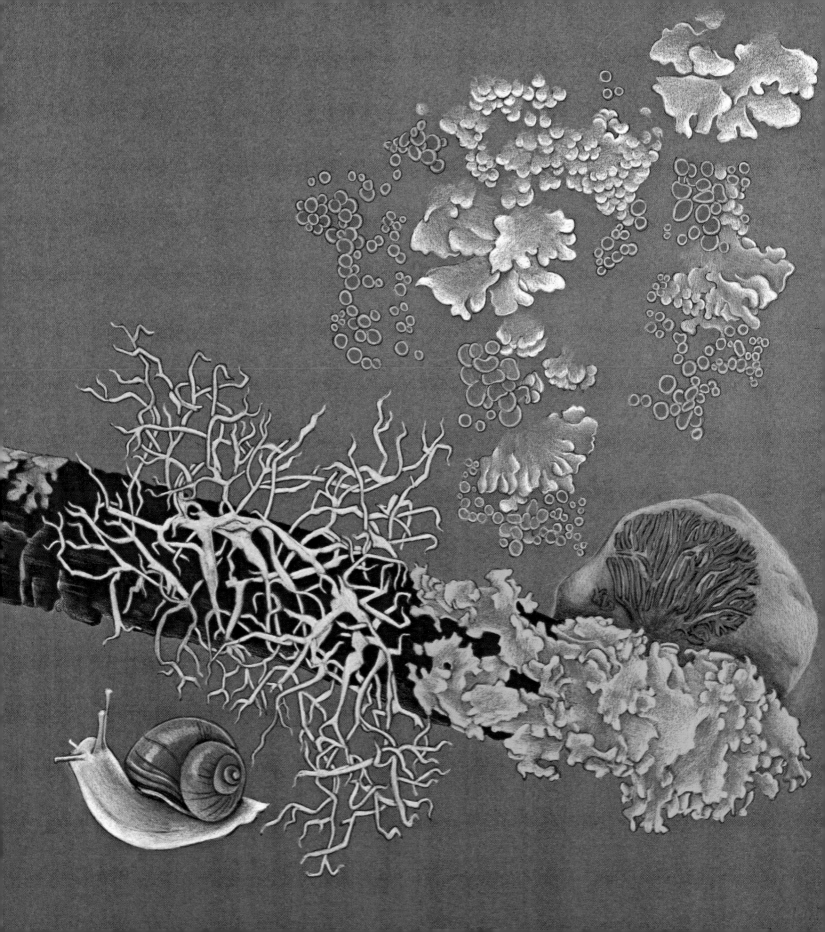

Lush
MOSS

that
clings
to trees...

and LIVERWORTS like these

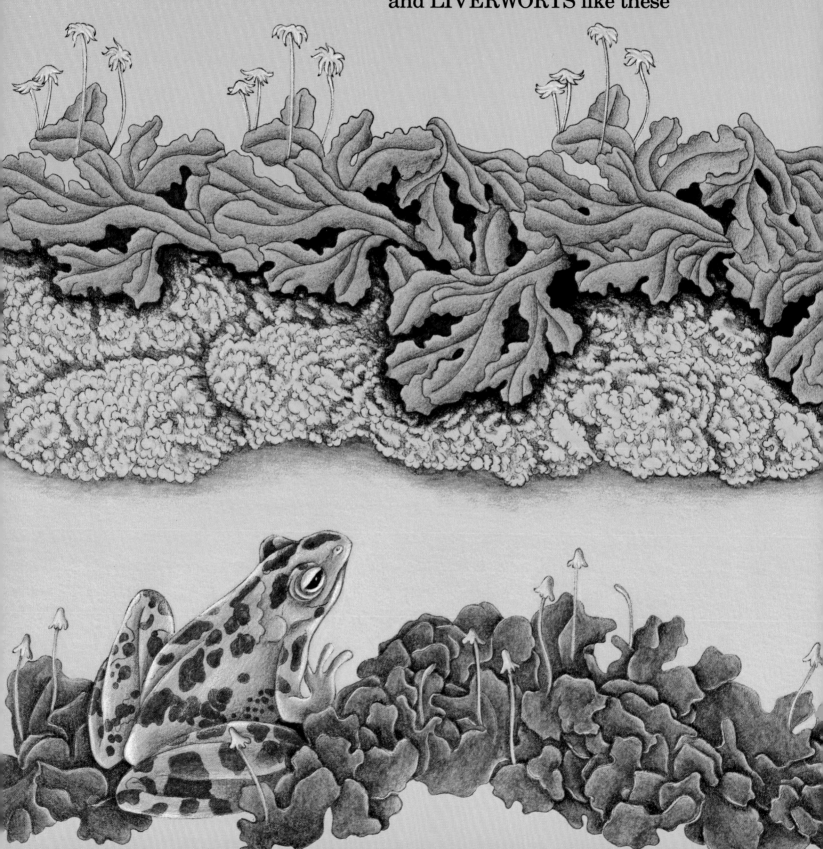

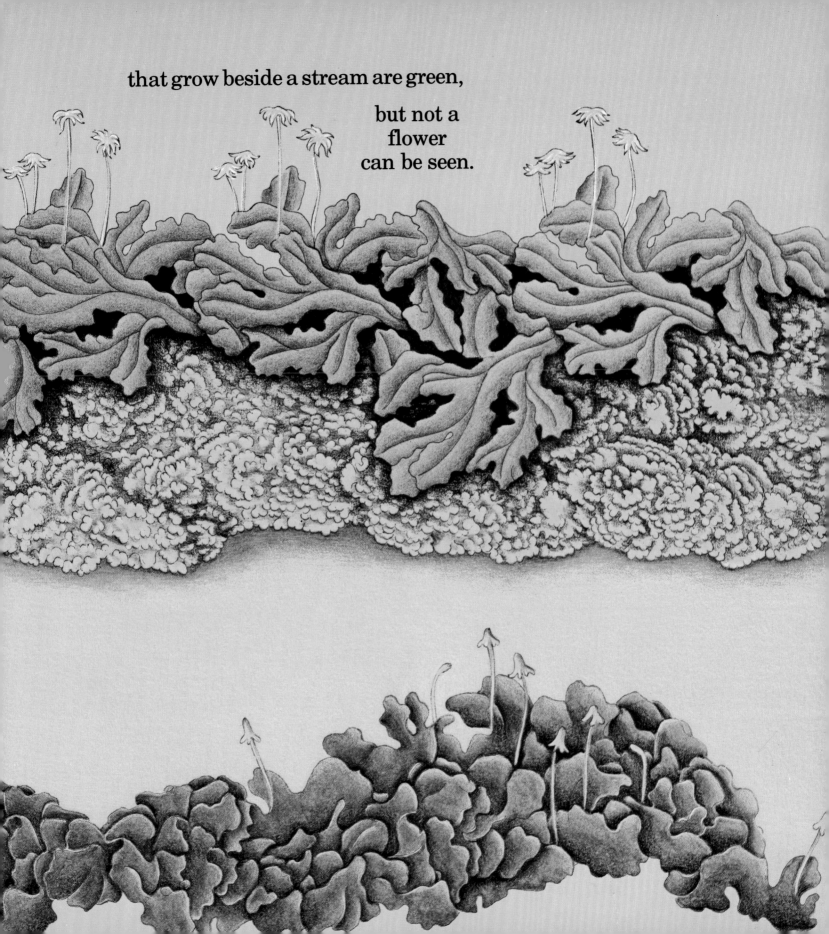

that grow beside a stream are green,

but not a
flower
can be seen.

FERNS…

from
fiddleheads
unfurl.

Their
cousins
are
the
HORSETAILS

and
this
creeping
evergreen,

and not on any one of these
are flowers ever seen.

Two hundred million years ago
FERNS
were rather small.

Their cousins,
on the other hand,
grew
very,
very
tall.

None of these
have flowers,
and so
they have
no seeds.

They have no seeds,
as I have said,
they grow from
tiny SPORES instead.

But here are some exceptions. There always are a few.

Like
all
the
rest

they
never
bloom

but
from
a
seed
they
grew.

One
is
called
the
GINKGO,

another
is
the
YEW....

And
every
plant
that
bears
a
CONE

is
an
exception
too.

In
proper
scientific
terms
all
of
these
are
GYM·NO·SPERMS·

CARVINGS, CASTS & REPLICAS

DISTRIBUTED BY UNIVERSITY PRESS OF NEW ENGLAND

HANOVER AND LONDON

CARVINGS, CASTS & REPLICAS

Nineteenth-Century Sculpture from Europe & America

in New England Collections

❦

by John M. Hunisak

with an essay by Ruth Butler

MCMXCIV

MIDDLEBURY COLLEGE MUSEUM OF ART

MIDDLEBURY · VERMONT

An exhibition organized by the Middlebury College Museum of Art

Middlebury College Museum of Art, Middlebury, Vermont
September 20 – December 18, 1994

Museum of Art, Rhode Island School of Design, Providence, Rhode Island
February 10 – April 23, 1995

LIBRARY OF CONGRESS CATALOGING–IN–PUBLICATION DATA
Hunisak, John M., 1944–
Carvings, casts & replicas : nineteenth-century sculpture from Europe and America
in New England collections / by John M. Hunisak with an essay by Ruth Butler.
p.   cm.
"Published on the occasion of an exhibition, September 20 – December 18, 1994."
Includes bibliographical references and index.
ISBN 0-9625262-7-4 : $39.95
1. Sculpture, European–Exhibitions. 2. Sculpture, Modern–19th century–Europe–Exhibitions.
3. Sculpture–Collectors and collecting–New England–Exhibitions.
I. Butler, Ruth, 1931–   II. Title.   III. Title: Carvings, casts and replicas.
NB457.H86   1994
735´.22´0747435–dc20   94–11142
CIP

FRONT COVER: *The Ghost in Hamlet* by Thomas Gould (cat. no. 58)

FRONTISPIECE: *Ceres* by Augustus Saint-Gaudens (cat. no. 10)

CONTENTS

Maternal Joy by Jules Dalou (cat. no. 29)

FOREWORD & ACKNOWLEDGMENTS

*T*HE PRESENTATION of this exhibition and its accompanying catalogue are the fruits of a process that began, as many exhibitions do, as the subject of a casual conversation. Several years ago, John Hunisak, Professor of Art at Middlebury College, and I were discussing our recent acquisition of *Inkstand with Horse Pulling a Stone-Laden Cart*, the first work carved by the enigmatic American sculptor William Rimmer. Professor Hunisak remarked that one reason why such engaging and important works could still be purchased for relatively modest sums was that nineteenth-century sculpture continued to be far less appreciated than the painting of the same time. He noted that this was true even in New England, despite the collective wealth of our museums, which hold works of international importance that have been acquired over the past two centuries. When asked if he would like to explore the possibility of assembling an exhibition that would highlight these riches and also investigate the nature of nineteenth-century sculpture, he enthusiastically agreed. His introductory essay, which surveys the subject, contains one of the clearest expositions of nineteenth-century casting and reproductive techniques to be found in print. We were both delighted when Professor Ruth Butler, professor emerita of the Art Department of the University of Massachusetts, Boston, accepted the invitation to contribute an essay that expands the scope of our study with a fine discussion of the social history of collection building in New England.

This, the first exhibition that juxtaposes nineteenth-century European and American sculpture from the wealth of New England collections, marks the culmination of several years' work by the authors as well as the museum staff. Professor Hunisak traveled extensively about New England to examine the sculpture holdings of numerous institutions and private collections and to propose the works for the exhibition. We have been particularly gratified by the positive response that greeted our loan requests. This exhibit is truly an indication of the wealth of sculpture to be found in the region. It is the occasion for some little-known works to shine and for others to be conserved. We are particularly grateful to the Boston Public Library for allowing us to include two important works by Horatio Greenough – *Bust of Christ* and *Bust of Lucifer* – in exchange for their repair and cleaning. Similar cooperative conservation efforts were arranged for works from the Robert Hull Fleming Museum of the University of Vermont, the Yale University Art Gallery, and the Saint-Gaudens National Historic Site. Assisting in this effort have been the Center for Conservation and Technical Studies of Harvard University, the Williamstown Regional Art Conservation Laboratory, and the Art Conservation Technical Services in Baltimore.

It is entirely fitting that, after opening at Middlebury, the exhibition will travel to the Museum of Art of the Rhode Island School of Design, the home of many of the most important works of nineteenth-century sculpture in New England. Thomas W. Leavitt, former Director, and Daniel Rosenfeld, Chief Curator, have been early and enthusiastic supporters of the project.

Cooperative exhibitions are visible signs of the goodwill that exists among the staffs of New England's neighboring institutions. This exhibition is no exception, and for their assistance I would like to thank Martha Sandweiss, Director, Ross Fox, Curator of European Art, Linda Delone Best, Registrar, Mead Art Museum at Amherst College; Laura C. Luckey, former Director, Ruth Levin, Registrar, Bennington Museum; Rodney Armstrong, Director and Librarian, Michael Wentworth, Curator of American Art, Boston Athenaeum; Alan Shestack, former Director, Anne L. Poulet and Jeffrey Munger, Curators of European Decorative Arts, Linda L. Foss, Curator of American Decorative Arts, JoEllen Secondo, Curatorial Assistant, Kim Pashko, Registrar, Museum of Fine Arts, Boston; Katherine Dibble, Supervisor of Research, Boston Public Library; David Brooke, Director, Martha Asher, Registrar, Sterling and Francine Clark Art Institute; James Cuno, Elizabeth and John Moors Cabot Director, Ada Bortoluzzi, Coordinator of Loans, Fogg Art Museum, Harvard University; Jessica Nicoll, Curator of American Art, Michelle Butterfield, Registrar, Portland Museum of Art; Thomas W. Leavitt, former Director, Doreen Bolger, Director, and Daniel Rosenfeld, Chief Curator, Louann Drake, Registrar, Museum of Art, Rhode Island School of Design; John Dryfhout, Chief Curator, Judith Nyhus, Registrar, Saint-Gaudens National Historic Site; Brian Alexander, Managing Director, Pauline H. Mitchell, Registrar, Shelburne Museum; Suzannah Fabing, Director, Michael Goodison, Program Coordinator and Archivist, Louise A. Laplante, Registrar, Smith College Museum of Art; Salee Lawrence, Consulting Curator, St. Johnsbury Athenaeum; Ann Porter, Director, Janie Cohen, Curator, Christina Kelly, Registrar, Robert Hull Fleming Museum, University of Vermont; Patrick McCaughey, Director, Linda H. Roth, Associate Curator of European Decorative Arts, Martha Small, Registrar, Wadsworth Atheneum; Judith Hoos Fox, Curator, Lisa McDermott, Registrar, Davis Museum and Cultural Center, Wellesley College; Linda Shearer, Director, Diane Hart, Registrar, Williams College Museum of Art; Susan Strickler, Director of Curatorial Affairs, Joan-Elisabeth Reid, Registrar, Worcester Art Museum; Paul Stuehrenberg, Librarian, Yale Divinity School Library; and Mary Gardner Neill, former Director, John McDonald, Acting Director, Susan Frankenbach, Registrar, Yale University Art Gallery.

For their generosity, we would also like to thank Fred and Meg Licht and other anonymous private lenders to the exhibition.

The preparation and production of the catalogue involved many individuals near and far. Matthew Slaughter (Middlebury '93) worked as a research assistant during the early stages of the catalogue's conception, assembling bibliography and factual materials. June E. Hargrove, Professor of Art History, University of Maryland, and Frederick Ilchman, Columbia University, both read portions of the manuscript and made helpful suggestions. Fronia W. Simpson has provided superb editing of the text. Christopher Kuntze has developed the striking catalogue design, which has been admirably executed by The Stinehour Press.

Ultimately the success of an exhibition such as this rests on the abilities of the host institution's staff. The Middlebury College Museum of Art is particularly blessed in the professional skill and dedication of its entire staff: Jenny Wilker, Acting Assistant Director, Monica McCabe, Exhibitions and Collections Coordinator, and JoAnn Keeler, Museum Secretary, have worked together to organize the voluminous details of the exhibition and catalogue and to keep them moving forward in a timely manner. Darsie White and Jennifer Nelson provided them able assistance. Ken Pohlman, our Exhibitions Designer and Preparator, deserves special recognition for developing an installation that enhances the viewer's experience without dominating it. Above all, I wish to thank Emmie Donadio, Acting Director of the Museum for the 1993–94 academic year while I was on sabbatical. Without her superb ability to coordinate and supervise all the aspects of this complex exhibition, it would have been impossible for the institution to complete such a project.

Special thanks are also given to the Seybolt family for their ongoing generous support of the Middlebury College Museum of Art and particularly of its nineteenth-century sculpture collection.

It is a great pleasure to see this exhibition reach completion, as it exemplifies the mission of the Museum to enhance the academic program of Middlebury College and to provide the community and the region with a meaningful backward glance at its own history.

Richard H. Saunders
DIRECTOR

Bust of Madame Juliette Récamier by Joseph Chinard (cat. no. 39)

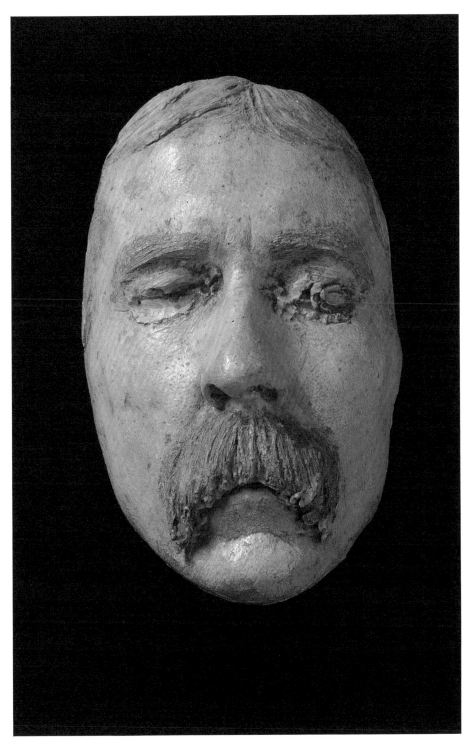

Life Mask of Talcott Williams by Thomas Eakins (cat. no. 42)

Head of Christ by John-Baptiste Clésinger (cat. no. 53)

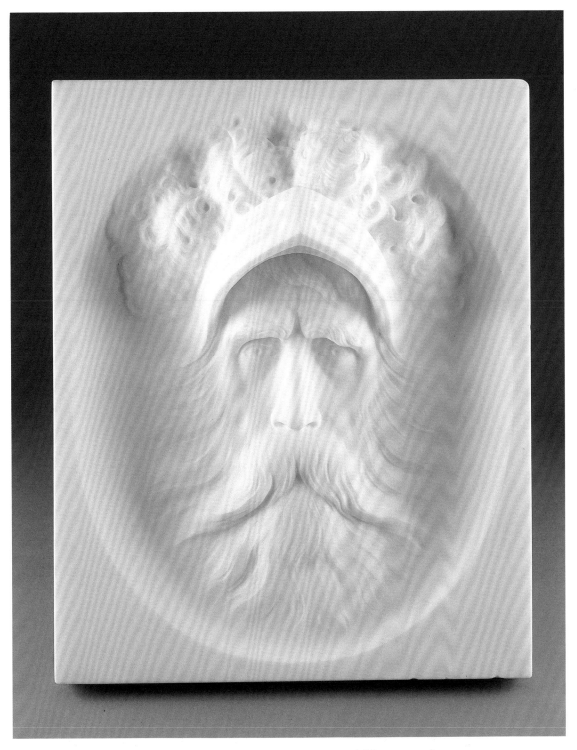

The Ghost in Hamlet by Thomas Gould (cat. no. 59)

Ideal Bust Representing Lucifer by Horatio Greenough (cat. no. 61)

Ceres by Auguste Rodin (cat. no. 64)

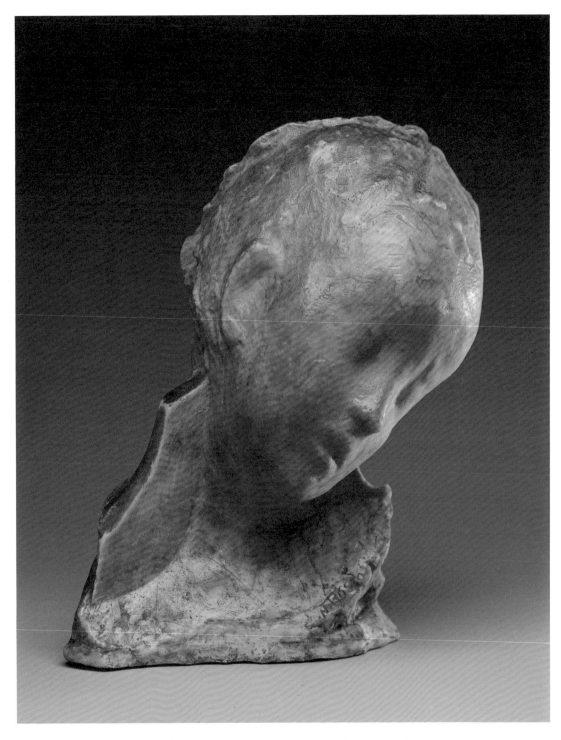

Sick Little Boy by Medardo Rosso (cat. no. 66)

NEW ENGLAND'S ACQUISITION OF NINETEENTH-CENTURY SCULPTURE: A TALE NOT TOLD BEFORE*

Ruth Butler

On July 11, 1809 Mr. John Stickney read his "article on Grecian pictures and statues" at the usual dinner shared by friends who had founded the Boston Athenaeum. It was accepted for the minutes. Mr. Buckminster objected, however: "too much nakedness." [1]

FREQUENTLY, a new group of students looks over an Art 100 syllabus, and some-one says: "I didn't know we would be studying sculpture." I think: "How odd, would a European student say that?" Perhaps we Americans have been so de-manding of sculpture to be useful, relying on sculptors to supply our portraits of great men, our gravestones, and our monuments, placing so much less emphasis on its role as art, that we somehow relegate sculptors to a less "artistic" stature than painters. By in-stalling American sculpture beside contemporaneous works from Europe, the Middle-bury exhibition of nineteenth-century sculpture focuses on this attitude as no previous show has done. That all the works – both European and American – come from New England collections gives us the opportunity to focus on one region – and surely the most cohesive and best documented one – of America, and how it accepted the value of sculpture as an art form.

There are only four institutions in New England with collections of more than a hun-dred works of nineteenth-century sculpture: the Museum of Fine Arts, Boston; the Boston Athenaeum; the combined collections of the Yale University Art Gallery and Yale University; and those of the Fogg Art Museum and Harvard University. The figures are even less impressive than they might appear, their sum being swollen by large numbers of portrait heads of individuals closely connected to these institutions; in their contexts they function more as useful objects than as works of art. Even artists thought this way. When a Philadelphian wanted to return a landscape to the painter Thomas Cole, Cole

*As the reader will soon discover, this is an against-great-odds tale. A word about methodology and the as-sertions I make about some object's being the first this or that in such-and-such collection. I arrived at my conclusions after going through all the object cards for nineteenth-century sculpture in the registrars' offices in the museums discussed in this essay. The slight flaw in this method is the margin for error residing in the pos-sibility of instances of deaccession that are unknown to me.

said it was out of the question: he would take a portrait back, but not a work of the imagination.[2] So when we know that the formation of sculpture collections was initially centered on the acquisition of portrait busts, we know we start with a problem.

The beginning of interest in sculpture in New England, and in nineteenth-century sculpture in particular, is first evident at the Boston Athenaeum. During the first fifteen years of its existence, from 1807 to 1822, when the Athenaeum was located on Tremont Street, it owned only three busts, those of Alexander Hamilton, John Adams, and the Reverend George Whitefield, all of them modeled by foreigners. Adams's portrait was the work of the Frenchman J. Binon, the first sculptor known to have worked in Boston.[3] More important, the Athenaeum owned casts of famous antiquities, the *Laocoön* and a gladiator, both given by the architect Solomon Willard. It also had a bas-relief of a horse, said to be from Herculaneum. In 1822 the Athenaeum moved to new quarters in Pearl Street, a move that was marked by a spectacular gift of casts of ancient statues from Augustus Thorndike. The proprietors continued to acquire busts, most of them fashioned by European artists such as Francis Chantrey, Henry Westmacott, Jean-Antoine Houdon, and Christian Rauch, and a few by American sculptors. Of special interest was a group of marbles of notable Bostonians – Nathaniel Bowditch, Daniel Webster, Thomas H. Perkins, John Lowell, William Prescott – and two U.S. Supreme Court justices – Joseph Story and John Marshall – carved by the New Jersey–New York sculptor John Frazee in 1833 and 1834. Frazee was the first American to carve busts in marble.

Visitors to the galleries in Pearl Street discovered an atmosphere of excellence and high ideals emanating from the antique casts and the classicizing busts of leaders of the young republic. But the Athenaeum was far from being open to the public; it was only the proprietors and their friends who could gain access. It was while copying Binon's *John Adams* that a young native Bostonian sculptor, Horatio Greenough, attracted enough attention to be introduced to the librarian of the Athenaeum, William S. Shaw, who gave him permission to copy its collection of casts and busts.[4] And so the man we regard as the first American sculptor came to work with this collection that, in the words of Ralph Waldo Emerson, was able to feed one's eyes "like nectar."

Greenough was the first American sculptor to seek training in Italy. When he had been living in Florence for a few years, he created a marble group called *Chanting Cherubs*, commissioned in 1829 by his close friend James Fenimore Cooper. It was not only Greenough's first Ideal work – that is, a work primarily based on an idea or a conception rather than a direct response to nature – but it was the first marble group by an American. When it was complete, Greenough sent it to Boston to be exhibited in rented quarters on Summer Street. Washington Allston walked in from Cambridge as soon as it went on view. In his opinion it was the work of a "brilliant, versatile genius."[5] Thousands saw it during the summer of 1831. It was praised in the press and by most who saw it, even if there were Bostonians who could not stomach the idea of a pair of naked cherubs, which they viewed as immoral. When Greenough heard of the latter remarks, he wrote: "I had thought the country beyond that. There is a nudity which is not impure."[6]

The trustees of the Athenaeum, perhaps taking a cue from the success of their protégé, decided to remodel the lecture hall as an exhibition space for sculpture. In the fall of 1839 eighty sculptures were displayed, an event hailed as "the first attempt in this country to make a gallery for sculpture."[7] The catalogue stated that with this new exhibition space the trustees were intent on forming "a general taste" for sculpture.

Although the taste being formed in Boston in the 1830s was based mostly on copies of ancient statues and togaed busts of great men, occasionally something could be seen that did not fit into these categories. One particularly popular work was *Uncle Toby and the Widow Wadman*, by the British – but now Boston-based – sculptor Robert Ball Hughes. This was the first three-dimensional work to be exhibited at the Athenaeum that was decidedly not classical (it was on loan from a New York collector) and presented the Athenaeum trustees with a challenge: they now recognized that exhibiting copies and portrait busts was not enough.

At the end of 1837 a brilliant young Boston lawyer, Charles Sumner, embarked on the grand tour. By the spring of 1839 he was in Rome, where he discovered a little-known sculptor, Thomas Crawford, "toiling in his studio, waiting for commissions, with narrow means and serious misgivings as to the future."[8] Crawford, a New Yorker, then in his twenties, was the first American sculptor to have established a studio in Rome. When Sumner found him he was absorbed in a great undertaking: a monumental group inspired by the tenth book of Ovid's *Metamorphoses* in which Orpheus descends into hell in search of his wife, Eurydice. Crawford wanted to show the moment when Orpheus, "having tamed the dog Cerberus, ceases playing upon the lyre and rushes triumphantly through the gate of hell."[9] Crawford's ambition was a synthesis of manliness – to be expressed through the anatomy – and human feelings – to be expressed in the lover's anxious face at the moment when he first glimpsed hell. And Crawford wanted to realize this with luminous clarity.

Sumner believed the sculptor had achieved his goal: "It is, without exception, the finest study I have seen in Rome, and if completed in corresponding style, – and I do not doubt that he will do this, – will be one of the most remarkable productions that has come from an artist of his years in modern times."[10] Sumner began a successful letter-writing campaign asking acquaintances in New York and Boston for funds to support the cost of transferring Crawford's plaster into marble. The effort resulted in a contract,

*Fig. 1. Thomas Crawford,
Orpheus and Cerberus, 1839–42.
Marble, 67½ x 36 x 54 in. Gift of
Mr. and Mrs. Cornelius Vermeule
III. Courtesy, Museum of Fine
Arts, Boston.*

which was signed in the American consul's office in Rome on March 31, 1841. Crawford was to carve the statue, designated for the Boston Athenaeum, in twenty months for $2,500 – an appallingly short time and small fee in the sculptor's view, but knowing it to be a magnificent opportunity, he went ahead with the project.

After two years the statue arrived in Boston (fig. 1). Sumner himself opened the box, but, to his horror, found that it had been broken in transport. He arranged for repairs, using the interim to convince the proprietors of the Athenaeum to build a small temporary viewing gallery on the lawn. Sumner selected plush red carpet, a deep mahogany brown for the walls, and thin crimson gauze to cover the windows. With a twenty-five-cent ticket a visitor could enter at time of payment; a fifty-cent ticket permitted admission at any time. Even though the Athenaeum sold thousands of tickets, there was not much of a profit. Nonetheless everyone gained, for this was neither a portrait nor a copy; it was a work of imagination, one that spoke in an ancient language but with a modern tongue, that is, with feeling and passion. The popularity of Crawford's *Orpheus* for mid-century Americans is inestimable. He became the "American Phidias." By the end of the

4

Fig. 2. Sculpture Gallery, Boston Athenaeum, mid-nineteenth century. Wood engraving. Reproduced with the permission of the Boston Athenaeum.

century, an anticlassicist like the sculptor Lorado Taft looked at *Orpheus* and pronounced it hopelessly "effeminate," the accompanying Cerberus "for all the world like a clumsy piece of furniture." But Taft had to admit that "this group marked an epoch in American sculpture," a judgment no one has ever doubted.[11]

In 1849 the Boston Athenaeum moved to its present building, at 10½ Beacon Street, and by 1851 had initiated sculpture exhibitions which were mounted in a specially designed sculpture gallery on the first floor (fig. 2). The room was established as a semi-permanent installation. Portrait busts were dispersed to other floors; the sculpture gallery was devoted to serious works of art based on the classics and on literature. The most celebrated new work, after Crawford's *Orpheus*, was actually a copy: Francesco Cecchi's cast from Houdon's figure of Washington in the State House in Virginia. This work, which still stands in the entrance of the Athenaeum, was viewed as a counterpart to *Orpheus*, a pairing of the mythological hero who penetrated the underworld and the native hero who stood tall in the sunshine of republican life. Other favorites in the Athenaeum gallery were Horatio Greenough's *Venus Victrix* (1837–40), the first female nude ever carved by an American; Robert Ball Hughes's plaster model for his bronze statue of Nathaniel Bowditch (c. 1839), the first bronze to be cast in America; and a cu-

5

rious work full of pathos by a sculptor of Maine origin, Edward Augustus Brackett, *Ship-wrecked Mother and Child*, a horizontal marble group at which the viewer looked down to see a nude woman and child who have just drowned (fig. 3). This latter work was particularly popular, in part because Brackett finished it less than a year after the death of the famous transcendentalist Margaret Fuller, who had drowned with her infant son in 1850, when their ship went down off Fire Island. Horatio Greenough was a great admirer of this work and wanted to help his younger colleague sell the sculpture so that it would remain on public view. He wrote an open letter intended for publication in which he spoke of the hours he had spent admiring what Brackett had done to "that block of stone," and of how Brackett had made it a "vehicle of so many sad and tender thoughts." Greenough pointed out that the large group had been created at great sacrifice, that Brackett had not had the advantage of going abroad but "studied here *at home*." He insisted: "I cannot but feel that the artist has a claim on his fellow citizens for the means to go on in the path he has chosen, and for which he seems so well fitted."12

Young Harriet Hosmer of Watertown was a frequent visitor to the Athenaeum gallery; she especially loved the effect on the sculpture created by the new gas lights: "I go . . . to

Fig. 3. Edward Augustus Brackett, Shipwrecked Mother and Child, *c. 1850. Marble, 74¼ x 34¼ in. Reproduced with the permission of the Worcester Art Museum.*

the Athenaeum and fill my eyes and mind with beauty."[13] It was in the atmosphere of the first-floor gallery that Hosmer came to believe sculpture to be superior to painting, in fact, "a thousand times more expressive."[14] She was not alone in seeing its value, and more and more people came to recognize that Boston was home to "the most useful collection of sculpture in America."[15]

Looking elsewhere for signs of appreciation of sculpture in midcentury New England takes us to Yale University. Yale acquired its first American work in 1804: a portrait of Benjamin Franklin, fashioned from life by the Philadelphian William Rush, the early wood-carver who had achieved the transition from craftsman to sculptor. Before the end of the century Yale would acquire twenty-eight more sculptures. No other New England college or university has such an impressive list, nor did any other educational institution show the interest in art that Yale did in the nineteenth century. The doors of Yale's Trumbull Gallery – the first college art museum in America – opened in 1832. Although most of Yale's early acquisitions were busts of favorite presidents and professors donated by alumni, students, and friends of the institution, three Ideal sculptures entered the collection in the nineteenth century. The first was a pair of statuettes by Hezekiah Augur, a self-taught local sculptor, based on a passage from the Old Testament depicting Jephthah and his daughter. The Yale Corporation organized a subscription and collected money from the citizens of New Haven in order to buy the work for the Trumbull Gallery. Just as at the Athenaeum, the exhibition of a work like this offered an opportunity for fund-raising, and Yale sold tickets that were to "command access to the Gallery while the Statues remain there, and afterwards to the Museum of Sculpture, where it is proposed ultimately to deposit them."[16] The Museum of Sculpture did not materialize, but we find a real enthusiasm for sculpture at Yale, not matched elsewhere in New England save at the Boston Athenaeum.

Two other Ideal works were shown in the Trumbull Gallery in the nineteenth century: *Dying Hercules*, by Samuel F. B. Morse, a gift of the Reverend E. Goodrich Smith in 1866; and *The Wept of Wish-ton-Wish*, by Joseph Mozier, given to Yale in 1889. Morse created *Hercules* in 1812 when he was studying in London. After it won a gold medal at the Royal Academy in 1813, he shipped it to America. Of a later generation, Mozier also executed his sculpture abroad. He was among the Americans who set up shop in Rome, carrying with him a rich store of memories from American novels. Nathaniel Hawthorne visited his studio in 1858 and saw the model for *The Wept of Wish-ton-Wish*, based on James Fenimore Cooper's 1829 novel about a white woman who chose to live among "savage" Indians rather than with "civilized" people. Even though Hawthorne did not like Mozier's work on the whole, he found this piece to have real merit.[17]

The other center in New England where we find some interest in sculpture at midcentury is the Wadsworth Atheneum in Hartford, Connecticut. When the Atheneum opened its doors in 1844, seventy-eight paintings, one miniature, two marble busts, and a bronze sculpture went on exhibition.[18] The busts were the work of a Connecticut sculptor, Chauncey B. Ives, one being of the museum's founder, Daniel Wadsworth, the other an Ideal portrait called *Meekness*. A few years later Wadsworth gave to the Atheneum a plaster cast of Canova's *Dancing Girl*. But the major reason for the interest in sculpture at the Wadsworth Atheneum was the participation, from the institution's earliest days, of Edward Sheffield Bartholomew.

Bartholomew went to Hartford as a boy, and, though naturally inclined toward art, he apprenticed to a bookbinder and then decided to become a dentist. When still a student, he read Benvenuto Cellini's autobiography, which, in his own words, "put the devil into him." He quit his job so that he could spend his time "looking at pictures"[19] and became close friends with the Hartford painter Frederic E. Church. Bartholomew then went to the life school of the National Academy of Design in New York. Returning home, he was hired at the newly founded Atheneum. Some sources call him the "first curator," others, "the janitor," but whatever his job description, he basically ran the Atheneum in its first years. There he nurtured himself as an artist. But to his dismay, in the same period he discovered his color blindness. It was then that he turned to sculpture. James Batterson, proprietor of a local marble yard, gave him direction about materials and carving, and, before long, nothing could satisfy Bartholomew but studying in Italy. Even after Bartholomew became an American "Roman," he did not lose contact with Hartford or the Atheneum. On his second return visit, in 1857, Hartford gave Bartholomew and Church a joint testimonial banquet. It was on this occasion that Bartholomew meditated on the richness of his experience in Europe, of visits to the galleries of the Louvre, the Uffizi, and the Vatican where no entrance fees were charged, as they were at the Wadsworth Atheneum. Bartholomew felt he must do something for the people of Hartford, so he wrote the trustees of the Atheneum to ask them to abolish admission charges: "by making the gallery free, we attract the public to visit it; and as soon as an interest is aroused, artists and people are encouraged to deposit pictures or loan them." He offered to subsidize all visitors to the Atheneum for one year, but the trustees turned him down.[20] After this disappointment Bartholomew returned to Rome, only to fall ill and die the following spring.

The city felt the loss of this man who had cared so much about the cultural life of Hartford and wished to respond to his generous offer of the previous year. A subscription was opened with a view of raising five thousand dollars to purchase the original models in his Rome studio, as well as to fund a marble copy of his *Repentant Eve*, owned by Joseph Harrison, Jr., of Philadelphia. Colonel Samuel Colt (inventor of the revolver) was head of the subscription committee and led off with a gift of five hundred dollars. James Batterson went to Rome to take an inventory of Bartholomew's studio and to arrange for packing and shipping. When Bartholomew's rich array of plasters and his thirteen marbles arrived at the Atheneum in 1859, the trustees found they had what was necessary for a sculpture room, different from, but parallel to, that of the Boston Athenaeum.

Meanwhile, at the Athenaeum, despite the success of the sculpture exhibitions in the early 1860s, space became a problem, and in 1868 the trustees voted to convert the sculpture gallery into a reading room. Although the Athenaeum Fine Arts Committee understood the reason behind the trustees' decision, its members could not but lament the fact that "the appropriation of the Sculpture Gallery . . . will break up our collection of valuable casts from the antique and marbles, the only one existing in New England."[21]

Although by 1860 the Wadsworth Atheneum had a sculpture room, the institution made no more acquisitions in the nineteenth century. Thus, with the dismantling of the sculpture gallery at the Boston Athenaeum, the first phase of collecting and exhibiting contemporary sculpture in New England was over. The effervescence of interest in sculpture in the first half of the century was stimulated by fiercely American patrons fired with an intense patriotism. With the exception of the neoclassical sculptors from whom American sculptors learned – especially Canova, Thorvaldsen, and Bartolini, and the Frenchman Houdon, the great chronicler of America's revolutionary leaders – Americans had little interest in European sculptors.

Their own sculptors, however, were national heroes. They were like men who had walked on the moon; they lived in Florence and Rome and proclaimed a message that Americans were as clever and as full of genius as Europeans. Further, they were forthright and entrepreneurial in a way that was admired by all; they sent back Ideal works that could be viewed for a fee and that were capable of building a climate of patronage in America. James Fenimore Cooper wrote to Horatio Greenough that he should send his "boys [*Chanting Cherubs*] to Charleston, New Orleans, and Cincinnati." He told him, "You may not gain in the way of money, but you will gain enormously in making yourself known, and you will get orders in consequence."[22] More and more American businessmen were making the grand tour and becoming "art infected." And what did they buy? Sculpture. The painter Thomas Cole took note of this disagreeable trend: "It seems to me sculpture has risen above par, of late. . . . This exaltation of sculpture above painting . . . is unjust, and has never been acknowledged in the past."[23]

The brief span from 1840 to 1870 was the golden age of American sculpture. Sculptors, relying not on the color used by painters but only on the pure, abstract qualities of line and surface, realized a noble ideal in figures and in groups that was in harmony with the young republic's image of herself. Her sculptors were descendants of the Greeks – a sculptor like Horatio Greenough would even sign his bust of President John Quincy Adams in Greek. Yet they were better, for they had found how to Christianize the Greeks. Viewers saw this clearly in Crawford's *Orpheus*. The sculptors proclaimed the greatness of the nation as they fashioned equestrian figures and placed statues in the halls of government. Thomas Crawford's work for the United States Capitol in the 1850s – bronze doors for the Senate and House wings, a pedimental relief showing the white man's advances over the Indian, and his colossal *Armed Freedom* for the Capitol dome – was the epitome of achievement of the first generation of American sculptors.

To follow this story of the growing appreciation of sculpture – and sculpture really is the issue, not just nineteenth-century sculpture – in New England in the years following the Civil War, we again focus on Boston, the largest and most prosperous of New England cities. It was being transformed from a snug little town on a peninsula, where leading families – the economic elite called Boston Brahmins – lived within highly defined boundaries, into a metropolis, by filling in its big Back Bay to create the most beautiful residential and cultural center in America. It was the hub of America's pioneer railways from which eight lines radiated, while Boston clippers and steamships plied the seas, east and west.

Boston's culture remained in the hands of a small group of connoisseurs and intellectuals, people ready and willing to support, through private donation, institutions such as the Boston Athenaeum. Donations to the Athenaeum sculpture collection did not cease altogether when the sculpture gallery closed. There was already talk of a new building. An 1869 bequest brought Richard Saltonstall Greenough's *Carthaginian Girl* to the Athenaeum. Horatio Greenough's younger brother was a favorite at the Athenaeum, where a group of patrons had organized a subscription in the mid-fifties to have his *Shepherd Boy with Eagle* cast in bronze (one of the first parlor-size works of bronze to be cast in America), and they continued to support him in the sixties when he had moved his studio from Rome to Paris, one of the first Americans to do so. Signs of this move are the vague echoes of the Louvre's *Vénus de Milo* to be seen in *Carthaginian Girl*.

In spite of the shortage of space, the Athenaeum could still acquire *Carthaginian Girl* in 1869. The following year, however, a bequest was made that was not possible to exhibit: the armor and weapons collection of Colonel Timothy Bigelow Lawrence. His widow was even ready "to fit up a room in suitable manner and style."[24] Next, she mentioned the possibility of giving one hundred thousand dollars for a building. This in turn started talk of a Museum of Fine Arts.

The man who took the lead in transforming the talk into reality was Charles Callahan Perkins, who had just returned from a long stay in Europe. Grandson of one of the great

China merchants of Boston, Perkins went to Europe to study art after his graduation from Harvard in 1843. It was a decision that was not particularly well received among Boston Brahmins, but he studied first in the circle of Thomas Crawford in Rome, then in 1846 with Ary Scheffer in Paris. He also studied etching with Félix Bracquemond. Although he did not develop a full-fledged career as an artist, he did write books, most of them on sculpture, sometimes illustrating them with his own etchings.[25] Perkins's idea of a museum was influenced more by London's South Kensington than by any other European museum he had visited. That is, he thought it should be encyclopedic in nature and educational in purpose. For sculpture this meant the inclusion of large numbers of plaster casts, since he believed original works of art were "out of our reach on account of their rarity and excessive costliness."[26]

The Act of Incorporation of the new museum was written in February 1870. By May the city of Boston had committed land on Copley Square, an area that was just beginning to take shape in the new Back Bay section. The following spring, architects were submitting designs in a competition which was won by John H. Sturgis and Charles Brigham. Sturgis and Brigham produced a gabled brick building with arches, columns, and string courses in yellow terra cotta. Its High Gothic style reflected that of South Kensington, and the building became famous in America as a good example of the new terra-cotta construction. By July 1876 the Museum of Fine Arts was ready to open its doors.

A generous patron, Thomas Gold Appleton, wrote the first guide to the museum, in which he described himself shepherding an imaginary companion whom he called "Starbuck." As they ascended the museum steps, Appleton pointed out, "Mr. Starbuck, you must know we are really proud of our modest yet brilliant beginning." Just as they entered (fig. 4) they came upon Crawford's *Orpheus*, about which Appleton remarked, "It is Greek, but filtered through a Yankee mind, and with somewhat of the energy of the New World." Nearby were Greenough's *Carthaginian Girl* and another recent gift, a marble figure of an impish naked babe astride an owl by Harriet Hosmer, which Appleton referred to as "Will-o'-the-Wisp."[27] Again Appleton's pride puffed up, remembering a visit, in Horatio Greenough's company, to "the brave little lady" and her father in their Watertown, Massachusetts, home. They went with the purpose of discussing with her father, Dr. Hosmer, the possibility that "her eccentricity might be genius." As everyone now knew, "she has held her own; America loves her as one of its pioneer women, who, instead of talking on platforms of what women have the right to do, simply went and did it."[28]

The visitors then turned to a life-size marble, "'Young Columbus', a very clever specimen of the new school of Italy" (fig. 5). Appleton explained how this school (he never

11

Fig. 4. Entrance to Copley Museum (old Museum of Fine Arts, Boston). Photograph. Courtesy, Museum of Fine Arts, Boston.

mentioned the creator of *Columbus*, Giulio Monteverde, by name) achieved popularity after "the success of a statue of the dying Napoleon," referring to Vincenzo Vela's *Napoleone morente*, which had been all the rage in Paris at the Exposition Universelle of 1867. Americans got to know the Italian school at the Centennial Exhibition in Philadelphia in 1876. As Appleton pointed out, "there, room after room showed the triumph of the Italian chisel over the sobriety of marble," and he wondered if Starbuck could see evidence of that miracle in the "boyish face of thought big with the birth of a world" that was before them.[29]

Young Columbus was the first modern nonportrait sculpture by a European to enter a public collection in New England. Augustus Porter Chamberlaine, a Concord physician who spent more time traveling abroad than at home, discovered it in Monteverde's Roman studio. What could make a more perfect gift for a museum whose opening would mark the centennial of the United States than an image of the young explorer? Seated on a mooring post, foot resting on a large iron ring – implying the nearness of the sea – Columbus holds a book in his lap, looks away, and dreams his faraway dreams. As soon

12

Fig. 5. Giulio Monteverde, Young Columbus (Il Colombo Giovanetto), *1871. Marble, 56¾ x 26 x 21½ in. Gift of Augustus Porter Chamberlaine. Courtesy, Museum of Fine Arts, Boston.*

as Chamberlaine knew the museum was to become a reality, he offered the sculpture to Perkins, who was chairman of the Committee on the Museum. When the museum made no arrangements to have the sculpture shipped from Rome, Chamberlaine was surprised and wrote as much to Perkins in November 1871. Perkins had given him the impression that the museum would be delighted with the gift, never having considered the possibility that a work of modern sculpture might not be welcome. But such a notion was clearly in the air when Perkins anxiously wrote to Martin Brimmer, president of the museum, to urge him to write immediately, "before any thought of such a prohibition" became a reality.[30] Monteverde's *Columbus*, which depends on one of the nineteenth century's favorite themes – the childhood of a great man – became one of the most popular works at the Boston Museum of Fine Arts in its first decades.

Perkins's letter is the first sign we have that the policy of the new museum would be different from that of the Athenaeum. The Athenaeum maintained a balance between exhibiting casts of antique sculptures and encouraging modern sculptors. The new museum, heavily influenced by South Kensington, went forward enthusiastically with building a large collection of plaster casts. In keeping with prevailing notions of modesty, fig leaves were added to some of the casts. When the museum published its catalogue ten years later, ninety-six pages were devoted to the cast collection (Greek, Roman, architectural – medieval, Moorish, and Renaissance – and Renaissance sculptures) and three pages to modern sculpture.[31]

As the Museum of Fine Arts ended its first decade, it was joined on Copley Square by an important neighbor: the Boston Public Library, the first free municipal library in the world (founded 1854). The cornerstone for the new building was laid on July 23, 1888. At the opening ceremony Oliver Wendell Holmes posed the question: "Can freedom breathe if ignorance reign?" His emphatic answer was: "Let in the light! . . . no lackeys cringe, no courtiers wait – this palace is the people's own!" The important idea embodied by the new Boston Public Library was that it would be a palace for the people, and the architects, McKim, Mead and White, were eager to develop this concept.

From the beginning Charles McKim had a strong sense of the interrelatedness of the arts and the importance of including major painting and sculpture commissions in the design of such a monumental building. The artists McKim selected were the best: Puvis de Chavannes, the most-recognized mural painter in the world; John Singer Sargent, the illustrious portrait painter; James McNeill Whistler, the independent American artist who had dazzled London and Paris for a quarter of a century; and the two best sculptors in America, Augustus Saint-Gaudens and Daniel Chester French, both hard at work on major projects in Boston – French on the memorial to the sculptor Martin Milmore for Forest Hills Cemetery and Saint-Gaudens on the Shaw Memorial to be erected across from the State House.

A palatial modern library, constructed of rich materials with a handsome complement of major art works, had been McKim's vision. But many in Boston were not prepared for such opulence, and by 1891 the press was full of rumors reporting overspending and waste. The mayor appointed a committee to investigate; its members recommended that the statuary, bronze doors, and ornamental work be eliminated. It took the combined efforts of the architect Richard Morris Hunt, the philanthropist Henry Lee Higginson, and several others to convince Boston politicians of the necessity of painting and sculpture at the library. In the end, Whistler never did get a commission, and Saint-Gaudens was too ill to complete the allegories he had designed to flank the stairs of the main facade, although he carved the three seals of the Library, the City, and the Commonwealth that were placed above the arches of the main entrance. His brother, Louis Saint-Gaudens, carved the lions for the main staircase.

As the library neared completion, prominent Bostonians came forward with gifts of sculpture to line the rich marble corridors: a statuette of former governor John Andrews by Martin Milmore from S. R. Urbino; a bust of William Whitwell Greenough (president of the board of trustees from 1866 to 1888) by Richard S. Greenough, offered by W. W. Greenough's wife; and a bust of Benjamin Franklin by the Italian sculptor Giuseppe Ceracchi. Marble replicas of famous neoclassical figures – Canova's *Venus Italica* and Hiram Powers's *Greek Slave* – were given by Mrs. John Ellerton Lodge and Mrs. Margaret Otis respectively. Horatio Greenough's son (also Horatio), gave *Christ* and *Lucifer* (cat. nos. 60, 61), a pair of Ideal busts his father had created in the spirit of Milton's *Paradise Lost*. And Dr. Charles Goddard Weld, a well-known collector of Japanese art, gave a bronze statue of Sir Henry Vane, a seventeenth-century governor of Massachusetts, admired for his defense of religious tolerance and civic freedom. Still standing in the entrance hall, *Sir Henry Vane*, an exquisitely dressed young man of the seventeenth century, is nervous and alive and turns his body easily as he reaches with one hand to button the other into a glove. Lorado Taft called it "a young athlete on dress parade" and defended its creator, Frederick MacMonnies, against those who pointed out that the action depicted was "trivial."[32]

In the mid-1890s, MacMonnies, still in his early thirties, was viewed as one of the most exciting young sculptors on the American scene. Protégé of Saint-Gaudens, he had studied in Paris with Gérôme, Falguière, and Mercié, that is, with the best of the academic masters. He had charmed visitors to the 1893 World's Columbian Exposition in Chicago with his *Barge of State*, one of the major decorative works at the exposition.

Charles McKim met MacMonnies when the sculptor was a seventeen-year-old assistant in Saint-Gaudens's New York studio and, along with his partner Stanford White, became a patron of the young artist. When MacMonnies became famous, as a sign of appreciation, he gave McKim the group he had shown in the Paris Salon of 1894. It was a dancing bacchante holding a child in one arm while lifting with the other hand a bunch of grapes high above their heads (cat. no. 20). Coming as it did just at the moment when the construction of the library was drawing to a close, and wishing to donate something of a personal nature to the library, McKim (with the sculptor's approval) offered the group to the trustees, hoping it would crown the fountain in the courtyard. When the gift was announced, a New York critic wrote, "In giving it, Mr. McKim and Mr. Macmonnies [*sic*] will give Boston one of the few admirable examples of imaginative sculpture in public places in America."[33] Although the trustees tentatively accepted the gift, it had to be approved by an art commission composed of local men of good taste. In the summer of 1896 they examined a reduced model and, after considerable debate, recommended that the group be turned down. Most adamant against the sculpture was Charles Eliot Norton. As the man who had introduced fine arts into the Harvard curriculum, Norton was considered one of the most prominent tastemakers of Boston. A former mayor of Boston on the commission, Frederick O. Prince, made the mistake of telling the *Advertiser* that the commission did not question the artistic merit of MacMonnies's group – it did not even object to the nudity; the problem was the sculpture's apparent celebration of "inebriety," which seemed totally wrong for a library.[34]

Supporters of the sculpture quickly pointed out that the members of the commission had never actually seen the group they rejected. The commission then agreed to have the *Bacchante* brought from New York and installed in the library courtyard in order to judge it in situ. On a Sunday morning in November, "the rejected Bacchante was set up in the Library court with the fountain playing about it, and the solemn Art Commission with its experts in tow assembled there for deliberate inspection."[35] Almost everyone thought that it actually looked quite good. Norton still denounced it as being opposed to the ideals of a public library and its contents. In spite of Norton, the commission accepted the *Bacchante*. But by this time, the matter had become too public, and the clergy now swung into action. The Reverend James B. Brady of the People's Temple called the *Bacchante* a "treason" against sobriety, virtue, and Almighty God. The Congregational Club passed a resolution that the statue was "not simply nude, it is glaring and obtrusively naked," and at a temperance meeting at Faneuil Hall on November 26, 1896, there was a call for the trustees to "break up the dirty thing and destroy forever the influence of its shame."[36]

McKim did not destroy the *Bacchante*, but, at this point, he withdrew his gift, offering it to the Metropolitan Museum of Art in New York, which accepted it with gratitude. McKim wrote MacMonnies in Paris: "Your gift has passed out of my hands and has been made over in good faith to the Metropolitan Museum. Removed from Puritan surroundings to this Metropolis, where she belongs, I think we may regard the question of her virtue as settled for all time."[37]

In rejecting MacMonnies's *Bacchante*, Boston had rejected the most Parisian of modern American sculptures. After the brilliant success of the *Bacchante* in the Salon of 1894, the French were eager for a cast to be placed in Paris's contemporary art museum, the Luxembourg. But there was a Bostonian in Paris in the nineties who would bring modern French taste to the city of his birth in no uncertain terms. At the end of the summer of 1895, Henry Adams had just finished touring France's northern cathedrals. In a quick change of tempo, when he returned to Paris, he set off on a visit to the studio of the world's most controversial modern sculptor, Auguste Rodin. Even before he went, Adams had decided he would buy something from Rodin. After his first visit, he wrote his friend Elizabeth Cameron about a marble group, *Venus and the Dead Adonis*, he had seen in the studio: "too utter and decadent," he exclaimed; he found it impossible to hide his eagerness to purchase a work yet could not bring himself to do so. His letter to Mrs. Cameron was a mournful lament: "Why can we decadents never take the comfort and satisfaction of our decadence? Surely the meanest life on earth is that of an age that has not a standard left on any form of morality or art, except the British sovereign. I prefer Rodin's decadent sensualities, but I must not have them."[38] Adams never did buy a Rodin – for himself – but in the interests of others he became a devoted Rodin client, starting with a 2½-foot marble, *Psyche Carrying Her Lamp*, purchased at Rodin's 1900 retrospective for his niece, Louisa Hooper. By 1902 Adams was in Paris brokering a serious purchase of Rodins for the archetypal proper Bostonian Henry Lee Higginson (founder of the Boston Symphony). Adams carried on negotiations through June and July, working assiduously to shave down Rodin's prices and using tactics that were eminently successful. To his amazement, not only did Rodin lower his prices, but the sculptor arrived in person at Adams's home in Paris to deliver a bronze: "either he mistrusted me, or had some clumsy French notion of politeness . . . for he wasted a couple of hours on a stupid errand which any sculptor in America would have sent an Irishman on."[39]

A small announcement in the *Museum of Fine Arts Bulletin* in May 1903 read, "Owing to the kindness of Henry Lee Higginson the Museum is able to show five Rodins: *Flight of Love* (marble), *Head of Ceres* (marble) [cat. no. 10], *Brother and Sister* (bronze), *Death of Alcestis* (bronze), and *Vulcan Creating Pandora* (bronze)."[40] The following year Louisa Hooper lent *Psyche Carrying Her Lamp*, making the Boston Museum of Fine Arts the only museum in America that could show a real collection of Rodins.[41]

The headline "Eleven Works of Auguste Rodin, the Most Famous Living Sculptor" in the *Boston Transcript* heralded the opening of a Monet/Rodin exhibition at Copley Hall in March 1905. According to the critic, Rodin was the only modern sculptor capable of expression in a way that equaled that of the Renaissance masters. Rodin's friend Truman H. Bartlett, professor of sculpture at MIT, had other thoughts about this show: "Living artists do not count in Boston. . . . Your works were badly placed. After an artist is dead, Boston goes crazy for him. . . . I am sorry to say this is true, but nothing more can be expected. Americans buy what they can with money and then not always intelligently."[42]

We can compare Henry Adams's visits to Rodin's studio in the 1890s and the resulting purchases with Charles Sumner's 1839 visit to Crawford's studio in Rome and Sumner's decision to secure *Orpheus* for Boston. Both were visionary acts of connoisseurship, putting Boston in the forefront of American taste vis-à-vis modern sculpture.

Sumner's patronage, however, fell on more fertile ground, for the *Orpheus*, a neoclassical sculpture that entered a classically inspired collection, became a major cultural event in nineteenth-century Boston and New England. When the Rodins came to the Museum of Fine Arts in the early twentieth century, they came, without great fanfare, into a collection that offered little context for their reception. As the twentieth century began, the men who directed the future of the Museum of Fine Arts were putting all their energy into the classical collection, the new discoveries in archaeology, and into a fine Japanese collection which had no equal in the Western world.

In the decades between Chamberlaine's gift of Monteverde's *Columbus* in 1871 and Higginson's gift of the Rodin in 1906, there were only four additions to the modern European sculpture collection in the museum. The most notable was an over-life-size double bust, *Dante and Virgil*, by the romantic sculptor Baron Henri de Triqueti (gift of Mrs. Edward Lee Childe in 1876).[43] Thomas Gold Appleton, a trustee who was also a major collector, gave John Gibson's *Love as a Shepherd* in 1884, and Mrs. Francis A. Hall donated a bust of Sir Thomas Lawrence by Robert William Sievier in 1891. Mrs. Samuel D. Warren gave the museum its first Barye, an *Elephant and Tiger*, in 1892, the year her husband joined the board of trustees. The great American collections of the famous French animalier's work had been formed in the 1860s, 1870s, and 1880s in Baltimore and Washington; his groups and single figures continued to attract collectors into the twentieth century, but hardly at all in Boston.

It was Rodin who would become by far the most popular modern French sculptor in America, and Boston was in a leading position in the formative years of the new taste, which had replaced nineteenth-century neoclassicism. The MFA held an important exhibition of bronzes from the Renaissance to modern times in 1908; 10 of the 150 works were Rodins. That same year, the museum's buyer of classical antiquities, Edward Perry Warren, who was a friend of Rodin's, gave the museum a cast of the very daring *Iris*. Four years later, when the members of the Société de Peintres et de Sculpteurs of Paris, an organization of which Rodin was president, showed at the Museum of Fine Arts, Bostonians saw eleven of his works, plus a selection of drawings, three of which were owned by the museum. From this show the museum acquired his *Bust of Dalou*. Denman Ross had lent a male figure from *The Gates of Hell* in 1910, and Julia Isham donated three Rodin marbles in 1917. So by the year in which Rodin died, 1917, we find the Boston museum with a significant collection of his work, yet this collection has spent more time in storage than on exhibition. In 1953 the museum orchestrated an exchange with the dealer Curt Valentin in New York of the *Iris* and a group of *Lovers* that had come with the Henry Lee Higginson bequest in 1921, both of which were considered indecent and unsuitable for exhibition.[44] Then in 1961 the museum sold one of the original Adams/

Higginson gifts, *Flight of Love*, along with a nude female figure, also in marble.[45] As with MacMonnies's *Bacchante*, works by Rodin turned out to be New York, not Boston, taste; the Metropolitan Museum boasted about its Rodin collection, opening a beautiful hall uniquely devoted to his sculpture in 1912.

At the close of the century the Wadsworth Atheneum had not installed a new work of modern sculpture in almost fifty years, and the collection was basically composed of works by the two Connecticut sculptors Edward Bartholomew and Chauncey Ives. In the opening year of the new century, however, two distinguished gifts appeared: a version of Thorvaldsen's *Venus* (gift of Caleb P. Marsh) and a four-foot replica of Harriet Hosmer's colossal queen of Palmyra, the popular *Zenobia in Chains* (gift of Mrs. Josephine M. J. Dodge).

Due to three outstanding acts of philanthropy on the part of Elizabeth Hart Jarvis Colt (widow of the inventor of the revolver); J. Pierpont Morgan, Jr.; and Samuel P. Avery, Jr., the fortunes of the Wadsworth Atheneum turned around in the early twentieth century. All three gave large numbers of works, including a few nineteenth-century sculptures.[46] Even more important, they gave funds for additional gallery spaces. The most impressive gift of sculpture came from Avery, whose father, the noted New York dealer and collector, had been especially interested in modern French sculpture. Avery lent his collection of twenty-four Baryes to the Atheneum in 1919, as well as his bronze cast of Rodin's study for the *Monument to Bastien-Lepage*. It had been purchased by George Lucas in Rodin's studio in 1888 and was the first work of Rodin's to be acquired by an American.[47] These works became a permanent part of the Atheneum when Avery died in 1920.

In the early twentieth century, as Hartford built its new treasure house, another New England city found the means to develop a comprehensive museum of art and archaeology. In 1896 the leading citizen of Worcester, Massachusetts, Stephen Salisbury III, invited fifty prominent citizens to his home to join with him in planning a museum. It opened in 1898, even though there was little to be seen beyond works by local artists and casts of antique sculptures. Salisbury's personal collection came to the museum at his death in 1905. Slowly the people of Worcester built their museum into the considerable collection we find today, one that includes most periods of Western and Eastern art.

The Worcester Museum never showed interest in, nor received many gifts of, nineteenth-century sculpture. Nevertheless, two early gifts must be noted. In 1899, the year after the museum opened its doors, a bronze portrait of the French painter Gérôme by Jean-Baptiste Carpeaux entered the collection (cat. no. 37), from the estate of a relative of Stephen Salisbury, Joseph Tuckerman. One of the Tuckerman sons had studied painting with Gérôme in Paris, so we must assume this sculpture was purchased more for reasons of the sitter's identity than for the sculptor's. But the presence of this vividly personal portrait, so full of movement and tension, and in such stark contrast to the ponderous, down-to-earth portraits in the majority of New England collections, must have been a jolt to visitors to the young museum. At this date France's great Second Empire sculptor was virtually unknown in America; his work was not seen in public collections until the 1930s and was not popular with curators until the 1960s.

The other early gift of nineteenth-century sculpture to come to Worcester was Edward Brackett's *Shipwrecked Mother and Child*, the group that had made such a hit at the Boston Athenaeum in the middle of the century. It was a gift from Brackett himself, now no longer a sculptor but the retired Massachusetts Commissioner of Fish and Game. Although a subscription to purchase Brackett's work was initiated at the Boston Athenaeum in 1849, it was never brought to a successful conclusion. By the end of the century the marble group was in a crate that was being used as a bench at the Athenaeum. That his work was reduced to such a use annoyed Brackett so much that he became agitated, and finally, in 1902, the Athenaeum returned it to him. He, in turn, gave it to the new museum in Worcester.[48] It was probably disappointments such as this that led Brackett to seek a second career in conservation, wildlife, and husbandry.

The remainder of this slight tale about New England's reception of nineteenth-century sculpture lies primarily in college and university museums. As I have said, the idea of the college museum in America originated at Yale, and ever since the acquisition of Augur's *Jephthah and His Daughter* in 1835, the Yale Gallery has been building a sculpture collection. The year 1900 was a banner year at Yale, with nine sculptures entering the collection. Three were busts after the antique (*Homer*, *Cicero*, and *Demosthenes*) made by Thomas Crawford in 1837, gifts of Edward Elbridge Salisbury, professor of Arabic and Sanskrit, the first patron of American sculpture to give his collection to Yale.[49] There were two busts by Chauncey Ives, the son of a Hamden, Connecticut, farmer, who had recently died in Rome. Ives had had a long and successful career creating portraits in which he amalgamated the simple naturalism so appealing to Americans and the neoclassicism he thrived on during his Italian years. Ives also created a large number of sweet, Ideal works so well suited to Victorian parlors (cat. no. 18). Yale owns sixteen works by Ives. Perhaps the most interesting work admitted to the collection in 1900 was the sentimental *Sleeping Children* by the Baltimorean William Rinehart. And the most modern among the group was the gift of Frederic Remington, an alumnus of the Yale School of Fine Arts. He donated a cast of a sculpture finished four years earlier, *The Wounded Bunkie*, showing two figures on horseback in full gallop. A work replete with accurate detail, movement, and momentary feeling, it was one of the most popular works ever modeled by Remington. Then, in 1910, Yale accepted a gift from the French government: *Charity*, a Sèvres porcelain reduction of a figure Paul Dubois had modeled to serve as an allegory on the *Monument to the Memory of General Lamoricière* (1876) in Nantes, the first of several French sculptures to enter the Yale Gallery (cat. no. 1).

Other New England colleges followed Yale's lead. Although all art collections come into existence owing more to patrons' whims than to directions established by museum personnel, in colleges and universities the serendipitous nature of collection building is even more manifest than in municipal museums. A good example is found at Williams College. In 1887, following the death of her husband, Mrs. John White Field gave Williams eighty-five works of art, a gift that included two bas-reliefs by Thorvaldsen,[50] two bronzes by Barye, and a marble group, *Theseus and Andromeda*, by Thomas Waldo Story. The Fields had no connection to Williams College but they summered in nearby Ashfield, where Charles Eliot Norton was a friend and neighbor. Two years after making the gift, Mrs. Field wrote to the president of Williams expressing her wish to donate funds to provide a "lodgement for the pictures." She said this was not to be considered a memorial to her husband, but she simply wanted the "things of value we enjoyed – to be an agreeable feature in the lives of young students."[51] Despite the presence of the Field collection, a true museum of art was not founded at the college until 1926.

Bowdoin College, in Brunswick, Maine, was the site of the second college museum in New England. Although the works of art inventoried by its first director in 1885 had been in the possession of the college since James Bowdoin III's death in 1811, it is only at the later date that we can recognize a real museum. It became even more concrete when Harriet and Sophia Walker hired Charles McKim to create a building, which was dedicated in 1894. Bowdoin, rich in American painting, decorative arts, drawings, and prints, has never had much of a sculpture collection. In the year of the dedication, however, the Walker sisters gave the museum one of the most beautiful Baryes in America, *The Young Man Mastering a Horse*, a sketch betraying a vividness of movement and freedom of modeling that is a marvel to behold.

Wellesley College introduced the teaching of studio art in 1879 and art history in 1885. When the Farnsworth Art Building opened in 1889, the college was able to display a fine collection of casts and other copies. By the end of the century Wellesley owned over two thousand objects, many of them original works of art. As the director, Alice Van Vechten Brown, said in 1901, the Wellesley museum could now look "toward the day when the Art building shall become a well-equipped museum, which shall serve its neighborhood."[52] Two of the museum's most interesting recent acquisitions were modern sculptures: *Roma* (1869) (cat. no. 3) by Anne Whitney, gift of the Class of 1886, and Richard Saltonstall Greenough's *The Dreamer* (1863), gift of Ellen and Ida Mason. Anne Whitney, of Watertown, Massachusetts, was something of a heroine in the Wellesley community since she gave her eight-foot seated marble figure of Harriet Martineau, the philosopher, economist, and leader in the international woman's rights movement to the college in 1885 (destroyed by fire in 1914). In *Roma* Whitney allegorized the ancient city in the guise of a dejected old beggar woman. She wanted to portray the miserable conditions of peasant life in Rome and she also aimed a subtle criticism at the modern papacy.

Thus far, we have been looking at works of nineteenth-century sculpture that entered New England collections when they were considered "modern." In the post–Armory Show period, the years after World War I, Americans began to understand that naturalism was not the only way artists could work, and, more and more, the art of the previous century looked outdated. The idea of collecting nineteenth-century sculpture became even less interesting than it had been. In spite of this, there were a few notable undertakings in the period between the world wars with regard to nineteenth-century sculpture. The most important was Jules E. Mastbaum's donation in Philadelphia and the opening of the Rodin Museum in that city in 1929.[53]

On a smaller scale we find some gifts to the museum at the Rhode Island School of Design in Providence. This museum had been shepherded into existence in the 1890s by Mrs. Helen Adelia Rowe Metcalf, wife of Jesse Metcalf, founder of the Wanskuk Mills. First came the school, then the museum, both being housed in the Waterman Building by 1893. With the support of the Metcalfs, school and museum grew rapidly. Following the death of Helen and Jesse Metcalf's son Manton B. Metcalf in 1923, plans were set in motion for a proper museum building to be named after his sister, Eliza Greene Radeke. When the Radeke Museum opened in 1926, visitors saw some newly acquired works of nineteenth-century French sculpture that were very impressive: Rodin's *Man with a Broken Nose*, an early cast purchased from Rodin in 1882 by a London collector, and *The Hand of God*, purchased from Rodin by a Rhode Island millionaire, Samuel P. Colt, president of U.S. Rubber Co. In addition, the Metcalfs gave a bronze cast of Edgar Degas's *Grand Arabesque, Second Time*, probably the first Degas sculpture to enter a New England collection. (The Museum of Fine Arts, Boston, did not purchase their *Little Fourteen-Year-Old Dancer* until 1939.)

In Cambridge, the first sculpture owned by Harvard University was a plaster bust of William Pitt by the British sculptor Joseph Wilton. Benjamin Franklin had bought it in London and presented it to the Harvard Corporation in 1769.[54] Aside from busts, Harvard owned virtually no nineteenth-century sculpture until well after World War I, when Harry Sacks gave the Fogg Art Museum a reduced version of Randolph Rogers's popular *Nydia* in 1922. But in 1943 Grenville Lindall Winthrop, a descendant of Governor Winthrop of Massachusetts but of a branch of the family long since settled in New

York, left his collection, over 3,700 objects of extraordinary breadth – Buddhist sculpture to Peruvian gold, German Renaissance prints to American painting and sculpture – to the Fogg. The collection (especially rich in nineteenth-century French art) included forty-four nineteenth-century sculptures. The only nineteenth-century European sculptures Harvard had owned before 1943 were four Baryes and a *Cupid* by John Gibson. Overnight Harvard had one of the strongest collections in New England, and the very best collection of Rodins. Winthrop owned twenty-four works by this artist in bronze, marble, plaster, and terra cotta, plus six drawings. Most were purchased at auction in Paris in the 1920s and 1930s, many with impeccable provenance back to Rodin's studio.[55] But post-Renaissance sculpture is seldom taught at Harvard, which has meant that these sculptures are rarely exhibited and have never been shown as a group.

The other great collection to benefit a New England college town was that of Robert Sterling Clark, one of the heirs to the Singer sewing machine fortune, whose father and grandfather had served as trustees of Williams College. After collecting for over four decades, Clark looked for a safe home for his collection and felt it lay in Williamstown. When the Clark Art Institute opened in 1955 western Massachusetts was suddenly blessed with a magisterial collection, primarily of late-nineteenth-century paintings. But Clark had also bought some fine Carpeauxs, Rodins, and Degases, along with a Barye, a Dalou, and a Mène, so that the collection comes together in beautifully balanced galleries at the Clark. Like Grenville Winthrop, the Clarks bought their sculptures in Paris in the 1920s and 1930s.

The final chapter in this story, the one in which the present exhibition at Middlebury is lodged, begins in the period of the Clarks' museum – the 1950s. It is then that we find small seeds being planted that will give birth to a new interest in sculpture in general. Sir Herbert Read's 1954 Mellon lectures at the National Gallery of Art can be used as an indicator. Read spoke of a new concept of sculpture beginning with Rodin, one that saw "sculpture as a three-dimensional mass occupying space . . . to be apprehended by senses that are alive to its volume and ponderability."[56] Looking at sculpture through this prism, Read set out to reexamine the whole history of sculpture.

The appreciation of Rodin's place as the father of modern sculpture was established as a modernist canon in this period. New York in the fifties was home to a renewed appreciation of his sculpture. Curt Valentin's gallery played a major role, mounting Rodin exhibitions in 1950 and 1954, and Albert Elsen had begun working on a dissertation at Columbia University on Rodin's *Gates of Hell* in 1949.[57] Throughout his career Elsen has considered Rodin as the beginning of modernism and has devoted much study to Rodin's twentieth-century successors.

At New York University, H. W. Janson took up the subject from another point of view.

He studied the nineteenth century as a whole and considered Rodin's work in relation to the past, seeing it as much as a culmination as a beginning. He probably taught the only course on nineteenth-century sculpture in America in the 1950s and 1960s. My own work on Rodin began with Janson at the Institute of Fine Arts in the fifties, and John Hunisak was among the students benefiting from Janson's lessons in the sixties.

The atmosphere in American museums changed a great deal in the years following World War II. A new beginning in Boston came with the arrival of Perry Townsend Rathbone in 1955 as the museum's sixth director. In his first published statement of purpose Rathbone pointed out that "a generation ago museums in America had begun to liberalize their policies and were less often jeeringly referred to as warehouses of art; but the transition from static depository to dynamic institution is a recent accomplishment."[58] The museum had a membership organization for the first time, published calendars of events, and mounted special exhibitions with an enthusiasm not known before. The collecting of sculpture acquired true respectability in the Rathbone years when the Department of Decorative Arts became the Department of Decorative Arts and Sculpture under the direction of an unusual curator with a highly personal vision, Hanns Swarzenski. Swarzenski was a medievalist and concentrated his best efforts in broadening the collection in the centuries before 1800. But he was also interested in modern sculpture, favoring acquisitions that read as "modern" as opposed to "dead" academic nineteenth-century works. He purchased sculptures such as Gauguin's *Soyez Amoureuses, Vous Serez Heureuses* (in 1957), which attracted the gift of another Gauguin polychromed relief, *La Guerre et la Paix* (from Mr. and Mrs. Laurence K. Marshall, 1963). Swarzenski chose two Carpeauxs (*Le Silence* and *Ugolino*), a small version of Renoir's *Venus Victorious*, and Rodin's *Les Premières Funérailles*, a complicated bronze group that grew out of *The Gates of Hell*, which has a peculiar quality of abstract mystery. These works were installed with the museum's fine collection of late-nineteenth-century paintings, richly enlarging the scope of those galleries. In 1960 some of the Rodin marbles from the Adams/Higginson purchase were brought out of storage along with two other Rodin bronzes and given a place of honor in a heavily trafficked area on the ground floor of the museum.[59]

The Boston Museum of Fine Arts did not have a Department of American Decorative Arts and Sculpture until 1970. After that date we find a vigorous program of acquisition. Among the most notable additions are Horatio Greenough's exquisitely modeled portrait of his dog, *Arno* (1973); two life-size marbles by William Wetmore Story, *Sappho* (1977) and *Medea* (1984); and a cast of John Quincy Adams Ward's most popular work, *The Indian Hunter* (1979). Until that time Ward was not represented in the Boston collection. Saint-Gaudens, by contrast, was well represented, and between 1975 and 1980 the American department added five Saint-Gaudenses, amplifying an already rich collection.

The college and university museums became far more professional in the postwar era, hiring staff who had been trained for museum work and making real plans for funding acquisitions rather than relying chiefly on donations and bequests. The case of the Smith College Museum is interesting. Its first director, Alfred Vance Churchill, *purchased* a work by Rodin – *Children with Lizard* – in 1914, the first work of European art to enter the museum. The following year an alumna, Mrs. Jessie Rand Goldthwait, donated Daniel Chester French's *The May Queen*, the first marble in the collection. Between these early gifts and the 1950s, only three works of nineteenth-century sculpture appeared. But in the fifties, Smith was regularly buying American sculptures; in the sixties and seventies European works entered in a steady stream: a cast of Rodin's over-life-size *Walking Man*, Meunier's *Prodigal Son*, Carpeaux's *Bust of a Chinese Man*, and Barye's *Theseus Combating the Centaur* (see cat. no. 11 for another version) were among the outstanding purchases. The galleries at the Smith College Museum are among the most satisfying in New England in their collective cohesiveness and perfect integration of painting and sculpture. Smith had two advantages in putting this collection together. One was the decision by Churchill to focus on the nineteenth and twentieth centuries; the other was James Holderbaum, an art historian at Smith who specialized in Renaissance sculpture but who recognized, in the way that H. W. Janson had, that nineteenth-century bronzes offered some of the attraction of the beautiful modeled work of the Renaissance, but at affordable prices.

The nearby Mead Art Museum at Amherst College has also purchased a number of nineteenth-century works in the second half of the twentieth century, starting with the acquisition of Rodin's *Man with the Broken Nose* in 1958. The collection has developed into a well-rounded assemblage of works by Saint-Gaudens, Meunier, Von Stuck, Klinger, Dalou, and David d'Angers, as well as the perennial favorites, Barye and Rodin. As Frank Trapp noted in a monograph on European sculpture at the Mead, "the strength of sculptural representations in the Amherst College collection is unusual for a museum of its size."[60]

Wellesley's new Davis Museum is another college museum whose nineteenth-century gallery displays an attractive balance between painting and sculpture, thanks to Ann Gabhart, director of the museum from 1972 to 1982, and her interest in nineteenth-century sculpture. Before she arrived the museum owned only nine works in the area.

> In 1973, when College benefactor Dorothy Johnston Towne (class of 1923) asked her to propose an acquisition, Gabhart selected a Beaux Arts bronze [*La*

Renomée by Louis-Ernest Barrias] to begin consolidating a nucleus of nineteenth-century French sculpture. By the end of her tenure she had acquired a group of sculptures whose extent and quality are rare in college or university museum collections.[61]

This is 1993 praise; Gabhart's decisions must have perplexed more than a few people in the 1970s when nineteenth-century sculptures were still not an obvious thing to buy for a serious collection.

Yale has continued its commitment to sculpture, although the majority of its modern acquisitions have been of contemporary work, hardly unexpected given the excellence of the Yale training for modern sculptors.[62] Yet in 1960 Yale purchased a beautiful terra cotta, *Study for the "Genius of the Dance"* by Carpeaux, the first of three Carpeauxs bought in recent years. Several Rodins were donated in the fifties and sixties, but the strength of Yale is the American collection, which achieves a truly satisfactory balance between painting and sculpture. Yale's most significant recent purchase of nineteenth-century sculpture has been the full-length version of Hiram Powers's *Greek Slave* (1962). This particularly fine carving was once in the collection of Prince Paul Demidoff on his Villa San Donato in Florence.

In 1970 A. Richard Turner, then chair of the Art Department and director of the Christian A. Johnson Memorial Gallery at Middlebury College, wrote to the Salomon-Hutzler Foundation, which was about to help Middlebury purchase a bust of the *Greek Slave*, saying that this was an "appropriate acquisition as Powers was Vermont's most famous native artist."[63] Thus began Middlebury's varied and highly satisfying collection of nineteenth-century sculpture purchased during the past two decades. It has been Middlebury's fortune to have Professor John Hunisak to guide its purchases and to attract donors to a subject he knows so well. The rich spirit of the collection comes from a teacher who has clearly wanted to open a field by selecting a wide variety of artists, subjects, and techniques. There are unusual sculptures at Middlebury of a kind seldom viewed elsewhere – works like William Rimmer's soapstone *Inkstand with Horse Pulling a Stone-Laden Cart* (cat no. 15), Medardo Rosso's luminous *Sick Little Boy* modeled in wax over plaster (cat. no. 66), and George Minne's plaster group, *Three Mourning Figures* (cat. no. 7).

My tale has spotlighted the early decades in the nineteenth century when sculptors were heralded heroes lifting up the reputation of America abroad and discovering the secret of how to join America's cherished republicanism with the modern neoclassical style. Next we looked at more depressed times in the second half of the last and the early parts of this one; those who wished to place modern sculpture in gallery exhibitions as "art" had few patrons in America. Sculptors were fine as long as they celebrated public events and people in city squares or memorialized the dead in cemeteries. But for a long time, "art" was painting. Then we glanced at the slow reevaluation of sculpture that brought a varied and rich group of objects into our museums over the past few decades. It seems strangely right that Middlebury, the most recent among college museums to acquire a nineteenth-century sculpture collection, should have taken on the task of assembling an exhibition of European and American sculptures for the first time. By 1994, nineteenth-century sculpture has solidly entered the ranks of what is "correct" for a museum purchase. And it is particularly favorable for college museums. Given the abundance of the material, and the fact that attics still hold some works we do not yet know, we can expect prices to remain relatively affordable – even though the days of buying a beautiful Barye *Theseus Combating the Centaur,* as Smith did in 1973 for $2,500, or Falguière's *Pegasus Carrying the Poet* (cat. no. 14), purchased in 1974 for $3,000 by Amherst, or his *Bust of Diana* (cat. no. 54), acquired by Middlebury for $2,200 in 1979, will never come again. Nineteenth-century sculpture has so much to teach in a liberal arts, humanistic context: lessons of history, leadership, myth, a whole realm of aspirations of the Western world, right alongside the basic lessons of sculptural technique and practice. A fascinating period in the Western tradition has rightfully established its place in our collections.

NOTES

1. Mabel Munson Swan, *The Athenaeum Gallery, 1827–1860: The Boston Athenaeum as an Early Patron of Art* (Boston, 1940), 1.

2. Neil Harris, *The Artist in American Society: The Formative Years, 1790–1860* (Chicago, 1982), 257.

3. The citizens of Boston had commissioned the original in marble for Faneuil Hall. When Binon asked Adams for permission to take plaster replicas in order to make some money, Adams declared the undertaking would not be profitable: "The age of sculpture & painting has not arrived in this country and I hope it will not arrive very soon." Letter of February 1919 in the Athenaeum, reproduced in Jonathan P. Harding, *The Boston Athenaeum Collection: Pre-Twentieth-Century American and European Painting and Sculpture* (Boston, 1984), 74.

4. Nathalia Wright, *Horatio Greenough: The First American Sculptor* (Philadelphia, 1963), 22–23.

5. Allston to the Charleston sculptor John Cogdell, in ibid., 72.

6. Greenough to Washington Allston, in ibid.

7. *Daily Advertiser and Patriot,* September 26, 1839. Quoted in Rosemary Booth, "A Taste for Sculpture," in *A Climate for Art: The History of the Boston Athenaeum Gallery, 1827–1873,* exh. cat., Boston Athenaeum (Boston, 1980), 23.

8. Edward L. Pierce, *Memoir and Letters of Charles Sumner,* 4 vols. (Boston, 1877), 2:94.

9. Crawford to his sister Jenny, May 1839. Quoted in George S. Hillard, "Thomas Crawford: A Eulogy," *Atlantic Monthly* 24 (July 1869): 45.

10. Sumner to George S. Hillard, July 26, 1838, in ibid., 105.

11. Lorado Taft, *The History of American Sculpture* (New York, 1903), 73–74.

12. Greenough to Richard H. Dana, February 23, 1852, in *Catalogue of the Exhibition of Sculpture at the Athenaeum Gallery* (Boston, 1852), 15.

13. Harriet Hosmer, *Letters and Memories,* ed. Cornelia Carr (New York, 1912), 14.

14. Undated letter of 1851 or 1852, Schlesinger Library on the History of Women in America, Radcliffe College, Cambridge, Mass.

15. *Putnam's Monthly* (September 1855): 331. Quoted in Booth, "A Taste for Sculpture," 32.

16. Memorandum of 1838. Quoted in Paula B. Freedman, *A Checklist of American Sculpture at Yale University* (New Haven, Conn., 1992), 15.

17. Nathaniel Hawthorne, *The French and Italian Notebooks*, ed. Thomas Woodson (Columbus, Ohio, 1980), 153.

18. Eugene R. Gaddis, "'Foremost upon This Continent': A History of the Wadsworth Atheneum," *"The Spirit of Genius": Art at the Wadsworth Atheneum* (Hartford, Conn., 1992), 11. No one seems to know what the "bronze sculpture" was, and it does not appear to be in the Atheneum today.

19. Henry T. Tuckerman, *Book of the Artists: American Artist Life* (New York, 1867), 609.

20. Letter of November 2, 1857, published in the *Hartford Evening Press*, November 9, 1857. Quoted in Gaddis, "'Foremost upon This Continent,'" 15.

21. Quoted in Walter Muir Whitehill, *Museum of Fine Arts: A Centennial History*, 2 vols. (Cambridge, Mass., 1970), 1:6.

22. Cooper to Greenough, December 24, 1831. Quoted in Sylvia E. Crane, *White Silence: Greenough, Powers, and Crawford: American Sculptors in Nineteenth-Century Italy* (Coral Gables, Fla., 1972), 49.

23. L. L. Noble, *The Course of Empire*, 1853. Quoted in Albert Ten Eyck Gardner, *Yankee Stonecutters: The First American School of Sculpture, 1800–1850* (New York, 1945), 15.

24. Whitehill, *Museum of Fine Arts*, 1:17.

25. Among Perkins's books are *Tuscan Sculptors* (1864), *Italian Sculptors* (1868), *Raphael and Michelangelo* (1878), *Handbook of Italian Sculpture* (1883), and *Ghiberti et son école* (1886).

26. Whitehill, *Museum of Fine Arts*, 1:10.

27. In the nineteenth-century Museum of Fine Arts catalogues Hosmer's figure is called *Will-o'-the-Wisp*, but it does not look like the cross-legged imp seen in the two versions in the Chrysler Museum which are called *Will-o'-the-Wisp*. The Museum of Fine Arts returned the statue to the Athenaeum in the twentieth century, where it is called *Puck and the Owl*. See Harding, *The Boston Athenaeum Collection*, 41.

28. Thomas Gold Appleton, *Boston Museum of the Fine Arts, A Companion to the Catalogue* (Boston, 1877), 11.

29. Ibid., 10.

30. The two letters, one of November 7, 1871, from Chamberlaine to Perkins, sent from Aigle, Vaud (France), and Perkins's letter of December 1871, are in the files of the Department of European Decorative Arts and Sculpture at the Museum of Fine Arts.

31. Museum of Fine Arts, *Catalogue of Works of Art Exhibited*, part 1, *Sculpture and Antiquities* (Boston, 1886).

32. Taft, *The History of American Sculpture*, 346–47.

33. H. T. Parker, writing from New York for the *Boston Transcript*, May 23, 1895. Quoted in Walter Muir Whitehill, "The Vicissitudes of *Bacchante* in Boston," *The New England Quarterly* 28, no. 4 (December 1954): 438.

34. Whitehill, "The Vicissitudes of *Bacchante*," 439.

35. *Passages from the Journal of Thomas Russell Sullivan*, 185–86. Quoted in Whitehill, "The Vicissitudes of *Bacchante*," 446.

36. Whitehill, "The Vicissitudes of *Bacchante*," 450–51.

37. Charles Moore, *The Life and Times of Charles Follen McKim* (1929; reprint, New York, 1970), 93. MacMonnies's *Bacchante* has become one of the most loved nineteenth-century sculptures in New England. There are versions in the Bennington Museum, the Berkshire Museum, the Boston Museum of Fine Arts, the Clark Art Institute, the Wadsworth Atheneum, and the Benton Museum at the University of Connecticut. As the Boston Public Library undergoes a thorough restoration, plans include a new cast to be placed where McKim had envisioned it – in the center of the courtyard fountain.

38. Adams to Elizabeth Cameron, August 30, 1895. Quoted in *The Letters of Henry Adams*, 6 vols. (Cambridge, Mass., 1988), 4:313.

39. Adams to Higginson, July 13, 1902. *Letters of Henry Adams*, 5:393.

40. Higginson gave the *Ceres* to the museum in 1906; the other four were in his bequest of 1921.

41. Samuel P. Avery gave the Metropolitan Museum Rodin's *Head of St. John the Baptist* in 1893, the same year that S.M.H. Ellis made it possible for the Art Institute of Chicago to keep the life-size *Burgher of Calais* that was shown at the Columbian Exposition. By 1898 a plaster version of the *Age of Bronze* was owned by the Philadelphia Academy of the Fine Arts. These were the only Rodins in public collections in America before 1900.

Louisa Hooper's *Psyche with Her Lamp* was not owned by the Boston Museum until 1975.

42. Bartlett to Rodin, June 1905. Archives, Musée Rodin, Paris.

43. In 1971, when I curated *Nineteenth-Century French Sculpture: Monuments for the Middle Class* for the J. B. Speed Art Museum in Louisville, I asked to borrow the Triqueti. The loan was approved, but the curator requested it be identified as an "anonymous loan." In the end, though not ready to boast about it, the curator relented and allowed it to be in the show with its full credit line.

44. The *Iris* is now in the Hirshhorn Museum and Sculpture Garden in Washington, D.C.

45. This sale reflects the lack of respect for Rodin's marbles that was almost universal in the 1950s and 1960s: "they belong to those works that cannot be claimed as autographs," wrote the curator Hanns Swarzenski to the director as he explained his wish to sell (April 14, 1960). When Knoedler's suggested a price of $15,000 for *Flight of Love*, Swarzenski wrote back, "we would be prepared to take less" (February 8, 1961). Letters in curatorial files at the MFA.

46. Mrs. Colt gave a *Crouching Venus* by Moritz Giess, an *Infant Bacchus* by A. Hautmann, and an unattributed bust of Aïda, which she bought in Milan for 800 lira. They were the sort of objects picked up on European tours. In 1914 the Morgans gave two works by W. W. Story and two by Hiram Powers.

47. Lucas, "At Rodins & bought statuette Bastien Lepage for 400 fs." Quoted in Lilian M. C. Randall, *The Diary of George A. Lucas: An American Art Agent in Paris, 1857–1909*, 2 vols. (Princeton, N.J., 1979), 2:662. Lucas gave (or sold) it to Avery.

48. This is all made clear in a letter from Albert Thorndike of the Boston Athenaeum (April 22, 1902) to Brackett in the object file of the Worcester Museum.

49. Freedman, *American Sculpture at Yale*, 18.

50. The Thorvaldsens have since been deaccessioned.

51. Information in curatorial files at Williams is the result of research done by Sarah Cash in 1979.

52. Lucy Flint-Gohlke, *Davis Museum and Cultural Center: History and Holdings* (Wellesley, Mass., 1993), 15.

53. Jules Mastbaum owned the largest corporative group of movie houses in America in the 1920s and had the necessary wealth to build an art collection. In Paris in 1923 he bought his first Rodin. This activity grew into a kind of mania, and by the time of his death, in 1926, he had a large collection, including the first bronze cast of *The Gates of Hell*. He gave the whole collection to the city of Philadelphia. See John L. Tancock, *The Sculptures of Auguste Rodin* (Philadelphia, 1976), 11–12.

54. H. Wade White, "Nineteenth-Century Sculpture at Harvard," *Harvard Library Bulletin* 18, no. 4 (October 1970): 359.

55. Although, according to Jeanne Wasserman, former curator of nineteenth- and twentieth-century sculpture at the Fogg, the authenticity of some of the Winthrop Rodins is now in doubt.

56. Herbert Read, *The Art of Sculpture* (New York, 1956), ix.

57. Elsen finished his dissertation in 1958, published as *Rodin's "Gates of Hell"* (Minneapolis, 1960). The new version of the book is *"The Gates of Hell" by Auguste Rodin* (Stanford, Calif., 1985).

58. Quoted in Whitehill, *Museum of Fine Arts*, 2:627.

59. Ibid., 2:771.

60. Introduction to *Masterworks of European Sculpture*, Mead Art Museum Monographs, vol. 4 (Summer 1983): iii.

61. Flint-Gohlke, *Davis Museum and Cultural Center*, 28.

62. Freedman, *American Sculpture at Yale*, includes 416 sculptures by known artists; more than half are from the twentieth century.

63. Letter in the curatorial files, Middlebury College Museum of Art.

LENDERS TO THE EXHIBITION

Mead Art Museum at Amherst College

Bennington Museum

Boston Athenaeum

Museum of Fine Arts, Boston

Boston Public Library

Chesterwood, a Museum Property of the National Trust for Historic Preservation

Sterling and Francine Clark Art Institute

Fogg Art Museum, Harvard University

Fred and Meg Licht

Portland Museum of Art

Museum of Art, Rhode Island School of Design

Saint-Gaudens National Historic Site

St. Johnsbury Athenaeum

Shelburne Museum

Smith College Museum of Art

Robert Hull Fleming Museum, University of Vermont

Wadsworth Atheneum

Davis Museum and Cultural Center, Wellesley College

Williams College Museum of Art

Worcester Art Museum

Yale Divinity School Library

Yale University Art Gallery

Anonymous private lenders

The Catalogue

INTRODUCTION

John M. Hunisak

*A*FTER ARCHITECTURE, sculpture has traditionally been the most public of art forms. Monuments celebrating either great individuals or beliefs which were held as a matter of societal consensus populate the urban landscapes of the Western world. Although early Christian discomfort with the idolatrous implications of three-dimensional images had led to the demise of large-scale sculpture between the fourth and eleventh centuries of the Common Era, the centuries before and after this hiatus witnessed its proliferation. Sculpture in public places has been a constant feature in Western culture, but citizens of the nineteenth century exceeded the zeal of their predecessors. They erected public monuments in such prolific quantity that their enthusiasm has been dubbed, as if it were a disease, "statuemania."

Scholars of nineteenth-century sculpture often concentrate their energies on the study of monuments, and for good reason. A vast amount of documentary evidence is available, and research into this kind of material can provide crucial insights, especially for those of us with an interest in social history. Monuments often convey with revelatory clarity the self-image of the individuals who commissioned them and the era that witnessed their creation.

Sculpture commissioned by monarchs, the church, and the old aristocracy diminished in quantity during the nineteenth century, but it continued to be made, and lavish sums were spent. Papal tombs, mortuary monuments like the one Victoria built for Albert and herself at Windsor Castle, and the bizarre, sui generis monument that Prince Demidoff erected to the glory of himself and his family along the Arno in the center of Florence are only a few among many tangible proofs of this continuity. At the same time, alteration in the patterns of patronage and the appearance of new buyers for sculpture permanently transformed the market, while improved technical procedures made it possible to satisfy a dramatic increase in demand for statuary.

In a democracy or constitutional monarchy, commissions for monuments are awarded with different notions of accountability than under an absolutist government. Public officials commission works of sculpture in the name of the citizens who foot the bill for the finished product. The public is not only an audience but ultimately the patron, as well. If this new patron does not approve or cannot understand a monument,

33

there will be a public outcry; the official in charge and the artist responsible will suffer adverse criticism. If the hostility is extreme enough, the official may be dismissed, the monument dismantled, and the artist deprived of future commissions. An important exhibition of French sculpture held at the J. B. Speed Art Museum in Louisville, Kentucky, late in 1971, was subtitled *Monuments for the Middle Class*; this phrase brilliantly encapsulates the new conditions under which sculpture came into being during the nineteenth century.

Members of the middle class not only pronounced judgments on public monuments; they also purchased sculpture for their own delectation. Royalty, churchmen, and those with great earned or inherited wealth ceased to be the exclusive buyers and owners. Figures for the garden, statues based on literary themes for parlors and libraries, busts of private individuals – as well as those of famous men and women, past and present – for pedestals and tabletops, tomb sculptures, and reduced versions of monuments or renowned statues became objects that a statistically small, but nevertheless significant, percentage of the population could own. "A marble or bronze on every mantelpiece" superseded "a chicken in every pot" as a cultural ideal among the bourgeoisie.

There can be no doubt that monuments, tombs, and equestrian statues constitute the most prominent and visible sculptural expression of any era prior to our own, including the nineteenth century. They are also among the richest resources for gaining insight into the relationships between art and society. Throughout the century, sculptors coveted commissions in these three categories above all others. But such works are only part of the whole story, and an exclusive focus on them tends to distort our understanding by overshadowing the extensive production of sculpture between 1800 and 1900 that was more modest in scale and less public in intention.

From the planning stages of this exhibition, I decided that those three preeminent categories of statuary, by far the most studied and best known, would be excluded. There would be no reduced versions of any monument in its final format, no tomb effigies, and no equestrian George Washingtons, Bismarcks, or Joans of Arc. What is left, after the three most obvious and visible categories are eliminated? A great deal of superb sculpture that provides a somewhat altered, but no less accurate, accounting of nineteenth-century taste and sensibility. This exhibition unites a large body of sculpture that is more intimate in scale and communicative capacity than statues conceived as monuments. Such works tend to address the viewer in a conversational mode, rather than with the rhetorical flourish of a soliloquy. They might well appear in public places, but not on piazzas, esplanades, parade grounds, or in cemeteries. Their natural environments are museums, educational institutions, public libraries, or homes. Even the largest and most aggressive statue included, the *Balzac Nude* by Rodin (cat. no. 24), is an early stage in the conception of a monument, not the monument itself; furthermore, it is smaller than life size, but not the reduction of a larger statue.

Other working rules were established to guide in the choice of objects and in the structure of the accompanying catalogue. All works are from New England collections, and the original conception of each piece (but not necessarily its physical execution in the material seen here) dates from 1800 to 1900. I wanted to avoid both the exclusive concentration on French sculptors that informed the exhibitions *Monuments for the Middle Class* and *The Romantics to Rodin* (Los Angeles County Museum of Art, 1980) and objects that appeared in either of them. (There are four exceptions to this rule, as well as a few that may be the same image, but not the same object, or that differ in size or material from the piece that appeared in those exhibitions.)

Most previous exhibitions of sculpture have been devoted to the work of a single artist or national group; I decided to juxtapose European and American sculpture according to categories of subject matter. Forty-two sculptors have been included. There are fifteen French and fifteen Americans; there are two Belgians, two Germans, three English, four Italians, and one Swiss-Italian. With the regrettable absence of any work by the great Italian, Antonio Canova, or the Dane, Bertel Thorvaldsen, this breakdown by national group reflects the collecting patterns that were followed on the eastern coast of the United States, and particularly in New England, during the nineteenth century itself and through our own century. It has not been possible to include every sculptor of major importance, but most of the luminaries are present with at least one work. Juxtaposing the sculpture of several European nations and the United States provides compelling evidence for the internationalism of approach which prevailed during the era.

Exhibition catalogues traditionally present aspects of and attitudes about the history of art, but often the objects exhibited do not coincide with the essays printed in the catalogue. Every effort has been made to tell the story of nineteenth-century sculpture through the objects that will be on view in the exhibition.

A crucial and difficult issue must be confronted at once. What constitutes an original work of sculpture in the nineteenth century? In earlier times the question could be answered with greater assurance and fewer qualifications. An original had always been an object that the artist made – in large part – by himself, and the final appearance was the composite result of his will and his touch. (The masculine pronoun is appropriate; before the nineteenth century, women are virtually nonexistent among the ranks of professional sculptors.) Works of sculpture were almost always made because they had been commissioned, and in consultative dialogue with patrons. Although we, who live in the twentieth century and have been conditioned by numerous photographs of sculptors alone in their studios, tend to overestimate the personal involvement of old-master sculptors in the execution of their works, the fact remains that they were more intimately connected with the final product than their nineteenth-century counterparts usually were.

Regardless of the materials used, old-master sculptors were expert craftsmen who modeled wax or clay, carved wood or marble, and sometimes even cast bronze, in their studios. Filippo Baldinucci, the biographer of Gianlorenzo Bernini (1598–1680), recounts that, in old age, the sculptor continued to spend long hours carving marble while standing on a scaffold; when his assistants urged him to quit at the end of a day, he would respond: "Let me stay here; I'm enthralled." Benvenuto Cellini (1500–1571) wrote an autobiographical account of casting his bronze *Perseus* that is one of the most thrilling episodes ever narrated in the history of art. After the metal had solidified and cooled, he – just like his predecessors and just like those who would follow him during the next two to three centuries – set to work with chisels and abrasives, manually and laboriously bringing the surfaces and details of the rough statue to a state of lustrous perfection. Such images of physical interaction between a sculptor and his materials tend to get elevated to mythic proportions. It is easy to forget that both of these great sculptors practiced their art in the company of numerous assistants, who were also intimately involved with the mechanical processes of carving and casting, polishing and chasing.

There can be no question about what constitutes one of Cellini's original works, however. His sculptures were not only his conceptions but in large part his realizations, as well; work done by assistants was supervised by him. During Cellini's era, there are also known instances in which replicas of certain pieces were made in response to specific requests. Each one of these amounts to a special case as far as the artist's personal involvement is concerned, but a replica is – by definition – a piece that came from the workshop of the artist who produced the original; at least some supervision by the creator is implied when the term is used. We also have documented instances from the Renaissance in which copies of famous pieces, both ancient and modern, were commissioned. Baccio Bandinelli (d. 1560) made a fine copy of the then recently rediscovered Hellenistic masterpiece, the Laocoön group, for Cardinal Giulio de' Medici; it can still be seen in the Uffizi. When the French Maréchal de Gié wanted a copy of Donatello's bronze David, no less an artist than Michelangelo was entrusted with the task by the Florentine Republic. Although this work has disappeared, it seems that Michelangelo produced a free invention based on Donatello's masterpiece, rather than the copy that was requested.

With nineteenth-century sculpture, the terms *original, copy,* and *replica* take on slightly different meanings, and the concept of *multiple* has to be added to our working vocabulary. If we ask, "Where is Michelangelo's *David?*" or "Where is Puget's *Diogenes?*"

there are concrete, unambiguous answers. Puget's monumental relief is in the Louvre – in Paris – and Michelangelo's colossal nude is in the Accademia – in Florence. No one is likely to be fooled into thinking that the clunky marble reproduction that stands today in front of the Palazzo Vecchio or the bronze reproduction installed in the Piazzale Michelangelo overlooking Florence is the "real" thing.

But if we ask, "Where is Rodin's group *The Burghers of Calais*?" the answer is anything but simple. Of course, it is in Calais on the place Richelieu, where it was inaugurated with great fanfare in 1895. But what of the cast that stands outside the Houses of Parliament in London? Is that an "original," too? How could it be anything else, since it was purchased in 1911 from Rodin, who supervised its installation on the site? I, for one, find it quite difficult to remember all the places I have encountered full-size bronze casts of the monument, most of them qualitatively interchangeable. In the United States, it can be seen in New York, Washington, Pasadena, and Philadelphia; furthermore, one can have the same experience in Paris, Brussels, Copenhagen, Basel, and Tokyo. There are also full-size plasters of the group in Meudon and Venice.

None of these is a fake or an illegal rip-off. All are "authorized" casts, made under the supervision of either Rodin or the Musée Rodin in Paris, according to the provisions of the artist's will. Furthermore, this proliferation is absolutely in keeping with Rodin's desire that his work be known by firsthand experience throughout the world. All of the casts are "authentic" according to nineteenth-century thinking, even though a Renaissance artist or connoisseur, miraculously transported to the present, would surely be confused by such extensive multiplication of a single work.

Clearly, a change in attitude about what constitutes an original work had taken place, and it was directly related to a reordering of priorities in the relative value assigned to an artistic idea and its realization during the later eighteenth and early nineteenth centuries. I hasten to admit that it is much easier to articulate the issue, which has long been recognized, than it is to explain why this happened. Whatever the reason, from the sixteenth century onward there had been increasing interest in the preliminary stages of artistic creation, which were closer to the initial inspiration than the final sculpture. Preliminary drawings and sketches in wax or clay have been greatly admired and collected by connoisseurs ever since. The acquisition of finished works by no means diminished, but by the nineteenth century most sculptors had distanced themselves from the actual execution of their works in permanent materials.

When a nineteenth-century sculptor finished the model for a sculpture (usually in clay), after a laborious process of working out the idea in sketches that progressively increased in size, complexity, and detail, he or she frequently regarded the creative process as finished. Most sculptors believed that the remaining work belonged to the mechanical, rather than to the creative, realm. In this exhibition, we have no such final models in terra cotta, but we do have a superb, and exceedingly rare, terra-cotta sketch, which bears the actual marks of the artist's touch. It is one of the early crystallizations of the idea for Dalou's *Maternal Joy* (cat. no. 29).

During the nineteenth century, most of the physical labor involved in producing finished works from artists' models was entrusted to specialists. When the definitive clay version was finished, it would usually be baked in a kiln, transforming it into more permanent terra cotta. This was still extremely fragile, so a negative mold would usually be made and then a plaster cast made from it. Sometimes the terra cotta would be lost in the process of making the mold, and the actual, autograph object would thereby cease to exist. During the course of the century, refinements in technique made such losses less and less likely. When the firm of A.-A. Hébrard undertook the casting of Degas's wax models between 1920 and 1932, they lost only four out of seventy-three in the process of making the molds.

The plaster became an extraordinarily important element in nineteenth-century sculptural practice. If a work was made on speculation, it would most likely be shown in a public exhibition or be kept in the artist's studio as a plaster, which prospective clients could examine firsthand, before reaching a decision to order a version in marble or bronze. Sometimes the plaster became the final stage in the work's evolution, as is true with Griffin's bust of his father (cat. no. 45), which was gilded but never executed in a more permanent material, and with Eakins's mask of Talcott Williams (cat. no. 42). Plasters were also sold as cheaper alternatives to bronzes or marbles, as was the case with Chantrey's plaster busts of Sir Walter Scott (cat. no. 38). Rimmer, the self-taught American who developed highly personal and idiosyncratic working methods, made his plaster *Torso* (cat. no. 23) as a finished work; there probably was never a clay model at all, only a block of plaster which the artist carved directly and smoothed with abrasive tools.

The term *original plaster* is frequently encountered in discussions of nineteenth-century sculpture and causes much confusion because its meaning is rather fluid. Any plaster that served as the "master" from which molds for bronze casting were made, or from which a marble was carved, is – by definition – an "original plaster." The probability is very high that the patinated plaster by Minne, *Three Mourning Figures* (cat. no. 7), served as such for bronze casts of the group. But what if several plaster casts were made, at the same time and with equal care, as was often the case? One might serve as the model for a marble replica, and another for a bronze edition. Frequently, a bronze would be cast in more than one size and by more than one firm. Each of them could have utilized a different plaster, each one of which could legitimately be regarded as an "original." Sometimes we know for a fact that a specific plaster was the one used by a particular firm to make its molds, and sometimes speculation can be made on the basis of high probability, even if proof is lacking. This is the case with Saint-Gaudens's plaster portrait relief of Mrs. Van Rensselaer (cat. no. 50), because the cast included in this exhibition is the very one that belonged to the sitter. To be authentic, an "original plaster" need not be unique.

During the nineteenth century, marble and bronze continued to be the two preferred materials for finished works of sculpture, as had been true ever since the Renaissance. At the beginning of the century, when classical taste prevailed, marble was more popular; afterward, bronze was used with greater frequency, but both remained options throughout the century. Although there are instances of nineteenth-century wood carving, it was a rare phenomenon. Composite works, made of mixed media, were popular after midcentury, but relatively few of these were made in comparison with the vast numbers of marbles and bronzes. Two are included in the exhibition. Degas's *Little Fourteen-Year-Old Dancer* (cat. no. 5) is a bronze cast, enhanced with linen, muslin, and satin. Saint-Gaudens's *Ceres* (cat. no. 10) is made of wood, copper, and semiprecious stones.

Marble carving probably has a greater mystique associated with it than any other interaction between artist and medium. Although the mental image of a sculptor alone in the studio with a block of marble, an abundance of inspiration, and a mallet and chisel is irresistible, it also bears little relation to sculptural practice during any age. The sheer physical labor involved in setting marble blocks in place and roughing out the intended image is daunting. An artist's touch is hardly necessary at these stages and would amount to time wasted for no good reason, since a skilled workman could accomplish the task equally as well. Models in wax or clay have been an integral part of the process of carving statues from the Renaissance onward. Although there are instances of sculptors carving directly in the stone without models, they are rare. Standard nineteenth-century practice involved a full-size model, usually in plaster, and the marble was meant to be an exact replica of it.

The process of transferring the image to the stone is, of course, the crux of the matter. Before the late eighteenth century, this was accomplished in a more dynamic, interactive manner, with the artist making decisions and improvising while carving. The greater the reliance on a detailed model (which is what became common practice), the less improvisatory the process. Eventually, it became almost purely a matter of mechanical transfer, with the model as the absolute authority and the artist engaged minimally, or not at all, in the manual process of carving. The exact procedure that was followed varied from sculptor to sculptor. Some were actively engaged as consultants who discussed the progress of the work with their professional carvers, made suggestions, and applied finishing touches themselves; others relied exclusively on the judgment of their paid assistants. Marble carving became an industry, with highly skilled workmen whose job it was to reproduce models with absolute fidelity. In both Europe and America, this profession was dominated by Italians, who were known as *practicians.*

The desired goal was exact reproduction of the model, but earlier in the century this transfer was accomplished with less precision than later became the norm. Plumb lines attached to identical grids were hung over the model and over the roughly shaped marble to serve as preliminary guides. Calipers were used to verify distances. But the process of pointing was essential. Holes of calibrated depth were drilled into the marble from all directions according to measurements established with the model, and they indicated to the practicians how much stone to carve away.

The first time one encounters an original plaster from the first half of the century – one that was actually used for carving a marble – can be disconcerting. The plaster looks like a pincushion, with small metal rods projecting in all directions, or like a statue with the pox, if those rods have been removed. These pins established the fixed distances for measurement in the pointing process. Sometimes, the holes in the marble were drilled to excess, and they appear as telltale blemishes on the surface of the highly polished final sculpture. Such scars are apparent on the *Bust of the Greek Slave* (cat. no. 62), if one looks closely.

Later in the century, a far more accurate pointing machine was developed, which looked rather like twin dentist drills attached to movable arms with a single, controlling mechanism between them. While one would move along the surface of the model, the other would simultaneously cut away marble until the resultant surface matched the slightest nuances of the original. (One of these machines is on exhibition at the Musée d'Orsay in Paris, with a plaster model and marbles at different stages of completion.) Such a machine made possible large editions of popular works in marble, and the same principle – when applied proportionately – resulted in precisely rendered, reduced or enlarged replicas of the original model.

We have in this exhibition three marble replicas, made under the artists' supervision, which were part of unusually large editions. Hosmer's *Puck on a Toadstool* (cat. no. 32) is one of at least thirty that were carved by practicians in her studio. Ives's *Pandora* (cat. no. 18) also belongs to an edition of at least thirty replicas. Rogers's *Nydia* (cat. no. 8), one of the most popular three-dimensional images of the century, was carved fifty-two times in two different sizes under the artist's supervision. There is a contemporary account of the appearance of Rogers's studio with a whole row of Nydias being carved at the same time by a small army of practicians.

During the nineteenth century, there were notable improvements in the mechanics of bronze casting, which lowered the cost of production and made bronzes more affordable than at any earlier time in the history of the Western world, and generally higher in quality than at any time since the Renaissance. Old-master sculptors had cast their bronzes by the method known as *cire perdue*, or lost wax. By the second quarter of the nineteenth century, this process was in large part superseded by an alternative method, sand casting, which was considerably less expensive and came to dominate the bronze-casting industry. Even though *cire perdue* casting was employed less frequently toward the end of the century, it had never completely died out.

There were always founders who specialized in this difficult and complex process during the intervening years, and sculptors who preferred the greater fidelity to their original models that resulted from *cire perdue*. In this exhibition, the *cire perdue* stamp appears on six bronzes: Dalou's *Angel with Child* (cat. no. 27); Degas's *Female Portrait with Head Resting on One Hand* (cat. no. 41), *Little Fourteen-Year-Old Dancer* (cat. no. 5), and *Rearing Horse* (cat. no. 13); Falguière's *Head of a Wounded Soldier* (cat. no. 55), and Matisse's *The Serf* (cat. no. 21). It is reasonable to believe that all the other bronzes included are sand casts.

Sand casting involves pressing the original plaster into a mixture of sand and other materials to create a negative impression into which the molten bronze will eventually be poured. This is a faster method than the more complex *cire perdue*, in which a ceramic or rubber negative is taken from the plaster, brushed with wax, and subsequently removed from the hardened wax, which can then be reworked by the artist. When this is repacked on the exterior with ceramic and inside with a core known as *investment* before firing – which removes the wax that will be replaced by molten bronze – a finer rendition of the artist's autograph intentions results. Although *cire perdue* has long been regarded as the superior method because of its greater fidelity to the original, the final results of nineteenth-century sand casts were often superb. The fundamental difference between the two processes is the fact that a nineteenth-century sand cast emerged from the mold in a coarser state and had to be extensively chiseled, smoothed, and reworked – usually by skilled artisans. Therefore, the final appearance of such casts, even when very fine, reflects an artisan's craftsmanship more than an artist's autograph handling as it was recorded in the original model.

One perplexing problem intrinsic to nineteenth-century sculpture is the fact that, even after we accept the concepts of the multiple, the role of mechanical reproduction, and the manual execution by craftsmen who are not the artists, we may never know when the piece that we look at, hold, or own was actually made. There are instances in which we know precisely when a piece was cast or a replica was carved, because the date is inscribed or external documentary evidence exists, but they are rare. Whitney's *Roma* (cat. no. 3) is inscribed with the date of the original model, 1869, but also bears a stamp with the date of casting – November 1890. We know that Ives's *Pandora* (cat. no. 18) was first modeled in 1851, and that the model was reworked in 1863, but the inscription *Romae 1875* is incised on the base, revealing the year in which this replica was carved. Likewise, Clésinger's *Head of Christ* (cat. no. 53) is inscribed *1867*, and Dalou's *Maternal Joy* in Sèvres porcelain (cat. no. 28) carries the date of its manufacture, 1912.

All of these instances are somewhat out of the ordinary. According to standard procedure during the nineteenth century, the date inscribed on a finished work is usually the date of the model and not of the object itself. Thus, Gould's *Bust of Christ* (cat. no. 56) and *Bust of Satan* (cat. no. 57) have the dates 1863 and 1862 inscribed on their respective marbles, even though we know that they were carved in Florence, under the artist's supervision, during 1878. Sometimes, but rarely, there is a terminus ante quem or terminus post quem established by external evidence. Chantrey's plaster *Bust of Scott* (cat. no. 38) is inscribed *1820*, the date of the model, but the fact that it was acquired by the Boston Athenaeum in 1827 proves beyond any doubt that it was cast during the 1820s. Lewis's *Bust of Longfellow* (cat. no. 46) carries the date of its model, 1871. A source of 1883 recounts that Lewis brought the plaster model back with her from Rome and that she herself carved the marble after a group of Longfellow's admirers raised the money because they wanted to donate the sculpture to Harvard.

According to standard practice, works intended for multiple sales were not all carved or cast at once, the way an edition of prints might be. An artist, a firm that had purchased reproduction rights, or a foundry that had a contract with the artist would keep an exemplar – probably a plaster, but perhaps a marble or bronze – on view in the shop where it could be examined by prospective customers. When a replica was commissioned, the process of manufacture began. The customer would specify material, size, and any special requests – like gilding or silvering. Unless a foundry's records survive, and an airtight provenance can be established between a statue that was delivered on a certain date and that same object today, it is virtually impossible to establish the precise date when a sculpture was made. If a foundry or institution owns reproduction rights, it can produce casts or replicas as long as there is a demand.

What becomes inescapable is that, in almost all instances, nineteenth-century sculptors regarded the date when the conception was realized in the final model as the significant date, and not the date of execution. This is another ramification of the century's emphasis on the initial aspects of the creative process. The work of art was regarded as a tangible, concrete manifestation of an inspired idea, but not necessarily the unique manifestation of it. It could be reproduced many times; the materials and size could change. But each time a viewer encountered one of these multiples, he or she would experience the original conception anew. Whoever stands in the presence of Rodin's

Burghers of Calais, whether in Basel, Pasadena, or Tokyo (or numerous places in between), is meant to marvel at the sculptor's ingenious solution to the problem of communicating human suffering, the pain of six individuals lost in their own worlds while sharing a common space, and the ambiguous sculptural forms which seem to heave and sigh. The fact that this is not a unique experience, which can be known only at a single site, is not supposed to matter. In truth, it matters little for most viewers, because of the powerful emotion that is communicated via sculptural form in each and every instance.

Every sculptor of the nineteenth century did not subscribe to these notions about the multiple, even though they were commonly believed. There were artists who followed their works from conception to realization and were manually involved at every step of the way, even for editions. There were sculptors who believed in the moral efficacy of unique objects from the artist's hand and disdained the notion of multiples. But these were also exceptions to the rule; they seemed prophetic when a twentieth-century backlash took place, demanding direct carving by a solitary artist and the purging of all elements that smacked of union between art and industry.

One has to leave aside many of the expectations of old-master connoisseurship and judge nineteenth-century sculpture with a different set of criteria. We frequently encounter brilliant pieces that delight us with their formal invention and exquisite craftsmanship, even when we know that they are not unique objects and that the workmanship we admire may be by the hand of an expert technician, rather than the artist. We should admit, without any embarrassment, that a great deal of the pleasure that nineteenth-century sculpture gives us is a direct outgrowth of its subject matter. In the past this was often seen as a fundamental weakness, but in the 1990s, viewers of art and museum goers seem more open to the pleasures of traditional subjects than they might have been even a decade ago. Telling a story well and finding the "significant moment" which conveyed the essential meaning of a narrative situation had, after all, been key criteria for judging quality since the Renaissance; nineteenth-century sculptors celebrated the twilight of this great tradition, often with stunning results. In recognition of the special significance of subjects, I have arranged the catalogue according to categories of subject matter which are frequently encountered in 19th-century sculpture. Those categories will also determine the installation of the sixty-seven works of sculpture that comprise the exhibition.

1

SEATED ALLEGORIES

PROGRESSIVE nineteenth-century thought drifted away from traditional allegory, but that did not prevent artists from creating numerous allegorical figures – especially sculptures made by more conservative artists for like-minded patrons. The most fundamental principle of allegorical representation in the visual arts is that an image has a symbolic meaning in addition to its literal and apparent one. Traditionally, such images were understood by literate and educated people because there was a common vocabulary of symbols meant to be universally comprehensible. There were "guidebooks" to allegory, such as the late-sixteenth-century compendium by Caesare Ripa, *Iconologia* (first ed. 1593), which explained what specific figures and their attributes meant.

During the course of the nineteenth century, there was a general disintegration, not of symbolic representation, but of its generally understood vocabulary. Traditional allegories lost much of their communicative capacity as the viewers of art works ceased to be educated – or felt the need to be educated – in this language. Artists began inventing their own allegorical imagery, which was and remains unintelligible to most viewers. One thinks immediately of Gustave Courbet's huge canvas *The Artist's Studio* (1854–55, Musée d'Orsay, Paris), which he baptized a "real allegory." This designation demands that we read the individuals and props inhabiting the pictorial space as carriers of symbolic meaning, rather than as mere physical presences. But unless we know a good deal about the intricacies of Courbet's life, politics, and aesthetic viewpoint, we are clueless when we confront this self-designated "allegory" and try to decipher it. Even those who understand him best can never be sure that they have unraveled the full meaning of his private symbolic language.

The three specifically allegorical figures, all clothed and seated, demonstrate a wide range of communicative capacity via symbol. Dubois's *Charity* (cat. no. 1) is the most comprehensible in traditional terms. For centuries in Western art, a modest, seated female figure with a head covering of some sort, holding at least two infants – and nursing one or more of them – had been recognized as the personification of the Christian virtue of Charity, precisely what Dubois intended this combination of images to mean.

Military Courage, also by Dubois (cat. no. 2), is not an allegorical concept with a comparable history of visual representation. In all likelihood, it was Dubois's invention, in response to the wishes of his patrons, but it is easily understood by anyone who has minimal familiarity with the conventions of allegorical language. The pose, which is a composite of various poses borrowed from Michelangelo, establishes the utmost seriousness of intention. The helmet, sword, and costume – evocative of ceremonial Roman armor – alert us to a military reference. The lion skin tied around the figure's shoulders and draped across his left thigh suggests an allusion to Hercules; the viewers of *Military Courage*, then, are expected to reflect on the manly virtues associated with the mythical figure: strength, fortitude, and courage.

Whitney's *Roma* (cat. no. 3) is the most personal allegorical invention among the three, and therefore the least easy to decipher. It is not based on any visual tradition with a comparable meaning, and the props do not carry a clear-cut symbolism. Without the title, we would have difficulty determining that this figure represents the city of Rome in 1869. The images embroidered on the hem of the figure's dress are famous works of ancient art that can be found in the city; the papal tiara that rests on the ground amid her drapery folds provides another clue that the figure alludes to Rome. But it is not until the figure is identified as Rome herself that we understand the artist's intention. Eternal Rome under the rule of the papacy has been reduced to the status of an old beggar woman. A fervent hope for Italian unification and the liberation of Rome from papal domination was in the air. Whitney, who lived in Rome at the time, felt the pulse of contemporary history and invented this allegory in direct response to it.

PAUL DUBOIS

1. *Charity*

    Sèvres porcelain, original model 1876

    height: 16½ inches

    width: 6½ inches

    depth: 8¾ inches

    Yale University Art Gallery. Gift of the French Government in 1910. 1910.22

2. *Military Courage*

    bronze, original model 1876

    height: 41 inches

    width: 12¾ inches

    depth: 11¾ inches

    Middlebury College Museum of Art. Purchase, with funds provided by the Electra Havemeyer Webb Memorial and Fine Arts Acquisition Funds. 1984.2

    Foundry mark: *F. Barbedienne/Fondeur/Paris* (right side of base)

    Stamped: *852* (back of base, left side); *reduction mécanique/A. Collas*

    Provenance: Estate of Adolf A. Weinman (1870–1952); Graham Gallery (New York)

2

These two figures were conceived as component parts of the impressive tomb of Général Juchault de Lamoricière for the north transept of the cathedral in his native city, Nantes, but they were first exhibited as independent sculptures and would subsequently earn great fame for their creator, separate from their places in the tomb ensemble. Before the tomb itself was exhibited, Dubois sent the plaster models of *Charity* and *Military Courage* to the Salon of 1876. Among the enthusiastic admirers of these two allegories was Henry James, who praised their "surpassing beauty" and called them "altogether the most eminent works in the Salon" (*New York Daily Tribune*, June 5, 1876). Eventually, both of these and the other two tomb allegories, *Faith* and *Meditation*, were offered for sale by the Barbedienne foundry in five different sizes, attesting to their immense popularity. As was also true for Dalou's *Maternal Joy* and *Old Peasant* (cat. nos. 28, 4), Sèvres produced porcelain versions of these popular images.

Général Lamoricière (1806–1865) was famous as a military leader and as a son of the church who led the papal army in 1860, so these allegories were meant to pay homage to both his personal virtue and his public accomplishments. To aggrandize the deceased general's stature, *Charity* and *Military Courage* invoke the authority of masterpieces of Italian Renaissance art. She is a variation on Michelangelo's *Bruges Madonna*, and he assimilates aspects of the same master's effigies of Lorenzo and Giuliano de' Medici from the wall tombs in the New Sacristy of San Lorenzo in Florence and his painted image of the Prophet Isaiah from the Sistine Chapel ceiling in the Vatican Palace complex.

ANNE WHITNEY

3.   *Roma*

> bronze, original model 1869; cast 1890
>
> height: 27 inches
>
> width: 15½ inches
>
> depth: 20 inches
>
> Davis Museum and Cultural Center, Wellesley College. Gift of the Class of 1886. 1891.1
>
> Signed, dated, and inscribed: *Anne Whitney Sc. Rome 1869* (base); inscribed and dated: *Roma MDCCCLXIX* (front of base)
>
> Foundry mark: *M. H. Mosman Founder/Chicopee Mass/Cast Nov 1890*

This impressive figure was executed by Whitney during an extended stay in Rome, from 1867 to 1871. The heavily draped, seated female figure is an oppressed and haggard old beggar woman who personifies Rome. Her historical antecedents can be found in Hellenistic and Roman sculptural representations of lower-class, aged women. Not the classical goddess, Roma, she is instead an allegory of contemporary Rome, ruled by the popes and awaiting the liberation that nationalist Italians and their supporters hoped would accompany unification. She holds a coin in her right hand and an oval medallion, which was her "license" to beg legally in Rome, in her left. With biting irony, Whitney included medallions on the hem of the beggar's drapery with artistic symbols of Rome's former greatness: the Apollo Belvedere, Laocoön, the Dying Gaul, and Hercules. Apparently, the antipapal intention was recognized and caused a stir; Whitney had originally placed a medallion with a recognizable portrait of a high-placed cardinal amid the

3

figure's drapery, just below her left hand. The sculptor later substituted the papal triple tiara for the portrait, but that seemed to be even more inflammatory. Whitney actually felt the need to ship the statue to an American official in Florence for safekeeping.

Roma was warmly received by Whitney's contemporaries; she exhibited it at three international exhibitions: London in 1871, Philadelphia in 1876, and Chicago in 1893. For the latter exposition she had the work expanded to colossal size and cast in plaster. This object, as well as two other plasters, another bronze, and a marble – all the same size as the Wellesley bronze – have disappeared.

STANDING FIGURES

The STANDING, FULL-LENGTH FIGURE has been a mainstay of the sculptor's art throughout history and was especially popular during the nineteenth century. Three of them – all clothed – were conceived as reliefs and are somewhat allegorical; they serve as a bridge between the three seated allegories and the four remaining figures. Saint-Gaudens's *Ceres* (cat. no. 10) is heavily swathed in draperies and richly embellished with semiprecious materials. She holds objects that suggest fecundity and abundance, which are appropriate for Mother Earth, and perhaps even more so for the dining room of a modern tycoon with unlimited wealth, the environment for which the panel was created. The same sculptor's *Amor Caritas* (cat. no. 9) has fewer clues that can be used to identify the figure. Although its origin is in a tomb design, it has become an independent object that serves as no more than a vague metaphor for Love Charity. If the title were not inscribed, we would probably not make any association between this standing, winged figure and the tradition to which Dubois's *Charity* so clearly belongs. The meaning of Minne's *Three Mourning Figures* (cat. no. 7) is even less clear. This free-standing figure group evinces only a generalized sense of mournfulness. The expressive drapery folds and the mysterious presence of the three enshrouded figures communicate the full extent of what can be known, and the vague title only confirms the elusiveness of their meaning. Three of the remaining clothed figures represent contemporary individuals who merely stand. Their poses derive from their respective professions, and the sculptures tell no stories. At face value, they are realist images derived from the artist's firsthand experience of actual people. They are themselves – and perhaps nothing more – but they could also be intended as "real allegories" with meanings not readily apparent. More than the other two, Meunier's *Hammerer* (cat. no. 6), with his classic contrapposto pose barely concealed by his shirt and leather apron, seems to hint at further meaning. Dalou's *Old Peasant* (cat. no. 4) and Degas's *Little Fourteen-Year-Old Dancer* (cat. no. 5) are truly modern works in that their poses are derived from life rather than some a priori formula. Characteristic of the work of these artists, both poses are the product of daily routines which the models habitually performed, even if Dalou's is more natural and Degas's more artificial. Vast numbers of nineteenth-century sculptures, whether clothed or nude, full or partial figures, depict narrative situations. In the case of Rogers's *Nydia* (cat. no. 8) we can locate the precise passages in a contemporary novel that explain her movement, her gestures, and the narrative props that the sculptor included. This kind of statue is based on an event that appears to be happening before our eyes, rather than attempting to capture a state of being or to communicate a symbolic meaning.

JULES DALOU

4. *Old Peasant*

bronze, original model 1898–99; reduced model 1904 or later

height: 38½ inches

width: 10¾ inches

depth: 10⅜ inches

Middlebury College Museum of Art. Purchase, with funds provided by The Reva B. Seybolt ('72) and The G. Crossan Seybolt ('77) Art Acquisition Funds. 1982.11

Inscribed: *DALOU Sclp/Susse Fres Edts/Paris* (back side of support)

Foundry mark: *Susse Fres Editeurs* (lower on support, left); illegible stamp (just to right of foundry mark)

Provenance: William Postar (Boston); Lewis A. Shepard (Worcester, Mass.)

Dalou's last years were filled with feverish creative activity, despite his poor health. In addition to numerous commissions for monuments and portraits, and service on various official committees, Dalou had a project on which he worked for his own satisfaction, without a commission: a visionary, private valedictory to monument making, a monument to workers. By the time of his death, he had modeled dozens of rapid clay sketches representing all sorts of manual workers; some of them had been developed into larger studies and given greater specificity of detail and costume. There were also three projects for the appearance of the monument as a whole. But even close friends who were the executors of Dalou's estate were not aware that he had modeled a life-size figure of a standing peasant who looks downward while rolling up his sleeve before setting to work. One of these friends, a Dr. Richer, discovered this plaster figure (which had been cast by Dalou's plaster caster, Bertault, in 1899) behind a curtain in Dalou's atelier after the sculptor's death.

A letter written by Léonce Bénédite, the director of the Luxembourg Museum, where a bronze cast of this plaster was installed in 1904, tells what he knew about Dalou's wishes, but not the source of the information. While Dalou was alive, he had refused to have any of his sculptures placed on view in the museum, but he was willing to have this standing peasant enter the collection posthumously. With this work, "he would accept being remembered by the younger generation who come to these galleries in order to absorb the teaching of their predecessors" (Archive du Louvre s 30).

The *Old Peasant* is a very moving image. This aging worker is presented with the greatest simplicity and dignity imaginable, but without any hint of the sentimentality or pretentiousness that mars many nineteenth-century images of peasants. Dalou felt the

51

4

greatest sympathy for manual workers and identified with them. This peasant and the whole visionary project for his monument to workers are tangible proofs of Dalou's deeply held beliefs about the moral efficacy of physical labor.

The firm of Susse Frères was entrusted with the bronze casting of the life-size figure, which was completed by the late summer of 1904. It also edited the work in various sizes, and Sèvres issued an edition in porcelain. The *Old Peasant* is one of Dalou's most characteristic and frequently encountered images.

5. *Little Fourteen-Year-Old Dancer*

bronze and mixed media (muslin, linen, and satin), original model 1878–81; cast 1921 or later

height: 37½ inches

width: 20 inches

depth: 20 inches

Courtesy of the Shelburne Museum, Shelburne, Vermont. 26-16

Signed: *Degas* (stamped replica)

Foundry mark: *A A Hébrard cire perdue/HEB/j*

Provenance: Mrs. J. Watson Webb

Degas's *Little Fourteen-Year-Old Dancer* was one of the few pieces of sculpture to be shown at the "impressionist" independent exhibitions of the 1870s and 1880s. Degas had planned to include it – or a preliminary version – in the fifth exhibition, held in 1880, but ultimately sent only the glass case in which the piece was to be displayed. In 1881 he again sent the case first and, after the opening had taken place, the figure itself. By that time a full decade had passed since Degas first made two-dimensional works devoted to ballet dancers, but his fullest exploration of ballet scenes still lay in the future.

The actual object exhibited in 1881 is now in the collection of Mr. and Mrs. Paul Mellon. The piece is unique in the annals of nineteenth-century sculpture that was conceived and exhibited as high art. The figure itself is made of wax modeled over a complex armature. The surfaces that represent flesh were tinted to resemble the real thing; the dancer wore actual clothing (stockings, bodice, slippers, and tutu) and a wig tied with a green ribbon. Another ribbon was tied around her neck.

Although this dancer is no more than two-thirds life size, and thus emphatically an art work that cannot be confused with reality, the coloration of her flesh and the clothing she wears serve to blur the distinction between art and life, as does her wig. Furthermore, Degas convinces us that in this work he has captured the physiognomic and physical particularities of an individual, Marie van Goethem, who was a ballet student at the Opéra and modeled many times for him as he developed the pose for this statue. Sixteen preparatory drawings and a wax sculpture of her in the nude, in the same position as in the finished statue, have survived. They document the care Degas took to capture her appearance, as well as her tense artificiality as she assumed a predetermined, and even painful, pose. No other sculpture by Degas was conceived and executed with the help of so many preliminary studies.

5

Other polychrome sculptures from the nineteenth century and earlier come to mind as comparisons, as do religious figures that have been dressed in actual clothing and wear wigs of real hair, and dolls or mannequins. We might even look to the more recent past and note the extent to which Degas's *Little Dancer* anticipates the figures of John De Andrea and Duane Hanson. None of these reference points constitutes an exact source or postscript, however. With virtually equal emphasis on the figure's artifice and its meticulous realism, Degas's *Little Dancer* occupies a unique place in the history of sculpture.

In 1881 the figure provoked great curiosity and clearly made many viewers and critics uncomfortable. The exhibition reviews refer to her ugliness, her viciousness, and her origins in the gutter – comments that seem very curious and beside the point of the statue. Degas chose an awkward, less-than-beautiful adolescent who was – as the title indicates – fourteen when she first modeled for him. She was precisely the sort of child from modest or poor backgrounds who came in great numbers to the ballet studios. For the moment, she was raw human potential who might possibly become – with the right, but unlikely, combination of natural talent, hard work, and luck – one of the fantasy sylphs who glide across the theater's stage. This professional route was one of the few that a nineteenth-century woman could follow with at least some minimal hope of success and independence. Far more likely, however, was the possibility of failure and, if she did not find a supporting admirer, of living a life of vice or working the streets. Degas's statue reveals his coldly objective recording of a specific dancer's appearance, but it seems to imply much more. She is not, and probably never will be, one of the fantasy creatures of the ballet stage.

Can we look this objectively at external appearances without considering social and human realities, as well? Degas's paintings suggest that he did not separate the two, and that objectivity in observing contexts was as important to him as capturing appearances. His scenes depicting the world of ballet often include the presence of well-dressed, top-hatted gentlemen in the halls and behind the scenes; they are observing the feminine "merchandise" and waiting for the end of a rehearsal or performance. Doesn't Degas's *Little Dancer* in three dimensions, with her awkward and strained pose, her wig, slippers, and costume, evoke this unsavory world even more vividly and assertively than his two-dimensional creations? If so, the unusual critical vocabulary suggesting "viciousness" and "the gutter" might well be coded references to what the artist's contemporaries recognized but refused to acknowledge about the lives of the dancers who were Degas's subjects.

The Hébrard bronzes that reproduce Degas's sculptures made of wax evoke the originals with great accuracy. At the National Gallery of Art, in Washington, D.C., waxes and bronzes are exhibited side by side, and – were it not for the oily slick the wax has secreted over time – it would be quite difficult to distinguish them by visual means alone, even from a short distance. That is not the case with the casts made after the mixed-media originals, however. The bronze versions of the *Little Fourteen-Year-Old Dancer* are also mixed-media pieces, but in abbreviated form. Each cast has a tutu and a hair ribbon (not always green) attached to it, but the hair itself, bodice, stockings, and slippers have been rendered in bronze. Patination of the surfaces creates different coloristic sensations, and the *cire-perdue* casting by Hébrard convincingly matches textural distinctions that exist in the original clothed figure, but much has still been lost. The shocking sense of tangible presence and the blurred distinctions between art and life are considerably diminished in these bronze versions.

CONSTANTIN MEUNIER

6.   *Hammerer, or the Man with the Pincers*

> bronze, original model 1884; cast possibly 1890
>
> height: 18³⁄₁₆ inches
>
> width: 8⅛ inches
>
> depth: 6¼ inches
>
> Williams College Museum of Art. Gift of William Hutton, Class of 1950, in memory of his father, G. V. D. Hutton, Class of 1920. 67.9
>
> Signed: *C. Meunier* (on base)
>
> Provenance: James Goodman, Inc. (Buffalo, N.Y.)

Meunier exhibited the life-size *Hammerer* in 1886, first in Ghent and later at the Salon in Paris. These exhibitions were, in fact, his local and international debuts as a sculptor, and the response was enthusiastic. Like his statue of a *Stevedore* – with which it is contemporary – the *Hammerer* wears the clothing of a contemporary worker, but he stands in classical contrapposto like a divinity or hero from the past. Although Meunier conceived his worker statues with the greatest sympathy, he sometimes miscalculated the effect of imbuing ordinary people with such extremes of heroism and pathos. As had been true for Jean-François Millet's painted peasants earlier in the century, their communicative capacity can be annulled by pretentiousness. That is decidedly not the case with the *Hammerer*, however. His contrapposto reads as a natural response, a workman taking a moment's rest and assuming a more relaxed pose than would be possible during his labor. The heavy apron and protective cap are convincingly integrated into the whole composition and create particularly inventive defining contours.

6

7. *Three Mourning Figures (Three Holy Women at the Tomb)*

painted plaster, original model 1896

height: 25½ inches

width: 18¾ inches

depth: 7¾ inches

Middlebury College Museum of Art. Purchase, with funds provided by The Reva B. Seybolt ('72), The G. Crossan Seybolt ('77) , and The Calvert H. Seybolt ('80) Art Acquisition Funds. 1990.18

Provenance: Léon de Smet (1881–1966), Mme de Smet; Mme de Ryck-Versele (sister of Mme de Smet); Mme Jacqueline de Ryck (daughter of Mme de Ryck-Versele); Luc de Booser Art Gallery (Knokke-Zoute, Belgium); Shepherd Gallery Associates (New York)

These heavily shrouded, mourning figures are the embodiment of anonymous sorrow. Their bodies, faces, and hands are obscured, and whatever can be learned about them can only be known by the evidence revealed by their draperies. In this respect they consciously recall the mourning, or *pleurant,* figures that appear in fifteenth-century Burgundian tombs. (In the fifteenth century, Burgundy and modern Belgium had been a single political entity, so this evocation makes historical sense in the context of later nineteenth-century Belgian nationalism, which deeply affected the generation of symbolist writers and artists.)

This trio of mourners is endlessly evocative, but never specific. Every aspect of their communicative power is ambiguous and elusive. To describe them with any accuracy, one has to resort to analogy. This is wholly appropriate in a symbolist context, where tangible reality was always the starting point, but a state of essence was the goal. Minne and his colleagues were more interested in effects than in things. As Gustave Kahn proclaimed in 1886: "Our essential aim is to objectify the subjective (the exteriorization of the idea)."

7

8.   *Nydia, the Blind Girl of Pompeii*

marble, original model 1855–56

height: 36½ inches (figure); 31 inches (pedestal)

diameter: 22 inches

Museum of Art, Rhode Island School of Design. Gift of Mrs. Mary Russell (Providence, Rhode Island) in memory of Mr. John Fiske Paine. 53.423

Rogers's *Nydia*, like Powers's *Greek Slave* (cat. no. 62), became one of the ubiquitous three-dimensional icons of the Victorian era. According to Rogers's account book, he had this narrative statue executed in marble for eager patrons fifty-two times, both life size and in reduction as it appears here. The figure struck a sympathetic chord in the sensibilities of those who gazed at it with emotion as they recalled the apocalyptic ending of Edward Bulwer-Lytton's extremely popular novel, *The Last Days of Pompeii*, published in 1834. Nydia is a blind, love-struck flower seller, who appears throughout the novel and, after having survived the eruption of Vesuvius and saved her beloved, Glaucus – only to restore him to his beloved, Ione – commits suicide by throwing herself into the sea.

Rogers's figure was inspired by specific passages in the ninth chapter of the novel. Against the tumult of the raging volcano, with its smoke and showers of ash, and terrified crowds of fleeing Pompeiians, the pathetic blind girl – suddenly empowered by her ability to negotiate her way in the darkness – becomes the center of the novelist's attention.

> In vain she raised that plaintive cry so peculiar to the blind; it was lost amidst a thousand shrieks of more selfish terror.
>
> Again and again she returned to the spot where they had been divided [she from Glaucus and Ione]. . . .
>
> At length it occurred to Nydia, that as it had been resolved to seek the sea-shore for escape, her most probable chance of rejoining her companions would be to persevere in that direction. Guiding her steps, then by the staff which she always carried, she continued, with incredible dexterity, to avoid the masses of ruin that encumbered the path . . . and unerringly (so blessed now was that accustomed darkness, so afflicting in ordinary life!) to take the nearest direction to the sea-side.
>
> Poor girl! – her courage was beautiful to behold! – and Fate seemed to

8

favour one so helpless! The boiling torrents touched her not . . . ; the huge fragments of scoria shivered the pavement before and beside her, but spared that frail form: and when the lesser ashes fell over her, she shook them away with a slight tremor, and dauntlessly resumed her course.

Rogers translated this literary passage into a sculpted narrative which appealed to the emotions of his contemporaries with its carefully calculated pathos. Nydia's blindness is made apparent by her closed eyes. Her staff allows her to negotiate her way through the "masses of ruin," suggested by a fallen Corinthian capital. Her left hand gestures to brush away ashes "with a slight tremor." The spiraling, unstable pose of Nydia's body, the movement implied by her agitated draperies, and the position of her walking stick all serve to animate this work and suggest that we are witnessing a moment of great urgency. Indeed, like many of the Italian baroque statues it emulates, *Nydia* seems to imply that other activity, although unseen, is taking place. The complex draperies alternate in function between revealing her body beneath and suggesting frantic, stumbling movement with its nervous rhythms and deeply undercut folds. This sense of urgency, communicated in large part by flowing draperies, also recalls baroque statues of pathetic young women placed in narrative contexts, such as Ercole Ferrata's *Saint Agnes on the Pyre* in the church of Sant'Agnese in Piazza Navona, Rome (1660).

AUGUSTUS SAINT-GAUDENS

9.   *Amor Caritas*

> bronze, original models 1880–98
> height: 40 inches
> width: 18 inches
> Museum of Art, Rhode Island School of Design. 48.352
> Signed and dated: *Augustus Saint-Gaudens/*MDCCCLXXX
> Inscribed on tablet: AMOR CARITAS
> Foundry mark: *E. Gruet, Jeune, Fondeur*

This figure is closely related to a number of elegantly draped female figures with up-raised arms which Saint-Gaudens used in a variety of circumstances at different times in his career. The earliest are the angels for the tomb commissioned by E. D. Morgan of Hartford, 1879–80, which was never realized. These were subsequently reworked as caryatids for a mantel, 1881–83 (now at the Metropolitan Museum), in the mansion built for Cornelius Vanderbilt II in New York at Fifth Avenue and Fifty-seventh Street, designed by George B. Post. Twice they were reused and slightly modified in the context of commissioned tombs: the Smith Tomb, Island Cemetery in Newport, Rhode Island, in 1887, and the Mitchell Memorial, St. Stephen's Church, Philadelphia, in 1902. Although the piece is best known as an independent relief, with the figure of the angel either life size (including a cast in the Musée d'Orsay in Paris, an extraordinary honor to be accorded an American sculptor) or – more commonly – in reduction as here, the fact that

9

Saint-Gaudens retained the date of 1880 for the inscription on all of these indicates that he associated his conception of *Amor Caritas* with the project for the Morgan Tomb.

This relief is based on a complex interaction between the standing figure; the architectural niche in which she stands; her wings, which overlap the confines of the niche and even break through the boundary implied by its outer reaches; and the rectangular, richly ornamented frame that encases the inscription in Latin, which translates, "Love Charity." This conceptual device, in which boundaries are exceeded and levels of reality overlap, can be traced back to Florentine quattrocento sculpture, particularly to Donatello in such works as the Cavalcanti *Annunciation* relief in the Church of Santa Croce, Florence. Saint-Gaudens understood the expressive urgency that results when boundaries are broken in this manner, and exploited it – knowingly, but with great restraint.

He also understood how to play ornament, drapery folds, and stark simplicity against each other to achieve maximum visual impressiveness. The angel's basically straightforward, symmetrical pose is animated by the infinitely complex treatment of drapery folds and the floral garlands encircling her head and hips. The angel's elegant, long neck and striking, classical beauty record the features of Davida Clark, who was both the model for the figure and Saint-Gaudens's mistress.

10.   *Ceres* [color plate, p. ii]

> mixed media (wood, copper, semiprecious stone), 1882
> height: 62¾ inches
> width: 25¼ inches
> U.S. Department of Interior National Park Service, Saint-Gaudens National Historic Site,
>   Cornish, N.H. Gift of the Augustus Saint-Gaudens Memorial, 1979. 2527

This splendid relief was made after a design by John La Farge for the palatial dining room of the Vanderbilt Mansion in Manhattan. It was moved to an upstairs billiards room during a renovation of the house. Moved to the Hungarian Embassy (Washington, D.C.) when the building was demolished in 1925, it reappeared on the art market in 1979. *Ceres* was one of four mixed-media reliefs of the same size made for the Vanderbilt dining room; the other three – representing Acteon, Bacchus, and Pomona – have all disappeared.

This relief proves that Saint-Gaudens could balance the competing demands of a predetermined design, the need to harmonize with a decorative ensemble, and the integrity of his artistic vision. He did not choose the four standing pagan deities (indeed, it is hard to imagine any iconographic concept – except the desire to astonish impressionable guests – that underlay their choice), and he did not design their general format, but he put his personal stamp on their appearance, nevertheless. The poses are generically classical, but the richness of surface nuances of both figure and background is recognizably his own. The various materials – different hues of wood, copper, semiprecious stones,

10

and mother-of-pearl – are combined according to a sensibility keenly attuned to coloristic effect. This is nineteenth-century multimedia work in three dimensions at its finest.

HORSES, NOT EQUESTRIANS

ORSES HAVE BEEN a frequent motif in Western sculpture from antiquity onward, but they are more likely to appear as impressive accoutrements for human beings than as creatures of intrinsic interest. In public sculpture, horses most often draw chariots or serve as the mounts for individuals of great importance. The unambiguous purpose of an equestrian statue is to commemorate the rider, while the horse is an enhancement to human fame and distinction. The best-known, large-scale horses that do not carry illustrious riders – the splendid gilt quartet that for centuries surmounted the entrance facade of Saint Mark's in Venice – were surely not conceived as an independent group (as they have been seen since they were brought as booty from Constantinople early in the thirteenth century) but as part of an ensemble that included a chariot and its driver.

During the romantic movement of the later eighteenth and early nineteenth centuries, there was an intense interest in horses, which continued throughout the century. Rather than well-trained, obedient beasts carrying the mighty and famous, horses often appear in a wild state, as victims of other animals, as components in ensembles of combat, or as highly anthropomorphic creatures. The ultimate anthropomorphism in equine representation occurs with that composite man-beast, the centaur. These creatures, so easily seen as metaphors for the conflicting bestial and spiritual aspects of human nature, were very popular as artistic motifs. Frequently shown in combat with men or ravishing women, they have an ancestry that can be traced back to the pediments and metopes of Greek temples. In this exhibition, we have one centaur who abducts a female victim (Carrier-Belleuse, *Abduction of Hippodamia*, cat. no. 12), another who is about to die at the hand of a hero (Barye, *Theseus Combating the Centaur Biénor*, cat. no. 11), and a third who appears alone in the aftermath of battle, wounded and about to expire (Von Stuck, *Wounded Centaur*, cat. no. 16).

There is a natural array of horse types, ranging from the most humble beast of burden to the most elegant and graceful purebred. Until the nineteenth century, the former category was unknown in the realm of sculpture. One of the most eloquent examples of this new motif has been included (Rimmer, *Inkstand with Horse Pulling a Stone-Laden Cart*, cat. no. 15). By contrast, a horse can be the embodiment of elegance and beauty, a candidate for idealistic representation and allegorical significance (Falguière, *Pegasus Carrying the Poet toward the Realm of Dreams*, cat. no. 14). Pegasus is shown in a pose of balletic refinement, about to leave earthly constraints behind and ascend into the heavens, taking an artist with him into the higher spheres. Degas's *Rearing Horse* (cat. no. 13) also raises two front legs while resting on two hind ones, but this sculpture is not about imminent ascent. The pose is so precarious that it could not be sustained beyond an instant and seems to presuppose a photographic source. This horse is physically lithe and beautiful, but the pose has the ungainliness that often accompanies hyper-realist depiction.

Antoine-Louis Barye

11. *Theseus Combating the Centaur Biénor*

bronze, original model before 1850
height: 13½ inches
width: 15¼ inches
depth: 7½ inches
Wadsworth Atheneum, Hartford. Gift of Samuel P. Avery. 20.980
Signed: *A. L. Barye* (left front of base)

11

Excluded from the Salon since the late 1830s, Barye participated once again in the official government exhibitions after the administrative reforms of 1848. He sent two contrasting pieces to the Salon of 1850: the *Jaguar Devouring a Hare* and *Theseus Combating the Centaur Biénor*. The former was a reprise of his first major success with a scene of animal violence, the *Tiger Devouring a Gavial of the Ganges* in 1831. Once again, the hunt and kill are over, and the predator is consuming his prey. For the *Theseus*, however, the struggle is presented at its climax. The protagonists are not animals, but a mortal fighting a creature that is half-man and half-beast.

With this work Barye made learned references to the histories of literature and sculpture. He chose the account from Ovid's *Metamorphoses* in which Theseus kills Biénor with a club while riding on his back during the battle of the Lapiths and Centaurs. Without quoting any of the Lapith-Centaur reliefs from the metopes of the Parthenon (the Elgin Marbles in the British Museum, London) directly, Barye nevertheless alludes to several of them in his dramatic composition. Theseus thrusts back Biénor's head and torso as he is about to deliver the death blow; the doomed centaur struggles in horror and opens his mouth with a scream of pain; in a futile gesture that implies surrender, Biénor raises his left front leg and curls his left hoof back toward his body. These details are borrowed from Giovanni da Bologna's *Hercules and the Centaur Nessus*, 1594, on the Loggia dei Lanzi in Florence.

The plaster *Theseus and Biénor* shown at the Salon of 1850 was fifty inches high, and a number of the subsequent bronze casts are that size. In his catalogue of 1855 Barye also offered for sale a smaller version, which he called "a study" that was the same size as the bronze cast included here. In fact, this version has the character of a study when compared with the final version, in which details are more fully realized and in which there is an elaborate cluster of evergreen on the rock beneath the centaur's body. This cast was one of twenty-four bronzes by Barye that Samuel Avery – a great enthusiast and collector of his work – gave to the Wadsworth Atheneum. He must have particularly admired the *Theseus*; he also gave a full-size cast of the same image to the Metropolitan Museum.

12.   *Abduction of Hippodamia*

bronze, original model after 1874
height: 25¼ inches
width: 21¾ inches
depth: 11⅚ inches
Collection of Fred and Meg Licht

12

This dramatic group, recalling the animated abduction imagery of the sixteenth and seventeenth centuries, is a variant on a model made earlier by Carrier-Belleuse, executed in solid silver by Christofle and awarded by the Jockey Club in 1874. These prizes given by the club were *pièces uniques* and could not subsequently be edited by the artist. Carrier-Belleuse therefore transformed aspects of the composition within the framework of its fundamental conception before editing it. Most significantly, Hippodamia was moved from a nearly vertical position, with her head higher than the centaur's, to a nearly horizontal pose at his right side. This modification necessitated a realignment of the centaur's arms and shoulders; the sculptor also reworked the man-beast's head and made the title less specific: *Abduction*, rather than *Abduction of Hippodamia*.

EDGAR DEGAS

13.   *Rearing Horse*

> bronze, original model probably late 1880s; cast, 1919–32
> height: 12⅛ inches
> width: 8¼ inches
> depth: 10¼ inches
> Sterling and Francine Clark Art Institute, Williamstown, Massachusetts. 569

This is the most animated of Degas's sculpted horses. The animal not only rears but also twists dramatically, creating a neo-baroque spiral about the central axis of its body and enlivening the space penetrated by its forms. The balance seems precarious, and the action depicted could not be sustained beyond an instant.

Among Degas's horses, this one must have required the most complex structural underpinnings to maintain its forms aloft. It is now generally believed that the horse sculptures were all done during the 1880s (although John Rewald has maintained that some were done as early as the 1860s). Charles Millard argued that they were made after Degas became aware of the motion studies of the American photographer Eadweard Muybridge, whose work on animal locomotion was known in France from 1878 onward. The horses may also provide an example of a minor artist providing the initial idea that a great one later brings to fruition. Joseph Cuvelier, who died in 1871, was a friend of Degas who specialized in wax figures of horses, which were exhibited at the Salon during the period 1865–70.

13

ALEXANDRE FALGUIÈRE

14.   *Pegasus Carrying the Poet toward the Realm of Dreams*

bronze, original model 1897

height: 32½ inches

width: 26½ inches

diameter of circular self-base: 15 inches

Mead Art Museum, Amherst College. Museum Purchase. 1974.2

Provenance: Heim Gallery Ltd. (London)

14

This is a reduction of the over-life-size group that dominates the square de l'Opéra, rue Boudreau, immediately to the west of the Palais Garnier, which was the primary opera house in Paris between 1875 and the recent opening of the Bastille Opéra. The group was first exhibited at the Salon of 1897 and installed in situ later that same year. It remains one of the most beautifully situated nineteenth-century sculptures in a public space in Paris, but it is an urban ornament and space modulator rather than a traditional monument to an idea or an individual.

This complex group grew from a conception that Falguière had first envisioned for the Monument to Victor Hugo on the place Victor Hugo in the sixteenth arrondissement of Paris (Ernest Barrias eventually received that commission). It belongs to the visual language of apotheosis frequently associated with Victor Hugo, especially after the writer's death in 1885. The specific image of a nude youth astride a winged horse balanced on its back legs seems to derive from Dalou, who had sent a very large plaster sketch for a proposed monument to Hugo to the Salon of 1886. In it he depicted the poet's corpse lying in state under a triumphal arch (echoing the placement of Hugo's remains under the Arc de Triomphe de l'Étoile the day before his state funeral) and a group with a winged horse and rider in virtually the same pose that Falguière would later use at the top center of the arch. In the memorial exhibition held at the École des Beaux-Arts two years after Falguière's death, two of his sketches for this projected Hugo monument were included (as nos. 120 and 158).

The identification of Pegasus' rider poses some difficulty. When exhibited in *Monuments for the Middle Class* in Louisville in 1971, he was called "Bellerophon" and entered Amherst's collection with the same name. When the group was first exhibited in 1897, however, it was entitled *Pegasus Carrying the Poet toward the Realm of Dreams*. The rider has also been identified as Apollo. Either of these makes more sense in the context of Pegasus and apotheosis than Bellerophon. The Muses, who inspired poets among other mortal creators, were entrusted with the care of Pegasus, and Apollo was the Muses' guardian, so either a "poet" or Apollo might well be represented astride the mythical beast. By contrast, Bellerophon's association with Pegasus was a problematic mixture of success and failure. He had captured the winged horse and rode him while killing the Chimera, but when he attempted to ascend to the heavens on the horse's back, Pegasus threw him off, and ascended alone. If Falguière had intended the rider to be Bellerophon, his creation's subject would have been imminent disaster rather than ascent or apotheosis, and this seems unlikely, given the circumstances under which it was conceived.

WILLIAM RIMMER

15.   *Inkstand with Horse Pulling a Stone-Laden Cart*

soapstone, c. 1830

height: 6¼ inches

width: 17 inches

depth: 9¼ inches

Middlebury College Museum of Art. Purchase, with funds provided by the Christian A. Johnson Memorial Fund. 1988.133

Signed: *W. Rimmer* (at back, below horse's right front leg)

Provenance: unknown private dealer (Boston); S. Grant Waters (Kingsville, Md.); Sotheby's, New York (auction, Dec. 1, 1988, lot 85)

15

The *Horse Pulling a Stone-Laden Cart* may well be Rimmer's first work of sculpture. It cannot be precisely dated, but it probably predates the *Seated Man* (see cat. no. 22). The format of inkwell sculpture is part of the craft tradition of the nineteenth century; it would later be carried to heights of imaginative extravagance by the famed actress-sculptor, Sarah Bernhardt. The very young Rimmer created a practical, utilitarian object, but the conceptual and dramatic brilliance of the piece raises it to a far higher plane of sophistication. This tabletop sculpture forms an environment, with the suggestion of a large rock (with a moveable top that conceals an inkwell, as does the burden loaded into the cart), muddy terrain, and even a body of water (the flat surface where pens could be laid).

The horse is the most intriguing aspect of this environment. He is a powerfully anthropomorphic presence with overtones of tragedy. He struggles with his burden like an equestrian Sisyphus, and that struggle seems wholly self-generated, since we detect no human presence that forces him onward. He labors heroically, as if that is his destiny – and he comprehends it.

74

Franz von Stuck

16. *Wounded Centaur*

bronze, original model c. 1890
height: 14 inches (figure), 4 inches (self-base)
width: 12¾ inches
depth: 4 inches
Mead Art Museum, Amherst College. Museum Purchase. 1973.5
Signed: *Franz von Stuck* (incised)
Founder's mark: *Guss C. Leyrer. Munchen*
Provenance: Shepherd Gallery Associates (New York)

16

The *Wounded Centaur* constituted Stuck's impressive debut as a sculptor. Although the work was conceived with a principal viewpoint as if it were a relief (none of the alternative views are as satisfactory), it nonetheless communicates a heightened sense of drama through three-dimensional form. The surfaces read as taut skin stretched over the straining muscles of this man-beast writhing in agony, and the twist of the human torso forcefully projects his pain into three dimensions. An interest in mythology and mythological composite creatures often manifested itself at the fin de siècle as artists influenced by symbolism sought to uncover universal meanings beneath surface appearances. This centaur's pathos and waning energy recall the drama of Arnold Böcklin's huge canvas the *Battle of the Centaurs* (1873, Kunstmuseum Basel), and we know that Stuck was impressed by Böcklin's work.

Stuck's *Centaur* was conceived as a unit with its base, which forms a volumetric near-equivalent to the figure itself. This support is a superbly designed architectural form which recalls that Stuck's interests crossed the usual boundaries of artistic media and welcomed synthesis among them. The rhythmic variations of pure horizontals and horizontals enlivened with repeated leaf forms are subtly integrated with the principal geometric volume of the base, and this whole serves as an effective foil for the dramatic figure which rests upon it.

NUDES

THE UNCLOTHED human body evokes a range of emotions and associations that seems limitless, and probably all of them have, at one time or another, entered into the conception of works of sculpture. Deprived of clothing, the body can be seen as repulsive or alluring, threatening or reassuring, a vessel of shame or a vehicle of celebration. Given such polarities, a particular response depends on the context, the individual, and the society in question.

What is crucial when confronting a specific work of art, which also happens to be the depiction of an unclothed body, is an understanding of the forces that are at work. Sometimes the subject itself demands partial or total undress. For example, full revelation of the body, including the sex organs, has been widely permitted and regarded as acceptable (even within churches) when depicting Adam and Eve before the Fall. It would be unthinkable to depict Christ undressed at the Last Supper during any era but equally unorthodox to show him clothed on the cross from the medieval era onward. When the text – especially a biblical text – from which a narrative situation is derived, requires full or partial revelation of the body, ample justification exists for creating such an image.

Once this generalization has been made, immediate qualification is in order. Even within the same culture and city, attitudes change. Eighteenth-century Florentines were so horrified by their ancestors' acceptance of the unclothed human form that the marble Adam and Eve that had long been displayed on the high altar of the cathedral were taken down, and in other churches offending pudenda were covered with painted fig leaves. In general, however, from the Renaissance onward, the Mediterranean world (excluding Spain) has been more tolerant than northern Europe, and France more so than England.

All undressed figures are not interchangeable. There are naked ones, and there are nude ones. This is one of the most crucial – but also one of the most difficult – distinctions in Western art. Total revelation of the human form has usually been regarded as acceptable when the figure is a nude, but frowned on – or even forbidden – if the unclothed state is perceived as nakedness. Basically, a nude has a sufficient degree of idealization to distinguish it from the appearance of a real-life figure who has disrobed. This idealized state of undress must be made to seem the figure's natural condition, and the artist's generalization of forms should make the figure conform to an intellectually determined norm of beauty. The resulting nude figure therefore exists outside the realm of lustful thoughts and erotic sensations. Needless to say, this theoretical distinction can prove wholly academic in the presence of a "nude" statue, and the justification made to seem like institutionalized hypocrisy. People do enjoy, and always have enjoyed, looking at other human beings undressed, especially if the person is beautiful, and viewing a nude statue can be a pleasurable surrogate experience.

The artistic issues associated with the nude expand with exponential complexity. Adam and Eve before the Fall should be shown nude, in a state of edenic purity, unaware of – and unfazed by – their lack of body covering. But after the Fall, their partially covered state should to some degree suggest that they are naked, because of their sin and resulting shame. In general, any figure shown unclothed demands an artistic treatment that is appropriate for the situation. There is the especially murky area of intrinsically erotic subjects, like representations of Venus, the goddess of love. If the artist idealizes her image too much and eradicates all traces of erotic allure, then he or she has denatured the subject; if the erotic possibilities are explored with too much relish, the resulting image is almost certain to cause offense. Artists themselves have responded to the nude in highly personal ways, some by avoiding the issue altogether and others by becoming specialists, but most with enthusiasm for occasionally undertaking one of the most enduring challenges in the art of sculpture.

Nineteenth-century sculptors treated the nude with an extraordinary variety of approaches, ranging from the typical circumspection of neoclassical idealization to an erotic frankness and explicitness which exceeded that of any previous era. Because nude statues carry so much historical and associational resonance, they were often used as the vehicle for especially daring experiments in formal invention and expressiveness. The old-master sculptors of the past had left a legacy of nude figures against which virtually all sculptors wished to measure their own accomplishments.

Two marble nudes, one male (Gibson's *Cupid Disguised as a Shepherd Boy*, cat. no. 17) and the other female (Ives's *Pandora*, cat. no. 18), are so similar in basic pose, material, and emotional remoteness that they form a logical starting point. Both can be characterized as "chaste nudes," with their idealized bodies and faces, the whiteness of material in which they were carved, and their downward gazes. Gibson and Ives consciously allied their work with the neoclassical aesthetic of the mid-eighteenth century, which had endured for more than a hundred years and inspired numerous artists throughout Europe and the United States.

By way of contrast, it is useful to compare a later idealized nude, Klinger's *Bathing Woman* (cat. no. 19). Even though the basic trend of nineteenth-century art was to break away from the formulaic solutions favored by neoclassicism, the principles of idealization lasted and were given new and sometimes surprising life later in the century. Here the forms themselves and the surfaces that contain them are no less generalized in the direction of ideal beauty than was true with Ives's *Pandora*, but their disposition proves that a new sensibility is at work, with the attenuation of limbs and torso and the unexpected urgency of pose.

Another original variant on the principle of idealization at the end of the century was the incorporation of archaic stylization. In Sargent's *Crucifix* for the Development of Religious Thought mural in the Boston Public Library (cat. no. 25), he subjected the nude corpus of Christ, as well as the bodies of Adam and Eve who collect his blood, to radical simplifications borrowed from Byzantine and medieval art, thereby evoking a particular era within Christianity's development.

Rimmer's *Seated Man* (cat. no. 22) is a milestone in American sculpture, almost certainly the first three-dimensional nude figure made in the United States. Because it was a private work and never exhibited during the artist's lifetime, it has ceded its precedence to nudes by Crawford and Powers. This seated male conveys such manic intensity and nervous energy that it has long been treated as if it had symbolic meaning. After it entered the collection of the Museum of Fine Arts, Boston, it acquired the spurious, but not inappropriate, title *Despair*.

With the anatomic specificity and wild abandon implied by MacMonnies's *Bacchante and Infant Faun* (cat. no. 20) we have an example of a nude that crossed the threshold from decorum to perceived indecency. In 1896 a cast of the life-size version was briefly installed in the courtyard of the new Boston Public Library, but had to be removed because of strenuous and vocal public protests. This nude is hardly chaste, idealized, or moralizing. Her face and body proclaim the specific features of a particular Parisian woman, a model with whom the sculptor was infatuated at the time he modeled her figure.

The three most aesthetically radical sculptures included in this exhibition are all male nudes. The earliest one (Rimmer's *Torso*, cat. no. 23) is the most astonishing. It is a self-sufficient fragment, created – or else recognized – as a finished work of sculpture by the artist, who signed and dated it. Without any awareness of Rodin's comparable explorations at the same time in Paris, Rimmer duplicated in Boston the most radical achievement of his day in redefining the art of sculpture. Rodin's *Balzac Nude* (cat. no. 24) broke virtually every rule applicable to nude statues. The heroic body and massive belly defy conventions of idealization, and ferocious energy – at once creative and sexual – seems to emanate from the figure and assault the viewer. By contrast, Matisse's *The Serf* (cat. no. 21) withdraws into itself and becomes a self-sufficient entity that bears little connection with its title or with mimetic imitation of an actual body.

17.   *Cupid (Disguised as a Shepherd Boy)*

marble, original model early 1830s

height: 51 inches

width: 17½ inches at widest point

Fogg Art Museum, Harvard University. Anonymous Gift. 1940.50

Provenance: purchase from artist by Mr. Farnum in 1850; Mary Ellis Farnum; private collection; on loan to the Metropolitan Museum of Art (New York) from 1883 until 1937

17

This is one of the numerous classical themes Gibson executed in Rome. The pose is frequently encountered in classical statues, but – in appropriating it – he made numerous small adjustments and enlivened the surfaces with hints of inner life. In this respect he revealed himself as Canova's heir to a greater degree than he was Thorvaldsen's. The figure type, the gently animated pose and surfaces, the curling cascade of hair in ringlets, and the dreamy sensuousness all foreshadow the *Narcissus* of 1838, his reception piece for the Royal Academy. *Cupid Disguised as a Shepherd* was so popular that Gibson had at least seven replicas carved in marble for eager patrons.

CHAUNCEY IVES

18. *Pandora*

> marble, 1875; original model 1851; reworked 1863
> height: 40 inches
> width: 11 inches
> depth: 10½ inches
> St. Johnsbury Athenaeum. Purchase. 73
> Signed, dated, and inscribed: C. B. IVES FECIT/ROMAE 1875 (right side of base)
> Provenance: Tiffany & Co. (New York)

The initial work on *Pandora* dates from the end of Ives's stay in Florence, but the marble versions of it were all made in Rome. The figure was much admired, and at least thirty replicas were carved, some life size and others half-life size, like this version. Contemporaries often compared *Pandora* favorably with Hiram Powers's *Greek Slave.* The nude is beautifully posed, and the contrasting drapery serves as enhancing counter-rhythm to the rounded curves of her body.

Ives isolated a moment filled with significance in the story of Pandora. So there could be no ambiguity about his intentions, he included the following text when the statue was exhibited:

> Pandora was sent by Jove to Prometheus, with a jar containing all the evils of life. . . . She was equipped by the gods with every charm. . . . Pandora was charged by Jove not to open the jar, but being seized with curiosity, she cautiously raised the lid, and at once there issued forth all the ills that beset mankind in body and in soul. Hastening to close the jar, she saved only hope which lay at the bottom, and thus, though a victim of every evil, man ever retains hope.

18

The "significant moment," then, is the one when Pandora decides to make the fateful gesture that will unleash the "ills that beset mankind." Although her pose is somewhat static, the statue is animated by this pregnant moment in the mythic narrative.

Max Klinger

19.   *Bathing Woman*

bronze, original model 1898

height: 24½ inches

width: 9⅛ inches

depth: 7½ inches

Mead Art Museum, Amherst College. Gift of Prof. Charles H. Morgan. 1973.4

Signed: MK (on support for right leg)

Foundry mark: *AKT[IEN]GES[ELLSCHAFT]/GLADENBECK/FRIEDRICHSHAGEN*
   (on self-base)

Provenance: Shepherd Gallery Associates (New York)

19

In this statue Klinger combined classical idealization of features and surfaces with expressive elongation and an unusual pose. The result of these contradictory impulses is a nude figure that communicates with considerable urgency. Klinger's work is never about simple repose or uncomplicated emotions, so this urgency can be seen as typical. The internal spiral around which the forms are organized recalls the complexities of Italian mannerist sculpture, and the compression that results from the nude's strange gesture of stretching one arm behind her to grasp the left hand is typical of contemporary symbolist sculpture.

She raises her right leg to an exaggerated height, once again emphasizing that everyday expectations have been exceeded. Although not as extreme as some of Rodin's poses, this figure does recall one on *The Gates of Hell*, about two-thirds of the way up the right door on the far right. As early as 1885, Klinger had expressed admiration for Rodin's work. It is tempting to think that here he adapted one of Rodin's poses to his very different expressive needs. This nude was first exhibited in Vienna, as a marble. The firm of Gladenbeck edited it in bronze of three different sizes; this is the intermediate one.

FREDERICK MACMONNIES

20. *Bacchante and Infant Faun*

> bronze, original model 1893
> height: 34⅜ inches
> diameter at self-base: 9½ inches
> Loaned by The Bennington Museum, Bennington, Vermont.
>   Bequest of Col. Joseph H. Colyer, Jr.
> Signed and dated: *F. MacMonnies/1894* (right side, top of base)
> Foundry mark: *E. Gruet, Paris* (back of base)

MacMonnies's *Bacchante* was a cause célèbre in late-nineteenth-century American art. In 1894 he exhibited the over-life-size group at the Salon in Paris (the French government purchased it later in the year, the first sculpture by an American so honored) and gave the first bronze cast of it to Charles McKim, the partner in McKim, Mead and White, the architectural firm that built the Boston Public Library. When McKim offered it to the library for installation in its neo-Renaissance courtyard, trouble developed. The statue was installed in 1896, but a public outcry over its alleged immorality forced its removal. McKim subsequently donated the cast to the Metropolitan Museum.

The *Bacchante* demonstrates MacMonnies's formal and conceptual exuberance at its

20

best. Just as his first full figure, a *Diana*, in 1889, had been a homage to his master Falguière's nude statue of the same goddess (marble exhibited at the Salon of 1887), his
Bacchante – balanced on one foot and caught in vigorous movement – evoked Falguière's first public success, the *Victor of the Cock Fight*, which had won honors at the
Salon of 1864. This group also demonstrates MacMonnies's infatuation with a Parisian
studio model, Eugénie Pasque, who had posed for it. Her very features were celebrated,

rather than hidden under a cloak of idealization; like Falguière, MacMonnies understood the appeal that the sculpted bodies of specific women, rather than chaste abstractions, held for late-nineteenth-century viewers. His characterization was wholly appropriate for a bacchante, but it did not amuse Boston's prudish guardians of morality. Bacchantes were, after all, followers of Dionysus and celebrants of wild revelry. She seems wholly inebriated, and the child she holds in one arm – while offering him grapes – has the glazed look of an imbiber, as well. This celebration of excessive drink and uninhibited, naked abandon has a giddy, pagan joy to it.

As has frequently been true in the modern era, objections to perceived immorality in art can backfire; controversies generate publicity, and the art work in question becomes widely known. In the case of the *Bacchante*, an already distinguished work was brought to the attention of a much wider audience than might otherwise have been aware of it. The many replicas of it attest to its popularity. At full size, it exists in bronze and marble. Multiple bronze casts of it exist in three reduced sizes; the cast exhibited here is the largest of those reductions.

Henri Matisse

21. *The Serf*

> bronze, original model 1900, with subsequent reworkings
> height: 36½ inches
> width: 12¾ inches
> depth: 11¼ inches
> Fogg Art Museum, Harvard University. Purchase, Alpheus Hyatt Fund. 1953.42
> Signed and inscribed: HM 10/10 (left rear, top of base); *Le Serf* (front center)
> Foundry mark: *Valsuani/cire perdue* (left rear)
> Provenance: Curt Valentin Gallery (New York)

At the turn of the century, Matisse was redefining his art, and this involved turning away from the landscapes and still lifes that had occupied him in the recent past and concentrating on the figure. This sculpture of a male nude was a significant aspect of the transformation. Although there are no preliminary, three-dimensional studies for *The Serf*, Matisse did a drawing and at least two oil paintings, using the same professional model who posed for the statue, an Italian immigrant named Bevilaqua. This man, previously known as Pignatelli, had been Rodin's model for *Saint John the Baptist* over twenty years before he posed for Matisse. Since the *Walking Man* by Rodin – with which Matisse's

21

Serf is regularly and fruitfully compared – is itself a variant on the *Saint John*, we have an instance of the same model posing for two seminal pieces of sculpture, the later one being at least in part a meditation on the former. The *Walking Man* was first shown at Rodin's place de l'Alma exhibition of 1900, and its dimensions were very close to the size Matisse chose to model his *Serf*.

Although Matisse named the sculpture and inscribed its title on the base, "The Serf" counts for little when we analyze the work and its content. The powerful body, unapologetically shown in late middle age, suggests a peasant who has done manual labor all his life, but there is no narrative or iconographic detail to connect the statue with its title (unlike Dalou's *Old Peasant* – cast in plaster the previous year – who is easily identifiable by his clothing, wooden clogs, work tool, and gesture of rolling up his sleeve before setting to work; cat. no. 4). This rupture between works of art and narrative or symbolic significance is one of the commonplaces of modern art. It happened earlier in painting, and Rodin had led the way in sculpture; for Matisse this severing of ties was crucial to the conception of *The Serf*.

This work does not make any associations with issues or ideas. The statue is not about serfdom, justice or injustice, the gods, or the affairs of men. It is about its own existence and its own expressiveness. Matisse once explained, referring to a model who was probably Bevilaqua: "If I have an Italian model who at first appearance suggests nothing but a purely animal existence, I nevertheless discover his essential qualities, I see amid the lines of his face those which suggest the deep gravity which persists in every human being. A work of art must carry within itself its complete significance and impose that upon the beholder even before he recognizes the subject." *The Serf* communicates "essentialness" without psychological probing or even any emphasis on "animal existence."

The pose is relaxed but unmistakably "arranged," and the body's relationship to gravity is wholly believable. Proportionally and anatomically, the figure seems normal; at first we do not notice the exaggerated size of the head relative to the body or the fact that his arms terminate above the nonexistent elbows. The muscular body is deprived of any heroic allusion by the emphatically nonheroic pose; the downward gaze, slouched shoulders, and thrust of the hips which emphasizes the belly all serve a single expressive purpose. It seems that Matisse has raised that "deep gravity" he described to the level of a principle and then found the formal means to communicate it. We know that the process of modeling this sculpture was inordinately long, as Matisse worked from the human figure and tried to grasp what was essential.

The starting point for the swelling sculptural forms and recesses is Bevilaqua's muscular body, but the surfaces do not read as skin, and the rounded protuberances do not emulate muscles or flesh. Matisse did not attempt mimetic exactitude, nor did he seek communication at the level of rhetoric. He achieved a wholeness in which forms are completely integrated, and the expressiveness is their sum total, nothing more or less.

It should be added that the truncated arms, which seem so essential to the statue's unity, were not part of the initial conception. In a photograph taken perhaps as late as 1908, Matisse posed in his studio next to *The Serf*, which still had fully modeled arms. Clearly, Matisse – following Rodin's example – believed that achieving a wholeness of integrated expression was a dynamic process and that truncation was a viable option, even long after apparent resolution had been achieved.

22. *Seated Man (Despair)*

gypsum with bronzed paint, 1831

height: 10¼ inches

width: 7¾ inches

depth: 4 inches

Museum of Fine Arts, Boston. Gift of Mrs. Henry Simonds. 20.210

Signed and dated: *W. Rimmer/1831* (back of base); *W. R.* (right side of base)

Provenance: C. H. Rimmer (Belmont, Mass.); E. R. D. Simonds (South Milford, Mass.); lent to
MFA in 1916

22

It is astonishing that a work as technically assured and emotionally complex as this one was carved by an untrained fifteen-year-old. The figure and his anguish were apparently inspired by young William's father, Thomas. This troubled man always believed that he was the Dauphin of France; his lifelong delusions and paranoia descended into madness prior to his death, nineteen years after this statuette was made.

This nude figure was made ten years before Hiram Powers began his *Greek Slave* and is almost certainly the first nude figure created by an American sculptor. Since it was not intended as a public piece and was never exhibited during Rimmer's lifetime, the *Seated Man* remained an unknown phenomenon and had no contemporary influence on other artists. The pose may be a reference to the damned soul at the lower right in Michelangelo's *Last Judgment* (Sistine Chapel), but if this is so, the composition has nevertheless been thoroughly assimilated and reinterpreted; it is no simple quotation. With the knees drawn inward toward the torso – the right more extremely than the left – and the arms tensely hugging the contours of the figure seen head-on, this pose anticipates the self-referential ones favored by symbolist sculptors, such as Minne, at the fin de siècle. The knotted muscles of the man's legs and bulging veins of his arms suggest hysterical tensions which reduce the figure to catatonic immobility. Young Rimmer seems to have comprehended, through intuition and by observation of his unfortunate father, that mental illness can manifest itself in frighteningly tangible ways.

23. *Torso*

> plaster, 1877
> height: 11¼ inches
> width: 14½ inches
> depth: 7½ inches
> Museum of Fine Arts, Boston. Bequest of Caroline Hunt Rimmer. 19.128
> Signed and dated: *W. Rimmer 1877* (top of base at front)
> Provenance: C. H. Rimmer (Belmont, Mass.)

This is Rimmer's final sculpture. At the time it was made, he was teaching anatomy at the newly founded School of Drawing and Painting associated with the Museum of Fine Arts, Boston. His treatise, *Art Anatomy*, illustrated with nine hundred of his own anatomical drawings, was also published in 1877. Whether this was an object that he intended as a teaching device in the lecture hall or as a finished work of sculpture is not entirely clear. The fact that he signed and dated it suggests that, even if it were not his original intention, he eventually understood the work's power and self-sufficiency as an art object.

This torso reverberates with art-historical references. Fragments of antique sculpture were common sights in the Western world's great museums, and plaster casts of them were staples of art-school paraphernalia during the nineteenth century. Rimmer's created fragment bears a striking resemblance to two of the famed Elgin Marbles from the Parthenon, brought to London earlier in the century. It also recalls the torso of Michelangelo's Adam from the Sistine Chapel ceiling. What separates the *Torso* from any of these antecedents, however, is the palpable, throbbing vitality that emanates from it. The surfaces are not refined and smooth but craggy and animated by the artist's touch. During 1877–78, Rodin also created his first roughly modeled, self-sufficient torso (bronze cast, Musée du Petit Palais, Paris); these two art-historical phenomena occurred independently, serving as harbingers of the future for the history of sculpture.

23

24.   *Balzac Nude (Study for the Monument to Balzac)*

bronze, original model 1892

height: 50¼ inches

width: 20½ inches

depth: 24¾ inches

Museum of Art, Rhode Island School of Design. Purchase, Museum Associates and donations
from Museum Members. 66.057

Foundry mark: *Rodin orig/Alexis Rudier/Fondeur/Paris* (right side of base)

Provenance: Galerie Beyler (Basel); G. David Thompson (New York); Parke-Bernet, New York
(auction, May 23–24, 1966, lot 18)

The story of the *Monument to Balzac* comprises one of the great litanies of modern art:
Rodin's commission in 1891 with the help of Zola – the president of the Société des Gens
de Lettres, the agonizingly slow and difficult creative process which followed, the masterpiece which resulted – only to be rejected in 1898 by the very society that had commissioned it. (All of this occurred with glaring publicity and became intertwined with
the explosive political and racial tensions that surrounded the Dreyfus Affair.) The final
monument, which Rodin never saw cast in bronze, has become a ubiquitous presence
for all those who study or create sculpture in its aftermath. There will be no attempt here
to recount that history one more time. An early stage in Rodin's creative process has
been chosen and isolated – the "nude Balzac with folded arms" – which is arguably the
most powerful of his conceptions for the statue prior to the final one.

Although Rodin presented this version to the Société for their examination in 1892,
he may never have intended that a nude statue be considered for the final monument.
The pose and physical type were paramount at this stage of the conception, and these
would be more clearly apparent without the distracting presence of modern dress or
some other sort of covering drapery. "Shocking" and "deformed" were words applied to
the image by the society's members. Rodin did not pursue this conception further, and
he abandoned the pose altogether. In the final figure presented in 1898, Balzac is clothed,
his body less corpulent, and his pose less pugnaciously physical.

It has long been recognized that the nude Balzac with his arms crossed is a brilliant
synthesis of naturalist description and symbolic characterization. As his champion Zola
did when preparing to write novels and short stories, Rodin gathered factual information as he conducted his "research." He knew Balzac's appearance from a daguerreotype
and from a long tradition of visual representations, but he also traveled to Balzac's na-

24

tive city of Tours, sought out men who had similar physical stature, and learned the precise dimensions of the writer's body by consulting his tailor, who was still alive. Rodin also immersed himself in Balzac's writings. He felt that he needed to know everything possible about the author as a physical and creative being in order to capture his essence in a statue.

Balzac was overweight, vain, and – by any conventional standard – ugly, but he communicated a great aura of physical presence. Rodin clearly wanted to find a correlative to that aura, but physical replication of appearance alone might have resulted in an image that was merely grotesque. Balzac was very large, but not muscular; his soft face and body and his elegant fingers made him appear rather feminine. Clearly, Rodin's rendition of him as an intensely physical nude is more of an interpretative analogue to Balzac's creative power than a recounting of his appearance. Albert Elsen has convincingly related this conception to the "athlete of virtue," which has a long iconographic tradition in Western art. The pose is aggressive and defiant, with wide-spread legs, powerful arms crossed and resting on a heroic belly, and a torsion-filled contrapposto that conveys ferocious latent energy. The skin that covers Balzac's body is stretched over his bulging muscles and fat with drumlike tautness, further emphasizing his superhuman status, as defined by his creativity.

The rough, pyramidal mound that rises from the base and attaches itself in places to Balzac's legs also culminates between his thighs and fuses with his sex organs. Surely Elsen is right when he claims that this was originally part of the mass of clay Rodin used to model the figure, but there is also an elemental, sexual suggestiveness to it. Erotic and creative potency were presented as interchangeable in other works by Rodin and in later versions of the Balzac, including the final one. That notion must be part of the conception of this figure, as well. Balzac's prodigious hunger for food and sex was as much part of his identity as was his prolific creativity. Rodin's statue belongs to that rare handful of sculptures in the Western tradition that communicate with elemental force the superhuman will or insatiable physical appetites of male subjects: Donatello's effigy of Coscia for the antipope's tomb in the Florence Baptistry, Michelangelo's bust of Brutus in the Bargello (Florence) or Moses for the Julius II tomb in San Pietro in Vincoli (Rome), and Bernini's bust of Scipione Borghese at Villa Borghese (Rome).

JOHN SINGER SARGENT

25. *Crucifix*

> bronze, original model 1898–99
>
> height: 29½ inches
>
> width: 20¼ inches
>
> depth: 2¼ inches
>
> U.S. Department of Interior National Park Service, Saint-Gaudens National Historical Site, Cornish, N.H. Gift of Mrs. Homer Saint-Gaudens, 1969. 1648

25

Sargent's three-dimensional rendition of a crucifix is the focal point of his mural *The Redemption*, on the third floor of the Boston Public Library. The style of the piece has a strong archaic aura, as he sought to evoke the Byzantine and medieval eras, but some of the iconography is so abstruse and private that it evokes the hermeticism of contemporary symbolist art. In 1895 Sargent wrote to a friend: "What a tiresome thing a perfectly clear symbol would be," and there was little danger that anyone would find his symbolism for this mural "tiresome."

95

Christ is attached to a cross that terminates in decorative quatrefoil shapes, like many crucifixes from the periods Sargent chose to evoke. Also typical is the presence of a pelican with its young, an age-old symbol for the blood sacrifice by which the redemption of humanity was won. Sargent, who had been born in Florence to expatriate American parents and who was trained and lived most of his life in Europe, knew these traditional motifs from continuous, firsthand experience in churches and museums. Two of them are quite unprecedented, however. Kneeling on either side of Christ are Adam and Eve, who hold chalices to collect the blood that issues forth from the hand wounds, a function invariably assigned to flying angels in traditional Christian art. The first man and woman are shown nude and in compressed, contorted poses, but there is a long shroud which entwines them and the Savior, uniting the three into a single rhythmic and thematic unit, encompassing the Fall and Redemption. A serpent is coiled at Christ's feet. This is surely Satan who has finally been overcome by Christ's sacrifice, but the motif is also an uncanny recollection of Horatio Greenough's paired busts of Christ and Satan, with serpents coiled about their plinths (these entered the collection of the Boston Public Library in 1895 just as Sargent was devising the iconography of the *Redemption* mural; see cat. nos. 60, 61). For the bust of Christ, Greenough had depicted the dead serpent with its head hanging downward, and Sargent borrowed this unusual motif for his crucifix.

We know that Saint-Gaudens had high regard for Sargent's atypical venture into the realm of three-dimensional art. He wrote to a friend in April 1899: "Sargent . . . came to see me about the enlargement of his Crucifixion for the Boston Library. It is in sculpture and is to go directly opposite the Moses. He has done a masterpiece." There are other bronze casts, including a nine-foot replica of the original, which was installed as Sargent's monument in the crypt of Saint Paul's, London. Saint-Gaudens's studio caster, Gaeton Ardison, was sent to London by the sculptor to assist Sargent in the work. Sargent responded by presenting one of the bronze reductions of the *Crucifix* to Saint-Gaudens.

CHILDREN AND NURSING MOTHERS

CHILDHOOD as an identifiable and separate state of human existence – interwoven with lofty sentiments concerning the child's innocence, purity, and vulnerability – was an intellectual construct of the nineteenth century. Images of children were produced in great numbers, and they cover a vast amount of emotional territory. Rarely does one encounter an ordinary child in sculpture before the later eighteenth century. There are endless cupids and putti, to be sure, but most treatments of children in earlier Western art involve archetypes, like the infant Jesus and Saint John the Baptist or the children nursed by Charity. Along with the nineteenth-century emphasis on children came a complementary concern for motherhood, resulting in numerous depictions of modern mothers and their children.

From the intimate, private joy at the birth of a child to the royal grief of Queen Victoria when her grandchildren died, the sentiments projected onto the depiction of children grew out of the sensibility of the era. Powers's paternal wonder after the birth of his first daughter was so great that he made a cast of her hand while she slept and modeled it emerging from a sunflower (*Loulie's Hand*, cat. no. 34). Today this work seems a bit surreal, and even creepy, but it is absolutely in keeping with the character of nineteenth-century emotional life. When Queen Victoria commissioned a private monument to commemorate her dead grandchildren, she chose Dalou to execute it. His first version, *Angel with Child* (cat. no. 27), depicts a single infant lovingly cradled by its angelic protector. As had been true in British funerary art since the later eighteenth century, there is no indication that the child is dead. The queen, whose name is synonymous with the age, preferred the euphemism of sleep, as was customary. The obverse of the celebration of sweetness and pathos was the indulgent depiction of mischievousness and childish misbehavior (within bounds, of course). The unruly sprite from *A Midsummer Night's Dream* was a popular motif, and no image of him is more engaging than Hosmer's *Puck on a Toadstool* (cat. no. 32).

A nursing mother is frequently encountered in the context of Madonna and Child imagery from the medieval era onward, but during the nineteenth century civilian mothers gained ascendency, even as representations of the Madonna became a rarity. Dalou was a prolific – and probably the greatest – creator of images of contemporary mothers who lovingly interact with their children; lactation is often his subject. His *Maternal Joy* (cat. no. 28) was an exceedingly popular statuary group during Dalou's lifetime, and long after. Charpentier's *Mother and Infant Boy* (cat. no. 26) suggests familiarity with Dalou's well-known work and serves as an inventive, personal variation on it. So universal was the belief in happy, fulfilling maternity that animal mothers were frequently

97

represented with their young as anthropomorphized equivalents of their human counterparts: Frémiet, *Cat Nursing Her Kittens* (cat. no. 30); Gott, *Greyhound with Her Two Puppies Suckling* (cat. no. 31); and Mène, *Sheep with Suckling Lamb* (cat. no. 33).

ALEXANDRE CHARPENTIER

26.   *Mother and Infant Boy*

        bronze, original model 1883, or later (modern frame)
        height: 18 inches
        width: 12½ inches
        Mead Art Museum, Amherst College. Wise Arts Council Purchase Fund. 1986.7
        Signed: *Alexandre Charpentier* (lower right)
        Provenance: David and Constance Yates (New York)

26

This is Charpentier's most engaging and communicative work. His point of departure seems to have been Dalou's contemporary nursing mothers done in England during the 1870s, but his rendering of the motif in relief constitutes a highly personal variation on a familiar theme. The foreshortening, especially that of the nursing baby, constitutes a virtuoso demonstration of Charpentier's sophistication in rendering illusionistic effects. His shallow relief was modulated with great concern for the optical sensations that would result. This is a rare instance in the later years of the nineteenth century of an artist – other than Saint-Gaudens – who explored such optical effects in relief.

At the Salon of 1883, Charpentier won an honorable mention for his plaster relief *Young Woman Nursing Her Child*, which was purchased by the state. On two other occasions Charpentier exhibited the piece again; in 1890 it was shown at the Salon in marble, and he again sent the plaster to the Exposition Universelle of 1900. In 1897 he also sent a plaster relief of a mother and child to the Salon, but it is not clear whether it was a variation on the relief exhibited in 1883. Nor is it is known whether the bronze casts were made from that original plaster or a variation of it.

JULES DALOU

27.   *Angel with Child*

> bronze, original model 1877–78
> height: 12¼ inches
> width: 4¾ inches
> depth: 4¹⁵⁄₁₆ inches
> Museum of Art, Rhode Island School of Design. Gift of Mrs. Henry D. Sharpe. 59.152
> Signed: *Dalou* (left side of base)
> Foundry mark: *CIRE/PERDUE/A. A. HEBRARD* (back of base)

This sculpture was the original conception for a monument commissioned by Queen Victoria to commemorate her dead grandchildren at the royal chapel in Windsor Castle. The sculptor had been recommended to the queen by her daughter Princess Louise, who was Dalou's pupil. He had clearly seen and remembered a terra-cotta sketch by Bernini for one of the angels intended for the Ponte Sant'Angelo in Rome, reversed the pose, and substituted Victorian Protestant reserve for baroque Catholic emotionalism. Apparently Victoria did not approve and wanted a more literal commemoration, not a single dead child to serve as the recollection of several. The final work installed at Windsor Castle,

27

which is far less moving and less formally satisfying than this earlier conception, is a terra-cotta group with a seated angel tending to five dead grandchildren: three in his arms, one standing between his knees, and another seated on the sculpture's base.

28.   *Maternal Joy*

> Sèvres porcelain, original 1872; reduced model somewhat later
> height: 20 inches
> width: 13⅛ inches
> depth: 13¹⁵⁄₁₆ inches
> Museum of Art, Rhode Island School of Design. Gift of Mrs. Zechariah Chafee. 34.1375
> Signed: DALOU (on right side of base)
> Foundry marks: *s/1912* and *Sevres I*

The first year that Dalou and his family spent in exile was a difficult one. He had to adapt to a new environment, culture, and climate of taste in London. He modeled picturesque peasant women from the area near Boulogne, allegorical reliefs, and portraits. What won the hearts of the British audience, however, was a life-size patinated plaster statue of an urban woman in modern dress, nursing her baby, *Maternal Joy*, which he sent to the Royal Academy exhibition of 1872. Critics were enthusiastic in their praise for the French sculptor making his debut and for his engaging, warmly communicative statue. During the next few years, he would make several variations on this theme: a peasant mother, a *boulonnaise* mother, other contemporary urban mothers – all raptly attentive to their young children. He preferred the life-size format, probably because it captured attention so effectively at the annual exhibition of the Royal Academy, but he also had reduced versions cast in plaster and terra cotta for eager patrons.

Dalou brought his reduced models with him when he moved back to Paris in 1880, and additional casts of *Maternal Joy* were made. Around 1884 an edition of unknown size was executed in stoneware by Haviland. Sèvres also edited the piece, in white porcelain, at least once during Dalou's lifetime; one of them was part of his estate when it was auctioned in 1906. This version was manufactured later and stamped "1912." *Maternal Joy* is one of Dalou's most popular images. Besides the examples in stoneware and porcelain, there are numerous bronzes, some probably cast in England during Dalou's lifetime, but most of them posthumously.

29.   *Maternal Joy* [color plate, p. vi]

> terra-cotta sketch, 1872
> height: 9¾ inches
> width: 4½ inches
> depth: 3¾ inches
> Middlebury College Museum of Art. Purchase, with funds provided by The G. Crossan Seybolt
> ('77) Art Acquisition Fund. 1987.5
> Provenance: Robert Schoelkopf Gallery (New York)

Dalou's creative process was laborious and meticulous. His artistic conceptions evolved over time according to an established pattern, as was typical for an academically trained artist. Initial ideas and observations were captured with pencil or pen-and-ink drawings and then developed more fully in three-dimensional clay sketches and more elaborate drawings. Dalou's process regularly began with a static disposition of forms, which he progressively energized as he increased their complexity. The juxtaposition of this terra-

28

cotta sketch and the reduced porcelain version of the final statue clearly demonstrates his characteristic working procedure.

Dalou began with the mother's feet both resting flat on supports: the base of the sculpture ("the floor") for her right and a footstool for her left. The baby rests on the

29

thigh of the raised leg; the mother's head is inclined toward the suckling child. This disposition of forms concentrates all the major sculptural "weight" on one side of the sketch and leaves the other side comparatively static and not fully integrated into the whole. As the process evolved, Dalou recognized the possibilities that lay in crossing the mother's right leg over her left one, creating not only a dynamic spiral of forms but also a complementary counterthrust to the baby, thus integrating both sides of the statue. As he developed the folds of drapery and the particularities of costume, physiognomies, and surfaces, he also realized the variety and urgency that resulted from excavating under the mass of the mother's body and skirt and leaving a large void formed by the space between the supporting legs of the modern chair.

Very few of Dalou's clay sketches from this stage in his creative process have survived. The sketches that were edited in bronze, stoneware, or porcelain tend to be much more finished and closer to the final versions. According to nineteenth-century sculptural practice, the freest and most experimental sketches – those closest to the original idea – are the smallest. The larger and more detailed the sketch, the closer it usually is to the final sculptural solution.

EMMANUEL FRÉMIET

30. *Cat Nursing Her Kittens*

> bronze, original model 1849, or earlier
>
> height: 3¾ inches
>
> width: 8⅜ inches
>
> depth: 4⅞ inches
>
> Smith College Museum of Art, Northampton, Massachusetts. Gift of George and Lincoln
> Kirstein in memory of their sister, Mina Kirstein Curtiss '18. 1986;60-36
>
> Signed: E. FRÉMIET (on blanket)

One of Frémiet's earliest successes came with the *Family of Cats*, which he exhibited at the Salon of 1849. Subsequently, the government commissioned the work in marble, which was exhibited with great success at the Exposition Universelle of 1855. Stanislas Lami published Frémiet's catalogue of works for sale; in it we learn that the group was offered life size or in reduction – like the one exhibited here (500 francs for a large bronze and 25 for a small one; 15 francs for a large plaster and 4 for a small one). This is an ingratiating image of domesticity and feline mother-love, which rivals those of Dalou and Charpentier that feature human mothers and their infants.

30

JOSEPH GOTT

31. *Greyhound with Her Two Puppies Suckling*

> marble, original model 1824–25
> height: 18 inches
> width: 32¾ inches
> depth: 17½ inches
> Wadsworth Atheneum. Purchase, with funds provided by the Henry D. Miller Fund. 1983.28
> Provenance: Charles Jerdein (London)

This sculpture was the result of Gott's first commission for an animal group. He had many replicas made; if signed and dated, they bear the date 1825. The original marble version is located at Chatsworth.

Gott was regarded by his contemporaries as an accomplished specialist in sculpting dogs. A guide to the studios of Roman artists, published in 1860, reported: "In his atelier is to be seen a very curious collection of fancy groups of dogs, of all races, in playful

31

attitudes, executed in marble." Gott understood the psychology of dogs and captured the greyhound mother's alertness with great urgency. Her pose of protective readiness is contrasted with the playful single-mindedness of the pups who nuzzle and suckle.

Harriet Goodhue Hosmer

32. *Puck on a Toadstool*

>   marble, original model 1855–56
>   height: 30 inches (statue); 46 inches (pedestal)
>   width: 15 inches
>   depth: 16 inches
>   Wadsworth Atheneum. Gift of A. C. and S. G. Dunham. 1914.2
>   Signed and inscribed: H HOSMER ROMAE (on front)

This witty personification of mischief was designed to be a crowd pleaser, and Hosmer succeeded brilliantly. She needed a measure of financial security after her father suffered

financial reverses and had to curtail his support. Shakespearean characters were very popular subjects with artists and patrons in the nineteenth century, and the sprite from *A Midsummer Night's Dream* was a wise choice from a commercial point of view. Hosmer called him "devil-born"; his bat wings and incipient horns bear this out. He holds a lizard and is on the verge of tossing a scorpion. Puck's ambivalent facial expression, pudgy baby fat, and straining toes are all calculated to delight, as are the mushrooms and other flora beneath the large toadstool which supports him. At least thirty replicas were carved in Hosmer's studio. One of them was purchased by the Prince of Wales for his rooms at Oxford.

33. *Sheep with Suckling Lamb*

bronze, original model 1845
height: 6 inches
width: 9¼ inches
depth: 4⅛ inches
Museum of Fine Arts, Boston. Gift of Misses Aimee and Rosamond Lamb (Boston). 67.1048
Signed and dated: *P. J. Mene 1845* (top of base)

Mène was an able, and sometimes inspired, interpreter of animals and their activities. Although he did a number of hunt scenes, he did not choose to emphasize savagery and bloodletting as Barye did; nor did he do scenes in which the animals are equal or superior to their human adversaries, as Frémiet often did. He modeled a number of animal mothers nursing their young; a cast of this *Sheep with Suckling Lamb* appeared at the Salon of 1845.

33

34.   *Loulie's Hand*

marble, original model 1839

height: 2¾ inches

diameter: 5½ inches

Fogg Art Museum, Harvard University. Gift of Professor James Hardy Ropes. 1928.115

Signed: *H. Powers* (on base)

Provenance: Charles Lawrence Peirson; gift to his nephew, James Hardy Ropes

34

"Loulie" was the sculptor's first daughter, Louisa Greenough Powers, who was born on September 10, 1838. During March of the following year, her father took a cast of the sleeping infant's left hand and forearm and used it as the basis for this very personal work of sculpture in which her hand seems to burst forth from a sunflower. Although he gave the first marble version of it as a gift to his wife, Powers had numerous replicas made in response to the demand of patrons. In his *French and Italian Notebooks* (1873), Nathaniel Hawthorne recounted that Powers had shown him the piece on June 13, 1858: "so many people . . . had insisted on having a copy, that there are now forty scattered about the world." The sentiment embodied in the piece is genuine, but dated. The Harvard art historian, Chandler Post, who specialized in the history of sculpture and of Spanish art – apparently without any dissent from his colleagues at the Fogg – put it to practical use; until his death in 1949, *Loulie's Hand* served as his ashtray.

PORTRAIT HEADS AND BUSTS

TENS OF THOUSANDS of portrait busts were made during the nineteenth century. It was commonplace for a member of the upper middle class to commission at least one during his or her lifetime; wealthy and famous individuals frequently sat for their portraits many times. Although full-length portraits were made in three dimensions, there are relatively few of them compared with the ubiquity of busts and heads. These were the most frequently encountered items at public exhibitions of sculpture during the nineteenth century. In addition to owning busts of oneself and one's family, private individuals – as well as educational or cultural institutions – often owned busts of illustrious personages from the past and present.

As is true for sculpture in general, portrait heads and busts tend to be more generalized early in the century and more literal at a later date, but this is only a rule of thumb. When they immortalized the appearance of their sitters, portraitists chose from a vast array of aesthetic possibilities. These varied from precise rendition of individual physiognomy to idealization of features, from lofty aloofness to intimate characterization, from textural richness to undifferentiated surfaces.

Four of the busts included indicate a preference for idealization, but none of them subscribes to full-blown, neoclassical remoteness. Even the historical portrait of Dante by Vela (cat. no. 51), with its late dugento costume and established set of features used to portray the poet, seems to be a contemporary individual rather than an icy abstraction. Lewis's bust of Longfellow (cat. no. 46) accepts the convention of nudity to evoke timelessness and conveys the aura of an antique philosopher, but the turn of this modern poet's head and the particularities of his features are at variance with his apparently sightless eyes. *Madame Récamier* by Chinard (cat. no. 39) displays a reticent charm as a result of the veiled forms with which the artist recorded her beautiful features. Bartolini's characterization of Anna Hull (cat. no. 36) honestly depicts her middle-aged features, while the allover textural uniformity harmonizes the bust as a whole.

Another group of portrait busts and heads aims for an even greater degree of particularity and a more intense sort of realist evocation of the sitter's presence. Emerson's verbal response at the first sight of his portrait by French (cat. no. 43) was, "That is the face that I shave." Some paraphrase of that statement might be invoked for each of the other six. The exactitude of Eakins's life mask of Talcott Williams (cat. no. 42) is almost clinical in its objectivity. Meissonier (by Gemito, cat. no. 44), Scott (by Chantrey, cat. no. 38), and Mendenhall (by Andreoni, cat. no. 35) all seem to be frozen in time and are eternally present when we experience their portrait busts. Saint-Gaudens's two portraits (Dr. Shiff, cat. no. 49, and Mrs. Van Rensselaer, cat. no. 50) amply illustrate why his portrait reliefs were and continue to be so highly prized. They are exceptionally vibrant evocations of the appearances and personalities of the sitters.

Four of the portraits probe even more deeply beneath the surface and seem to blur the distinction between art work and sitters. These are nineteenth-century equivalents of baroque "speaking likenesses." They conjure up an anecdote about Bernini's bust of Monsignor Mantoya (1622, Santa Maria di Montserrato, Rome). One day while the artist was working on this marble portrait, the sitter walked into the room. A witty spectator observed that the intruder was the art work and the marble in progress was the true Mantoya. Such works make us feel that the inert materials from which the portraits have been made are infused with the very essence of the sitter's presence and personality. The portraits in question are a closely related trio by the three greatest French sculptors of the nineteenth century: Carpeaux's *Gérôme* (cat. no. 37), Dalou's *Parent* (cat. no. 40), and Rodin's *Henley* (cat. no. 48), as well as a bust of the artist's father (cat. no. 45) by the American Walter Griffin.

Two female portraits violate our expectations and break new ground in terms of formal inventiveness. Degas's *Female Portrait with Head Resting on One Hand* (cat. no. 41) is like a portrait relief – but irregular in shape – with its outline corresponding to the limits of the sitter's body on right and left but wholly arbitrary in its cutoff along the bottom edge. This portrait does not rest on a base or socle, as portraits traditionally do; neither does it have a clear-cut relation to gravity or a visible means of support. Rodin's *Head of Camille Claudel* (cat. no. 47) has an unusual means of support, a phlange of metal from which the head emerges, but this base cannot be read in terms of a comprehensible, realistic equivalent. It is an abstract invention, which is formally and expressively effective but which cannot be explained rationally. Rodin dispensed with the conventions of portraiture and discovered a solution based on intuitive "rightness" when he wanted to create a memorable portrait of his mistress.

35. *Bust of Dorothy Reed Mendenhall (1874–1964; Smith '95)*

marble, 1887

height: 23 inches (34 inches with self-base)

width: 17 inches

depth: 11 inches

Smith College Museum of Art, Northampton, Massachusetts. Gift of Thomas Mendenhall,
    1993. EL 131:75

Signed, dated, and inscribed: *O Andreoni/Roma/1887* (on back of base)

Provenance: Dorothy Reed Mendenhall; Thomas C. Mendenhall

Dorothy Reed's cousin, Edmund Wilson, noted that from girlhood she exhibited "a very strong character and a decisive practical intelligence," and that she was "capable" and "handsome." Andreoni's characterization of his young sitter is wholly in keeping with Wilson's assessment. Dorothy seems exceptionally mature and self-possessed for a thirteen-year-old. The turn of her head and the posture of her shoulders suggest confidence, discipline, and determination. As a child she had been educated at home by a governess. In the future she would graduate from Smith College and The Johns Hopkins School of Medicine. Some fifty years after she sat for this portrait she wrote an autobiography which has never been published, but her son, Thomas Mendenhall, has provided the museum's files with photocopies of the pages pertinent to the events in her life at the time this bust was made, as well as a letter indicating his own memories concerning the bust.

During 1887 Dorothy accompanied her mother, her mother's traveling companion, Emma Kimball, and her mother's brother on a grand tour of Europe. They spent a block of time in Rome which included the Easter holiday. During this visit, Dorothy must have sat for the portrait bust by Andreoni. According to standard practice, he would have modeled her likeness in clay and, after the family's approval, had it carved in marble and shipped to America.

Dorothy Reed Mendenhall disliked this bust so much that, later in life, she disposed of it by having it thrown in a pond behind her home. Someone later retrieved it, and she was angered by this unanticipated rescue. The marble still bears some stains incurred during its watery exile.

Dorothy's distaste for what in fact is a very handsome, flattering portrait was probably a direct result of her experience in Rome during the Holy Week of 1887. On Good Friday after Dorothy had fallen asleep, her mother and uncle left her alone at their hotel

35

and went out to observe Roman rituals performed on the holy day. While they were gone, she awoke to find her room on fire. After she escaped with no more than blistered feet and a scorched nightgown, Dorothy closed the door to her room behind her (thus unintentionally containing the fire), wandered in a daze through corridors and staircases, and fell asleep again when she found an unoccupied bed in the servants' quarters. Had she not awakened in time, she almost certainly would have died. Apparently, Rome, the fire, and the bust all melded together in a single horrific memory that was responsible for her otherwise inexplicable dislike for a very fine portrait in marble. Andreoni's bust is distinguished by its evocation of a specific personality and the formal inventiveness with which he treats the specifics of physiognomy, coiffure, and costume. It compares favorably with the best late-nineteenth-century portrait busts of adolescents, such as those which Dalou made during the 1870s in London.

Lorenzo Bartolini

36.   *Bust of Anna McCurdy Hart Hull (1790–1874)*

marble, 1836–37

height: 27⅜ inches

width: 21³⁄₁₆ inches

depth: 13³⁄₁₆ inches

Boston Athenaeum. Gift of Frederick Nichols. U.H.24.1929

Provenance: Jeanette Hart Jarvis (Mrs. Osbert B. Loomis, New York), by 1874; Sarah Jarvis Dennis (Mrs. Elias J. Pattison, New York); Sarah Desier Pattison (Mrs. Frederick Nichols, Boston), by 1905

Anna Hull was a frequent and extensive world traveler. In 1813 she married Isaac Hull, an ambitious, upwardly mobile career man in the United States Navy who was then captain of the U.S.S. *Constitution.* He had a long and successful career ahead of him, which involved numerous voyages across the Atlantic and Pacific, and she regularly accompanied him. While commander of the American Mediterranean fleet, he was involved with the shipment of Horatio Greenough's colossal seated marble rendition of George Washington, which had to be transported from Florence to Washington, D.C., in 1840.

In 1836–37, twenty-three years after her marriage, Anna sat for her portrait bust by Bartolini while visiting Florence. In this portrait he captured both the particulars of her features in middle age and certain generalizations to suggest timelessness. Her neck, chin, and nose are highly individualized; the surfaces, by contrast, are lacking in textural variation and do not attempt to evoke the sensations of flesh, cloth, or hair. The drapery that covers her arms, shoulders, and chest has been subjected to a rigorous process of abstraction so that the folds conform to an a priori pattern rather than appearing to rest on an actual body; the curls of her coiffure evoke earlier art (late-first-century A.D. portraits of Roman matrons) more than human hair. One of Anna Hull's contemporaries, Admiral David Porter, described her as surpassing all the beautiful and brilliant women he had met in any country. Bartolini's reserved but insightful portrait suggests that he, too, recognized her exceptional qualities.

36

37. *Head of Jean-Léon Gérôme (1824–1904)*

bronze, original model 1871

height: 23⅞ inches

width: 10¼ inches

depth: 9¾ inches

Worcester Art Museum, Worcester, Massachusetts. Gift of the Grandchildren of Joseph Tuckerman through Stephen Salisbury III. 1899.1

Signed and inscribed: *al(')Sommo/pittore Gérome/Bt Carpeaux/London* (right side of base); GEROME (front of base)

Provenance: Ernest Tuckerman (Newport, R.I.)

Gérôme was one of the most successful academic painters of his day. He specialized in meticulously rendered historical genre scenes and images of the Near East and North Africa. He was a highly respected professor of painting at the École des Beaux-Arts from 1863 until the end of his life. He and Carpeaux were friends. When both found themselves in London during and after the Commune, Carpeaux modeled Gérôme's head and sent a bronze cast of it to the Salon of 1872, where it was received enthusiastically.

Although Carpeaux limited himself to his friend's head and a hint of his upper torso, he created a stunning evocation of Gérôme's presence, in the manner of a "speaking likeness" ultimately derived from Bernini's portraiture of the seventeenth century. The turn of the head, the deeply excavated eyes, the tousled hair and unruly moustache, and the masterful modeling of surfaces all contribute to the portrait's vitality. One reviewer suggested that the sculpture was "life itself." Carpeaux obviously felt great affection and affinity for the sitter and emphasized this fact with his inscription: "at the summit, the painter Gérôme." This superb head, which entered the museum's collections before the turn of the century, was ordered by Ernest Tuckerman, a wealthy American who had studied in Gérôme's atelier and wanted a tangible memento of his teacher's appearance.

37

38. *Bust of Sir Walter Scott (1771–1832)*

plaster, original model 1820

height: 30⅛ inches

width: 21¼ inches

depth: 12¹¹/₁₆ inches

Boston Athenaeum. Gift of Thomas Handasyd Perkins, 1827. U.H.142.1827

Signed, dated, and inscribed: *[WAL]TER SCOT[T]/CHANTRE[Y]/1820* (on back)

Over one hundred of Chantrey's portrait busts survive. His sitters belonged to the ranks of the most distinguished British citizens of the day, including four reigning sovereigns: George III, George IV, William IV, and Victoria. According to his own admission, Chantrey only once in his life invited someone to pose for a portrait, and that individual was Sir Walter Scott. The resultant bust was enthusiastically received by contemporaries, who commissioned Chantrey to make at least forty-five replicas of it.

The popularity of Scott's portrait is easily understood, because it numbers among Chantrey's finest. He greatly admired the portrait busts made by his distinguished predecessor, the transplanted Franco-Fleming, François Roubiliac, who practiced his art in London and was one of the greatest sculptors of the eighteenth century. Both sculptors aspired to the animation, informality, and psychological penetration that characterize the "speaking likenesses" created by Bernini in seventeenth-century papal Rome. A beholder feels that he is in the presence of Scott himself, and not a stone or plaster replica of his appearance. Scott is shown in the process of breaking into a smile, as his deeply excavated eyes peer out from under their heavy lids. He seems just to have turned his head in response to someone's presence; his hair is tousled and his hairline is receding. With a witty concession to his sitter's national origins, Chantrey incised a plaid pattern into the cloth which drapes so elegantly over Scott's shoulders and is held in place by a partially concealed ornamental clasp.

38

39. *Bust of Madame Juliette Récamier (1777–1849)* [color plate, p. x]

marble, original model c. 1801

height: 22¼ inches

width: 13 inches

depth: 10 inches

Museum of Art, Rhode Island School of Design. Gift of Mrs. Harold Brown. 37.201

Signed: *Chinard de Lyon* (right side of pedestal)

Provenance: Mme Récamier; Mme Lenormant (her niece and adopted daughter);
   Hôtel Drouot, Paris (auction, Nov. 29, 1893, lot 2); Marquis de Gontaut-Biron;
   Mrs. Harold Brown

Chinard's portrait of the fabled beauty Juliette Récamier is generally regarded as his finest work. This extraordinary woman lived at the pinnacle of French society at the time of the Revolution and the Empire. Wealth, charm, fashion, and the adulation of Paris were all hers. At the height of her fame and beauty, her portrait was done by David (1800), Chinard (c. 1801), and Gérard (1805); in middle age Canova (1813) and Dejuinne (after 1825) memorialized her features.

The original, fuller, marble portrait, now in the Musée des Beaux-Arts of Lyon, includes Madame Récamier's arms – which hold a shawl – and terminates at her midriff as the shawl continues, partially covering the socle. Her gesture at first appears to be one of great modesty, but the sheer fabric clings to one breast, and her fingers, toying with the cloth, have managed to expose the other. Chinard made her seem at once virginal and sensuous, modest and coy – all of which seems absolutely appropriate, given her real-life personality and temperament.

The Rhode Island marble included here is an excerpt from the original version in Lyon. The higher cut-off point is more traditional for a bust; it begins where arm and shoulder meet and extends only a few inches below the clavicle. Madame Récamier in abbreviated form is at least as beguiling and seductive as in the more complete version. The averted, down-turned glance alone communicates her perfumed, erotically charged reticence every bit as powerfully. The exquisite coiffure and headband actually increase in formal interest when they no longer have to compete with arms, breasts, and drapery for our attention. This excerpt is one of two in marble; it also exists in terra cotta.

39

40. *Head of Ulysse Parent (1828–1880)*

bronze, original model 1880
height: 20 inches
width: 10 inches
depth: 10 inches
Private collection
Signed: *J. Dalou* (lower right)
Foundry mark: *Lehmann Freres/Fondeurs/Paris* (lower left)
Provenance: Heim Gallery Ltd. (London)

When this bust appeared in the 1980 exhibition *The Romantics to Rodin*, the sitter was tentatively – and mistakenly – identified by this author as the French painter Jean-Paul Laurens. A plaster and another bronze cast of the same bust by a different founder, Egodard, are in the Musée Municipal de St.-Denis in the suburbs of Paris, where the sitter is properly identified as Ulysse Parent.

When Henriette Caillaux published her monograph on Dalou in 1935, she had access to Dalou's account book, which has since disappeared. A bust of Ulysse Parent was listed there as the first work after Dalou's return to Paris from London in 1880. There was no plaster or bronze version in Dalou's studio at the time of his death, and therefore no record of its appearance. It seems certain that this bust was one of many that he made out of gratitude for people who granted or facilitated a commission, or for some other kindness rendered. Dalou first did this in 1873 when he sculpted the bust of Mary Howard as a gift to the Howard family after her parents, Rosiland and George, had purchased one of his *boulonnaises* and commissioned their portraits.

Dalou had ample reason for goodwill and gratitude toward Parent. They shared political sympathies and had both participated in the Commune. It is known that Parent was an active Mason, and Dalou was either a member or had close association with that fraternal order, which was enormously influential in behind-the-scenes power brokering during the Third Republic. Parent had been a member of the committee that conducted the competition for the Monument to the Republic in 1879. Dalou desperately wanted that commission, but it was denied him by powerful opposition within the fourteen-member committee. Parent was part of the pro-Dalou faction. The mechanics of the deal are uncertain, but Parent and his allies were able to negotiate an extraordinary

40

compromise. Although Léopold Morice won the official competition and had his monument built on the place de la République, the City Council of Paris also agreed to erect
Dalou's monument, on the place de la Nation. Parent subsequently published a pam-
phlet about the city's acquisition of the competition model and Dalou's commission.

41. *Female Portrait with Head Resting on One Hand*

bronze, original model c. 1890
height: 4¾ inches
width: 6¾ inches
depth: 6½ inches
Museum of Fine Arts, Boston. Bequest of Margarett Sargent McKean. 1979.507
Signed: *Degas* (stamped replica)
Foundry mark: *cire perdue/A. A. Hebrard/62/H* (lower left)

The exact identification of the sitter for this unusual portrait is by no means certain. Mary Cassatt, Madame Paul Bartholomé, and Rose Caron have all been suggested with some degree of plausibility. Cassatt was an intimate of Degas's and the subject of several of his works. Madame Bartholomé was the wife of a close friend. Rose Caron, a singer at the Opéra, is mentioned in one of Degas's letters dating from 1892 and was also the subject of a pastel portrait (Albright-Knox Art Gallery, Buffalo). At an exhibition at Knoedler's in 1955 the piece was simply called *Head Resting on One Hand*. It has been published as Cassatt's portrait (Nancy Hale, *Biography of Mary Cassatt* [New York, 1975]). The authors of the 1988 Degas retrospective catalogue believed it was Madame Bartholomé. Charles Millard argued in favor of Rose Caron. The portrait resembles each of the three women somewhat, but the resemblance is not so compelling that we must choose one of them at the expense of the other two. The portrait may also depict some other, as yet unidentified, woman.

Whoever the sitter, the portrait is audacious in its departure from expectations for portrait sculpture. Unlike contemporary busts or heads, it has no base or plinth to identify it as a work of art and provide a means for its display. The features, hair, and clothing are dreamily out of focus and the lower cutoff is wholly arbitrary. It is as if Degas had excerpted a fragment from one of his contemporary pastels and projected it into three dimensions. The degree of informality, lack of traditional support, and sense of atmosphere which surrounds the figure make it similar to contemporary works by the Italian sculptor Medardo Rosso, who worked in Paris during 1884 and, again, from 1889 onward.

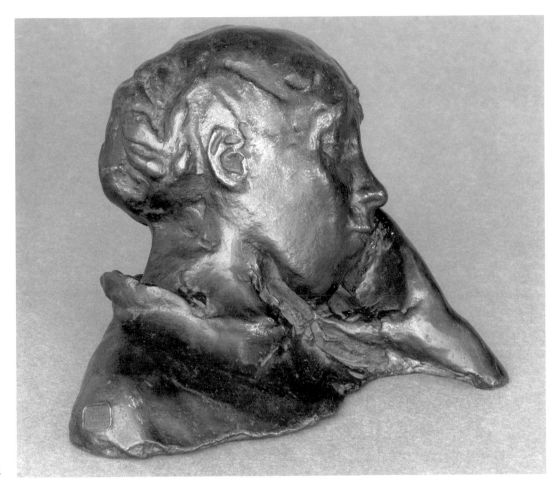

41

Thomas Eakins, with Samuel Murray

42. *Life Mask of Talcott Williams (1849–1928; Amherst '73)* [color plate, p.xi]

tinted plaster, 1889

height: 9 inches

width: 5 inches

Mead Art Museum/Frost Library, Amherst College. Gift of the Estate of Talcott Williams, Class of 1873. 1993.7

Provenance: Talcott Williams; Mrs. Talcott Williams

Talcott Williams was a journalist and editor of the *Philadelphia Press.* He knew Eakins, wrote about his work, and took him to Camden, New Jersey, where he introduced him to Walt Whitman, probably in 1887. Eakins photographed Williams and modeled this

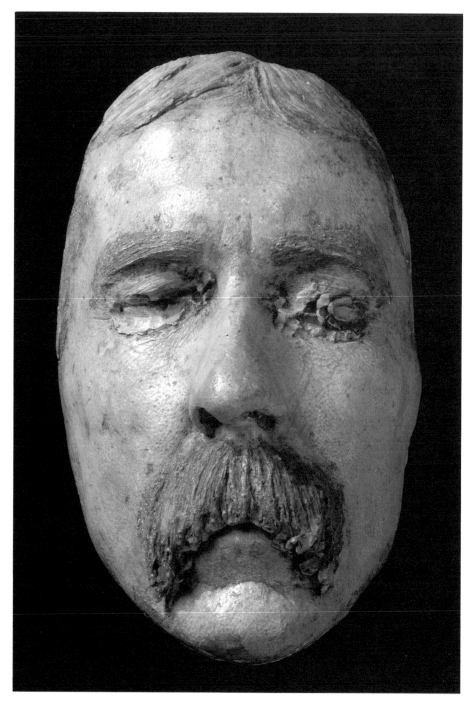

42

life mask with the assistance of Samuel Murray (1869/70–1941); presumably, both photograph and mask were made in order to study Williams's features with maximum objectivity prior to painting his portrait – which was an act of friendship, not a commission – in 1890 (National Portrait Gallery, Washington, D.C.). Photograph, mask, and painted portrait all feature Williams's luxuriant moustache and reveal the fine bone structure of his skull. The photograph (Hirshhorn Museum and Sculpture Garden, Washington, D.C.) shows him seated, with his hands and the right side of his head prominently lit, while other features and details are bathed in shadow. Much the same pose of the head and shoulders was kept for the painted portrait, but only his shoulders were included. With the hands and lower body eliminated, there was a greater focus on facial features; the lighting was reversed, so that Williams's right side was illuminated and the prominent left ear suppressed. Eakins showed Williams with his lips parted; this has repeatedly been interpreted as a reference to the gregarious journalist's nickname, "Talk-a-lot."

The powerful, three-dimensional study was surely an intermediary step between the photograph and painted portrait. With Williams's eyes closed and nothing else except the mask of his face, moustache, and wisps of hair at the top of his forehead included, Eakins was able to concentrate on the structure of facial features rendered in three dimensions, without exterior illumination or psychological nuance. In a letter of October 1889, Williams referred to the surprising effect of this objectivity: "Tuesday he took a cast of my face & very queer the cast looks today. It is so odd to see something which one would never recognize but for its resemblance to other members of the family." This objectifying mask is congruent with the procedures of an artist who prided himself on scientific accuracy, but it is also, so far as we know, something that Eakins had not done before and would never repeat for any of his later portraits. He did, however, collaborate with Murray on the death mask of Walt Whitman, which the young sculptor subsequently utilized for his posthumous bust of the poet.

Samuel Murray and Eakins had met in 1886, at the newly established Art Students' League (shortly after Eakins's dismissal from his teaching position at the Pennsylvania Academy of the Fine Arts). Eakins was forty-two at the time, and Murray was sixteen or seventeen. They had a fruitful student-teacher relationship, became intimate friends, and even shared a studio; Murray remained devoted to Eakins as long as his mentor lived, and to his memory thereafter. The younger man often accompanied Eakins when he worked on portraits. There are many photographs of Murray – at rest, at work, and at leisure – taken by Eakins, as well as images by unknown photographers of the two men together. Much of the Eakins material contained in the extensive holdings of the Hirshhorn Museum was once owned by Murray.

43. *Bust of Ralph Waldo Emerson (1803–1882)*

bronze, original model 1879

height: 22⅜ inches

width: 7½ inches

depth: 7½ inches

Chesterwood, a Museum Property of the National Trust for Historic Preservation, Stockbridge, Massachusetts. 69.38.246

Signed and dated: *D. C. French/1879* (on back)

Foundry mark: *Gorham Co. Founders* (on back of base); inscribed: *Emerson* (on front of base)

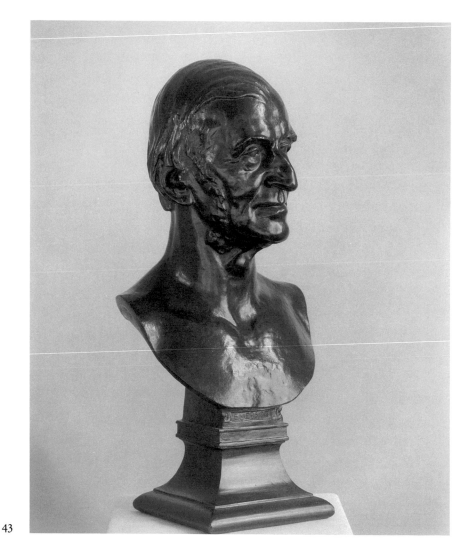

43

As a teenager, French must have occasionally encountered the great Ralph Waldo Emerson in Concord, Massachusetts, where they both lived. Years later, between his two study sojourns abroad, French asked the aged Emerson to sit for his portrait, and the philosopher agreed to do so. There was no commission; the situation was analogous to what had transpired earlier when Sir Walter Scott posed for Chantrey (cat. no. 38). The Emerson family called it the "best likeness" ever made of him. Upon first viewing it, the sitter himself praised its verisimilitude: "That is the face that I shave."

It is easy to understand the family's enthusiasm. French never made a finer portrait bust than this one. Limiting himself to Emerson's head and a truncated portion of his unclothed shoulders and chest, French achieved a stunning sense of the sitter's presence. The turn of the head and suggestion of external focus enliven the bust and would have us believe that we are in the company of a specific, vibrant, and penetrating personality. The depth of the folds and the creases of the aging flesh establish a craggy landscape which suggests wisdom and venerability.

French apparently planned from the beginning to market the bust. Given Emerson's popularity, this was a commercially viable idea. First he ordered a series of plaster replicas. Then, when patrons requested versions in more permanent materials, he had marbles carved and bronzes cast.

VINCENZO GEMITO

44.   *Bust of Ernest Meissonier (1815–1891)*

> bronze, original model 1878–79
> height: 9⁹⁄₁₆ inches
> width: 6½ inches
> depth: 5¹⁄₁₆ inches
> Collection of Fred and Meg Licht

After Meissonier, a highly successful French painter of historical genre, bought a cast of Gemito's *Neapolitan Fisherboy*, the two artists became friends. Gemito subsequently modeled a full-length portrait of Meissonier. This small bust is closely related to that project. It captures the painter, who was an impressive physical presence, in a moment of introspection. Gemito, whose portraiture often involved virtuoso handling of hair, was clearly inspired to considerable formal inventiveness by his friend's long and luxuriant beard, which dominates this striking likeness.

44

WALTER GRIFFIN

45. *Bust of Edward Souther Griffin (1834–1928)*

> plaster with gold leaf, 1881
> height: 13⅞ inches
> width: 9¼ inches
> depth: 6½ inches
> Portland Museum of Art, Portland, Maine. Anonymous Gift. 1935.1

Edward Souther Griffin was Walter's father and the owner of a successful wood-carving business in Portland, Maine. He himself carved many figureheads for ships built in

130

Maine, but his shop did wood carving of all kinds. It was there that young Walter had his earliest artistic training. Father and son also belonged to a local sketching and painting society, the Brush'uns.

Edward was forty-seven when his twenty-year-old son made this portrait, but he seems younger in this insightful and deeply affectionate characterization. The turn and slight tilt of the head, the deeply undercut iris and pupil of the eyes, and the casual in-

45

formality of hair and mustache, collar and cravat, all combine to create a sense of intense vitality, capturing an instant in the life of a vibrant individual. In this respect Griffin's achievement is comparable to the "speaking likenesses" which his French counterparts Carpeaux and Dalou created during the 1860s and 1870s. The gilding of the plaster heightens the dramatic effects of the bust, which is all the more stunning an accomplishment for being the only known sculpture by this artist.

The provenance of the bust is unknown, as is the situation under which it entered the Portland Museum of Art collections in 1935. That is also the year of Walter Griffin's death and of the memorial exhibition held at the museum from October 13 to November 30 (without a printed catalogue). It is probable that the bust was given in conjunction with these two events as a means of recalling father and son, both prominent natives of Portland.

EDMONIA LEWIS

46. *Bust of Henry Wadsworth Longfellow (1807–1882)*

> marble, original model 1871, carved by 1883
> height: 29 inches
> width: 16¼ inches
> depth: 12¼ inches
> Harvard University Portrait Collection. s52
> Signed, dated, and inscribed: EDMONIA LEWIS/ROMA 1871 (right side);
>   inscribed: H W LONGFELLOW (on back)

Lewis was a great admirer of Longfellow and especially of his poem "Song of Hiawatha." When she decided to make his bust, she did not ask him to sit for her. Rather, she observed him in Rome without his knowledge and modeled the image in secret. Almost finished, she contacted Longfellow's brother; he and the family inspected the bust and found only the nose unsatisfactory. Consequently, the poet himself sat while she executed the finishing touches, and he was pleased with the results. According to a nineteenth-century source, Lewis brought the plaster back to America with her. The bust was regarded as "one of the best ever taken" of Longfellow, and a group of his friends raised the funds necessary to have it carved in marble and donated to Harvard.

The bust is larger than life size and evokes images of Greek philosophers. It is a modified herm, with the lower extremities rounded to suggest a traditional bust. Lewis followed the neoclassical conventions of a nude upper body and blank eyeballs but did not hesitate to show such realistic details as flowing hair and beard, a receding hairline, and a bulging vein at the side of Longfellow's forehead.

46

47. *Head of Camille Claudel (1856–1943)*

bronze, original model 1884

height: 11 inches

width: 8 inches

depth: 7 inches

Smith College Museum of Art, Northampton, Massachusetts. Gift of the Cantor, Fitzgerald Art
    Foundation. 1975.39

Signed: *A. Rodin* (top of base, left side); *A. Rodin* (interior back); inscribed: *Musée Rodin 1957*
    (bottom, left edge)

Foundry mark: *Georges Rudier Fondeur. Paris* (back of base)

Provenance: Cast (Rudier cast #7) authorized by the Musée Rodin (Paris), 1957; Cantor,
    Fitzgerald Art Foundation (Beverly Hills, Ca.)

This is the first of several busts Rodin made of Camille Claudel, whom he met in the fall
of 1882. She became his mistress and collaborator shortly thereafter, and their passionate love affair lasted until 1893. When they met, she was one of several sculptors – all of
them young women – who regularly received criticism of their work from Alfred
Boucher. He won the Prix de Rome and left for Italy in the fall of 1882; before leaving, he
convinced Rodin to continue this informal arrangement in his place.

Claudel was a sculptor of considerable merit, and interest in her work has become
intense in the recent past. Casts of her distinguished portrait bust of Rodin are well
known, and a small number of her sculptures have long been on view at the Musée
Rodin at Hôtel Biron. With the appearance of Bruno Nuytten's fictionalized biographi-
cal film, *Camille Claudel*, in 1988 – starring Isabelle Adjani and Gérard Depardieu – she
and her tragic life became known to the general public. After Camille's affair with Rodin
ended, they nonetheless remained in contact until 1898, and he continued to assist her
whenever she would allow it after that. Her disintegrating emotional state became critical in 1913, and she was forcibly committed to an asylum, where she remained for the
rest of her life.

Whereas Rodin's images of his first love and lifelong companion, Rose Beuret, show
her head turned to one side from the axis of her body, his images of Camille are as rigidly
axial as any Romanesque Madonna. A widely published photograph of her taken in 1913
indicates that this was an habitual body posture for her. This unusual combination of
rigidity with extreme sensuality seems to have been part of Camille's erotic allure. It is

easy to believe from Rodin's repeated characterizations of her that he understood her intense seriousness as a sculptor as well as her passionate commitment to the life of the senses. Her features and characteristic posture also appear in later works that are not portraits but symbolic evocations: *Thought, Dawn,* and *La France.*

47

48. *Bust of William Ernest Henley (1849–1903)*

bronze, original model 1884–86

height: 16¼ inches

width: 11 inches

depth: 8½ inches

Mead Art Museum, Amherst College. Gift of Mrs. John W. Simpson and Jean W. Simpson.
  1942.87

Signed: *Rodin*

Foundry mark: *A. Rudier. Fondeur* (on back)

48

Rodin and Henley first met in 1882, when Rodin went to London at the invitation of his old friend, the expatriate French artist Alphonse Legros. At the time, Henley, who was both a poet and a critic, was also editor of the *Magazine of Art* (a post he held from 1881 until 1886), and a taste setter in England. They became friends, and Henley assumed the role of advocate for Rodin's art. In a characteristic gesture of thanks for his support, Rodin offered him a bust of Victor Hugo, but Henley replied that he would rather sit for his own portrait. Rodin complied and shipped the bust to Henley in 1886.

Rodin's male portraits often exhibit a strange but compelling combination of intimacy and distance, as if his knowledge of the person had revealed an essential aloofness at the core of the sitter's nature. This was surely the case with Rodin's busts of Hugo and Dalou, both of which appeared at the Salon of 1884. We know that Dalou was unhappy with his portrait despite the fact that it is one of Rodin's greatest. In it, Dalou has the same kind of icy reserve that borders on arrogance that we see in the Henley portrait, and this may have been the reason for his displeasure. Rodin's insight into human nature and male egos gives these portraits a force and communicative power that characterize the greatest portraiture from any era.

AUGUSTUS SAINT-GAUDENS

49. *Portrait Relief of Dr. Henry Shiff (1833 – c. 1906)*

bronze, 1880

height: 11¼ inches

width: 10¹¹⁄₁₆ inches

U.S. Department of Interior National Park Service, Saint-Gaudens National Historic Site, Cornish, N.H. 875

Signed, dated, and inscribed: *In Parigi nel mese di maggio dell(')anno* MDCCCLXXX *fece Augustus Saint-Gaudens*; *all[']amicone dottore Henry Shiff aetatis* XXXXVII *dei rospi di Roma e dei puzzi Roma ni amante di filosofia e di belle arti dilettante del tipo gattesco innamorato* (left side of relief)

This is one of Saint-Gaudens's most stunning portrait reliefs. It was made to commemorate the friendship between the sculptor and the expatriate American doctor, who was also a connoisseur and collector of Far Eastern bronzes. Beautifully crafted lettering covers the entire field between the back of the doctor's head and shoulders and the left frame of the relief. The inscription is a warm and gently teasing tribute to their intimacy (which was so strong that the sculptor named his son Homer Schiff Saint-Gaudens in

49

honor of Dr. Shiff – with a slight variation in the spelling). From it we learn that the relief was modeled in Paris when Shiff was forty-seven, that he was "a dilettante in philosophy and the fine arts," and a "lover of the smells of Rome." The reference to his being an "admirer of feline types" is, no doubt, some kind of cryptic in-joke between the two of them, but the "lover of toads" refers to the sitter's penchant for Oriental bronzes of frogs and toads, which he collected. The toad in relief on the right side makes this aspect of Dr. Shiff's interests unmistakable.

Every square inch of this remarkable relief – the blank right field and the left field covered by the inscription, the doctor's robe, skin, hair, and luxuriant beard – is animated by subtle surface modulations. Once before, in 1878, with his portrait relief of Dr. Walter Cary, Saint-Gaudens had featured such an ample beard, but he never would do so again. The frames that Stanford White designed for Saint-Gaudens's portrait reliefs are triumphs of sophisticated design; they are also perfect complements that display the reliefs to maximum advantage. This is arguably the apogee of the artists' collaborative achievement on a portrait relief and its frame.

50. *Portrait Relief of Mariana Griswold Van Rensselaer (1851–1934)*

coated plaster, original model 1888

height: 20¾ inches

width: 7¾ inches

Fogg Art Museum, Harvard University. Gift of Mrs. Schuyler Van Rensselaer. 1923.36

Signed: *AUGUSTUS SAINT-GAUDENS* (lower right); inscribed: *ANIMUS NON OPUS* (top center); *TO MARIANA GRISWOLD VAN RENSSELAER* (bottom center, beneath portrait); dated: *MDCCCLXXXVIII* (right center)

50

After the unveiling of Saint-Gaudens's standing *Lincoln* at Lincoln Park in Chicago, Mariana Griswold Van Rensselaer wrote a highly laudatory piece about it for the November 1887 issue of *Century Magazine.* As was frequently true with her writing about art, she was perceptive and insightful and found just the right words to characterize Saint-Gaudens's moving depiction of Lincoln. It was not the first time she had written about his work; he was obviously very pleased with her review and responded with an offer to model her portrait, which he completed in 1888. His inscriptions indicate that this portrait was done as an homage to the formidable lady – who became his friend – and not as a commission. The relief is dedicated to her, and the lofty phrase referring to "the spirit, not the work" seems to pay a gallant compliment, while the sculptor modestly defers to her intellectual powers and insight.

Mrs. Van Rensselaer was a prolific art critic and a notable presence on the American art scene. The same year her portrait was modeled by Saint-Gaudens, she published her monograph *Henry Hobson Richardson and His Works,* which was the first such book on an American architect to appear in print.

Characteristically, Saint-Gaudens modeled this portrait and its relief ground with the greatest subtlety. At thirty-seven, Mariana had a forceful and handsome profile, which Saint-Gaudens contrasted with the decorative exuberance of her collar and the curls and informal wisps of her hair. The sitter herself gave this plaster to the Fogg, so it is likely that it is the "original plaster" from which the mold was taken to make casts of the relief in bronze.

VINCENZO VELA

51. *Bust of Dante*

  bronze, original model 1865
  height: 23 inches
  width: 12½ inches
  depth: 8½ inches
  Yale University Divinity School. Gift of Rev. Charles A. Dinsmore (Yale, B.D. 1888, D.D. 1916).
    1933.11
  Signed: *V. Vela* (lower left side)
  Foundry Mark: *Ceriani e Fratli Barzaghi Milano Tusero 1865* (on back)
  Provenance: Mr. J. H. Whittmore (Naugatuck, Conn.); Mrs. J. H. Whittmore;
    the Reverend Dinsmore

51

No category of nineteenth-century sculpture is more characteristic of the sensibility of the age than the innumerable busts and statues of cultural heroes. There are precedents for this in antiquity and the Renaissance, but during the eighteenth century there was a transformation in frequency and intensity of such images that marked a significant turning point in the way Western society responded to the creators of its literature, art, and music. It is generally agreed that François Roubiliac's seated *Handel*, 1738, made for Vauxhall Gardens while Handel was still alive and at the height of his powers (now Victoria and Albert Museum, London), and Peter Scheemakers's standing *Shakespeare*,

1740, for the monument to "the bard" in Westminster Abby, are crucial moments in this transformation.

It was customary to emblazon the names of the then-canonical "greats" of any field of cultural endeavor across the facade of a museum, opera house, library, or concert hall during the later nineteenth century. Concurrently, monuments to "men of genius" became ubiquitous. On a more intimate scale, statues, statuettes, or busts of cultural heroes from the present, or from the recent and distant past, appeared everywhere. Creative giants on the order of Mozart, Milton, and Molière – as well as the rest of the pantheon – were regularly encountered as three-dimensional presences within cultural environments such as academies or libraries, and in the homes of individuals, even relatively modest ones of the cultivated middle class.

Vela's *Dante* belongs to this category of historical busts, based on an established iconography of the great Florentine poet's appearance and dress, that proliferated during the nineteenth century. It originally grew out of a project in 1859 for a gift to the French empress Eugénie contemplated by a group of great Milanese ladies; it then evolved into an ornamental bust, and eventually acquired its present format, a far more restrained head that terminates as a herm with an arbitrary horizontal cutoff, rather than resting on a socle or plinth. In 1865 – the same date inscribed on this bust – another *Dante* by Vela was exhibited at the International Exposition in Dublin and yet another entered the collection of the Civic Museum of Turin.

This characterization of Dante is imprinted with an unmistakable aura of the nineteenth century. The clothing may be that of Florence about 1300, and Vela may have given Dante a measure of austere idealization in keeping with his historical distance, but this is nonetheless a Dante of the present. He seems to have experienced more than any late medieval Florentine. He radiates a perhaps unintended degree of human warmth that is avuncular and familiar, and it would not surprise us at all if he began to discuss the poetry of Baudelaire.

HEADS AND BUSTS AS
INDEPENDENT CARRIERS OF MEANING

THE REMAINING sixteen heads or busts included in this exhibition are not conventional portraits. For want of a better term, I have called them "independent carriers of meaning," and they break down into at least three definable subcategories. Four of them are excerpts from full-length figures. Six are the embodiments of states of mind, and another five seem to be analogues for good and evil – personified by Christ and Satan. One other piece is gloriously ambiguous but is probably most closely aligned with the "states of mind" category.

By definition, a head or bust falls into the category of *pars pro toto*, a part that signifies the whole. This synecdochical condition is so common with portraits that very little thought is ever given to it. We do not regard portrait heads or busts as parts of severed or fragmented human bodies but as the essence of the sitters – presented under the guise of their greatest familiarity. A comparable situation exists with art works; heads or busts of famous sculptures serve as revered reminders of an original that could never be possessed, a replica or reproduction never afforded or accommodated in a domestic space. Particularly fascinating is the widely held conception that a head or bust can function as a disembodied essence – symbolizing a state of mind, a moral condition, or an abstract thought. During fin-de-siècle symbolism such intentions were rampant, but they also occur frequently earlier in the century.

Falguière's *Bust of Diana* (cat. no. 54), Rude's *Head of a Gaul* (cat. no. 67), Powers's *Bust of the Greek Slave* (cat. no. 62), and Rodin's *Head of Balzac* (cat. no. 63), are all excerpts from statues that were famous, full-length figures in three dimensions. During this exhibition, it will be possible to have the rare experience of witnessing Rodin's *Balzac Nude* adjacent to its excerpted head, the *pars* and *toto* reunited in close proximity.

Good and evil are such universal archetypes that it is hard to believe that it took until the nineteenth century before artists or their patrons thought to pair Christ and his infernal adversary in artistic union. So far as I know, Greenough's busts of Christ (cat. no. 60) and Lucifer (cat. no. 61), from the 1840s, are the first such pairing in history. Gould emulated his Bostonian predecessor's uniting of the two during the 1860s (*Bust of Christ*, cat. no. 56; and *Bust of Satan*, cat. no. 57). It is fascinating to note that, but hard to interpret why, both sculptors chose to invent their image of evil first. Unlike these two pairs, Clésinger's *Head of Christ* (cat. no. 53) is an independent creation. Despite its jeweler's perfection of detail, which tends to make it seem precious and distant, this is a broad-faced, fleshy, and intensely human image of Jesus, which suggests that it is an ex-

143

cerpt from a realist crucifix or crucifixion group, although no such work by Clésinger is known.

The "embodiments of states of mind" category is the most complex and elusive. When most straightforward (as in Carrier-Belleuse's *Awakening*, cat. no. 52), these images allude to common human experiences and provide aesthetic pleasure without demanding any emotional or intellectual investment from the viewer. Heads that attempt to summarize a dramatic or symbolic situation are somewhat more complex and provide a greater challenge to our interpretative skills and reactive capacity. Gould's *Ghost in Hamlet* (two versions, cat. nos. 58, 59) suggests the attempt by a Shakespearean enthusiast and critic to encapsulate the mysterious apparition and its implications by means of a disembodied head that seems to float in supernatural, aqueous nonspace. Falguière's *Head of a Wounded Soldier* (cat. no. 55) and Rodin's *Head of Sorrow* (cat. no. 65) are passionate and deeply moving images of suffering. In neither instance can we be sure about the cause of the evident pain, or the extent to which its source is physical or emotional. Rosso's *Sick Little Boy* (cat. no. 66) conveys an almost unbearable sense of pathos embodied in a desperately ill child, probably moments away from death, who can no longer hold his head erect and who is enveloped to the point of suffocation by the aura of his sickness. Rodin's *Ceres* (cat. no. 64) is particulary hard to grasp. The features of a known individual, Mariana Russell, are presented as a curious admixture of contemporaneity and the suggestion – via title – of temporal distance and symbolic significance.

ALBERT-ERNEST CARRIER-BELLEUSE

52.   *Awakening*

> cast brass, original model after 1865
> height: 22½ inches
> width: 12¼ inches
> depth: 9¾ inches
> Smith College Museum of Art, Northampton, Massachusetts. Purchased 1971. 1971.10
> Signed: *A. Carrier Belleuse* (on rear of socle)
> Provenance: Robert G. Allen (Antique Boutique, Provincetown, Mass.)

June Hargrove categorized *Awakening* and a number of related works as "fantasy busts." In 1865 Henri Ardant, director of the Limoges porcelain factory at Tharaud, gave a pair of them which he had previously commissioned – *Spring* and *Autumn* – to the Musée

Dubouché in Limoges. *Awakening* closely echoes the pose and erotic languor of *Autumn*, and on this basis Hargrove dates this sensuous personification of "awakening" somewhat later. It too had a pendant, *Sleep*.

Between March 20 and 23, 1893, works of Carrier-Belleuse, including molds for his sculpture and the rights of reproduction from them, were sold at Hôtel Drouot in Paris. Item number 104 was the mold in five pieces for *Awakening*, and a model, sixty centimeters high; purchase of these items included "all rights, except for the reproduction in bronze and in porcelain." Measurements of sculpture are notoriously inaccurate, and this may account for the nearly three-centimeter discrepancy between the model sold in 1893 and the *Awakening* from Smith, but the dimensions may also have been mechanically altered before casting took place. The change in metal from bronze to brass would be in keeping with the terms of the sale.

52

53. *Head of Christ* [color plate, p. xii]

bronze, 1867; original model 1858

height: 24⅞ inches

width: 15¾ inches

depth: 18⅜ inches

Museum of Fine Arts, Boston. Gift of Patricia Learmonth, to the memory of her husband, Raoul H. Fleischmann. 1983.158

Signed and dated: CLÉSINGER 1867 (right edge of truncation)

Foundry mark: POUSSIELGUE-RUSAND (right edge of truncation)

Provenance: Shepherd Gallery Associates (New York)

It may seem strange that an egomaniac like Clésinger, who welcomed notoriety when he exhibited one of the most blatantly erotic sculptures of the nineteenth century, was also capable of making distinguished religious sculpture, but this is so. His *Head of Christ* is as formally distinguished and emotionally engaging as Rude's *Crucifixion* group for the Parisian church of Saint-Vincent-de-Paul (Salon of 1852); Clésinger's Christ can be seen as a fleshier, more earthbound variant on Rude's.

His first bust of Christ was a marble done in 1847, the same year as the *Woman Bitten by a Serpent.* In 1858 while in Rome, he modeled a *Head of Christ,* which was both carved in marble (one of these entered the Vatican collections) and cast in bronze. A marble *Head of Christ* was also exhibited at the Salon of 1859. These heads are the same size as the bronze included here, even though this cast is dated 1867 (as is another cast – identical in size – but made of silvered bronze, which is in the Cleveland Museum of Art), whereas the earlier examples are signed and dated "Rome 1858." In addition to this Christ, Clésinger executed one major religious commission, a *Pietà* for the Chapel of the Souls in Purgatory in Saint-Sulpice, Paris (Salon of 1850). While in Rome, he also spent time in the company of cardinals and modeled a bust of Pope Pius IX.

Nineteenth-century images of Christ tend to emphasize the ideal and godlike (as do the other examples included in this exhibition, by Gould, Greenough, and Sargent) or the physical, as is true of Clésinger. The beautiful, broad face of the Savior is framed by flowing hair and beard and a crown of thorns that are as tactile as fine jeweler's work. The ancestors of this image are not only Rude but also great Italian sculptors and goldsmiths of the Renaissance, like Andrea del Verrocchio and Benvenuto Cellini.

53

54. *Bust of Diana*

bronze, original model 1882, or later

height: 17¾ inches

width: 18½ inches

depth: 15 inches

Middlebury College Museum of Art. Purchase, with funds provided by The Friends of Art Acquisition Fund. 1979.21

Signed: *A. Falguière* (engraved after casting); stamped: *4100* (under right shoulder)

Foundry mark: *Thiébaut frères/Fumière & Gavignot/Sre/Paris* (on back of self-base)

Provenance: Shepherd Gallery Associates (New York)

Falguière understood his public very well and on numerous occasions offered them provocatively posed female nudes to admire. He would introduce a life-size version of a sculpture at one Salon, and then send the same figure to a later Salon in another material. (This was common practice at nineteenth-century official exhibitions.) In 1882 he sent *Diana* in plaster and two years later his *Hunting Nymph*, in plaster as well. The latter figure also appeared as a bronze in 1885 and as a marble in 1888. In 1887 *Diana* returned as a marble. This kind of repetition was good for business; repeated viewings increased the likelihood of sales. In fact, Mr. Weld, a rich collector from Boston, purchased both marble versions (as well as a third marble nude, the *Woman with a Peacock* shown at the Salon of 1890) and eventually willed them all to the Musée des Augustins in Falguière's native city, Toulouse. These works were also edited in reduced versions of various sizes and were very popular.

Beside editing reductions of the full figure of *Diana*, Falguière excerpted her head and shoulders, and in so doing, produced one of his most aesthetically pleasing works. The *Bust of Diana*, which exists in more than one size in bronze, was also carved in marble and cast in terra cotta. The pose of the full figure is explained by the narrative situation. Diana, goddess of the hunt and of the moon, has just fired an arrow, and she now lowers the bow held in her left hand but still holds the right hand aloft in the aftermath of releasing her arrow. Her divine disdain is communicated by every nuance of body language and by the icy perfection of the surfaces that define her nude flesh. All of these characteristics seem heightened in the excerpt. The narrative situation disappears, and all that remains is the distilled essence of haughty aloofness. The lowered shoulder no

54

longer demands to be read in the context of Diana's bow, and the raised one now seems like an inspired formal decision rather than a necessary movement in the wake of firing an arrow.

55. *Head of a Wounded Soldier*

bronze, date of original model unknown
height: 5⅞ inches
width: 5½ inches
depth: 7¼ inches
Yale University Art Gallery. Director's Purchase. 1977.150
Signed and inscribed: *A. Falguière/cire perdue/A. Hebrard/179* (the number differs in size, font, and depth from the signature and inscription) (right side of neck)
Provenance: Galerie Fischer Kiener (Paris)

This striking head has a communicative power that exceeds what we normally expect from Falguière, but neither its context nor its date is known. It may have been modeled while Falguière was working on one of his monuments associated with the Revolution

55

(the Centenary Monument of 1892 for Chambéry, or various projects for a monument to be constructed in the apse of the Panthéon, 1890–96), but it also may have been created independently, in the wake of the Franco-Prussian War and the Commune. H. W. Janson suggested that it might be related to the monument that Falguière's native city of Toulouse commissioned him to make, *Switzerland Welcoming the French Army* (Salon of 1875); none of these possibilities can be embraced with any certainty.

Unlike Falguière's usual procedures, which emphasize that the object – no matter how convincing in terms of realism – is an art work, this head has no base and must rest directly and unceremoniously on whatever surface is available. The parted lips, closed eyes, and bandage all elicit sympathy, but the essence of its expressiveness seems to lie in the position of the head, inclined backward and suggesting extreme vulnerability. In this respect, it has a close affinity with Rodin's *Head of Sorrow* (cat. no. 65).

Thomas Gould

56. *Bust of Christ*

> marble, original model 1863, carved 1878
> height: 21⁹⁄₁₆ inches
> width: 15¼ inches
> depth: 14⅜ inches
> Boston Athenaeum. Gift of several subscribers, 1878. U.H.81.1878
> Signed and dated: *T. R. Gould/SC: 1863* (on back)

57. *Bust of Satan*

> marble, original model 1862, carved 1878
> height: 22⅛ inches
> width: 14⅝ inches
> depth: 11⅜ inches
> Boston Athenaeum. Gift of several subscribers, 1878. U.H.80.1878
> Signed and dated: *T. R. Gould/SC: 1862* (on back)

This pair was clearly inspired by Greenough's busts of Christ and Lucifer (cat. nos. 60, 61). Like Greenough, Gould accepted the neoclassical convention of the nude chest and shoulders for an ideal bust and the decision that Christ should wear a beard and Satan be clean-shaven, but he eschewed the luxuriant coiffures and the drama of serpents encircling the bases. The incline of Christ's head makes him seem more introspective, but

56

his ideal physiognomy is ultimately based – via Greenough – on that paragon of nine-teenth-century Protestant images of Christ, Bertel Thorvaldsen's over-life-size statue for the Church of Our Lady in Copenhagen. Satan is a more personal conception and is probably based on contemporary notions of physiognomy as revealer of personality traits. His face is broader and rounder; his nose is flattened and pugnacious; his thin lips are contorted in a sneer. Satan's eyebrows are luxuriant and would surely have been seen

by Gould's contemporaries as subhuman. His hair is considerably shorter than Christ's and seems tightly matted, almost like the pelt of an animal. In 1870 one writer published a contrasting characterization of the two: Gould's Christ manifested "godly sanctity and blessed humanity," while Satan revealed his "blasted cunning and infernal pride."

These busts made a strong impression on Gould's fellow Bostonians. From 1864 onward the plasters were exhibited at the Boston Athenaeum. After a group of enthusiastic subscribers raised the necessary one thousand dollars, the two busts were carved in marble under Gould's supervision in Florence during 1878 and presented to the Athenaeum the same year.

58.   *The Ghost in Hamlet* [cover]

marble, 1879
height: 20 inches
width: 16⅜ inches
Robert Hull Fleming Museum, University of Vermont. Gift of Mrs. A. T. Fenno. 1881.2.2LA

58

The Ghost in Hamlet [color plate, p. xiii]

marble, 1880
height: 20¼ inches
width: 16½ inches
Worcester Art Museum. Gift of Mrs. Kingsmill Marrs and Grenville H. Norcross. 1916.20
Signed, dated, and inscribed: *T. R. Gould/Inv. et fecit/Florence 1880* (left edge at bottom of
    rondel)

The *Ghost in Hamlet* is arguably Gould's finest work. The conception seems truly inspired, reducing the apparition from the first act of *Hamlet* to a disembodied head that

59

materializes within a concave oval, which in turn is framed within a rectangle. There is no rational explanation for the manner in which the long hair of the head and beard flows outward, as if submerged in some aqueous medium peculiar to the spirit world, rather than subject to the laws of gravity. The great visor of the helmet is surmounted by luxuriant plumage, which billows as if animated from within by the ghost's agitated state of mind. The deep undercuttings and richness of textural variations create a complex harmony of shadows, which contributes to the otherworldliness of the relief.

The *Ghost in Hamlet* was given to the Worcester Museum in 1916 and published in the museum's *Bulletin* of January 1920. Subsequently, Almira Fenno-Gendrot (who published *Artists I Have Known* in 1923, which includes her memories of Gould) wrote to the museum that its version, hitherto thought to be unique, was in fact the second that Gould had made. "The original ghost at one time was in our collection. The other [owned by Norcross, who donated it to the museum] was a replica, of which Mr. Gould told me, saying 'I feel I have added much to the replica, more intensity and mystery' – we donated ours to the Park Art Gallery, Burlington, Vt." (Archive, Worcester Museum). The first, "Fenno version" is, in fact, still in Burlington and belongs to the University of Vermont, but its existence had been forgotten after it was installed in a stairway in the Royall Tyler Theatre. In this exhibition the two marbles are juxtaposed, and Gould's subtle variations, intended to create "more intensity and mystery," can be examined and judged for the first time.

HORATIO GREENOUGH

60. *Ideal Bust Representing Christ*

marble, 1845–46
height: 32 inches
width: 16¾ inches
depth: 13½ inches
Courtesy of the Trustees of the Public Library of the City of Boston. Gift of Horatio
    S. Greenough in 1895.
Signed: *Christ by Horatio Greenough* (on pedestal of original)

61. *Ideal Bust Representing Lucifer* [color plate, p. xiv]

marble, 1841–42

height: 32 inches

width: 15¼ inches

depth: 12½ inches

Courtesy of the Trustees of the Public Library of the City of Boston. Gift of Horatio S.
    Greenough in 1895.

These two busts unite Christ and Lucifer as a complementary pair, and Greenough's iconographic intention in doing so is not entirely clear. Merely decorative paired busts are frequently encountered in eighteenth- and nineteenth-century sculpture; pairings of more serious subjects are also known, but they are less common and tend to be earlier. Cordieri's busts of Saint Peter and Saint Paul (c. 1610) at San Sebastiano in Rome pair the two saints to whom that church was once dedicated. Bernini's *Blessed Soul* and *Damned Soul* (c. 1620) in the Palazzo di Spagna (Rome) were conceived as polar opposites. Both sets were probably known to Greenough from firsthand study in Rome. Busts of Christ are rare in Western sculpture (and unknown in American sculpture prior to Greenough's); the pairing of a bust of Christ with one of Satan is unprecedented.

Greenough did not work on these two simultaneously. He completed Lucifer long before he began Christ, so their pairing may have been an inspired afterthought. Milton's *Paradise Lost* was almost certainly his point of departure. (In 1838–39 Greenough had made a statuette of the angel *Abdiel* [Yale University Art Gallery], whose identity could hardly have been known to him except through Milton.) In *Paradise Lost* Lucifer is not interchangeable with Satan; he is the demon of sinful pride. The equivalence of their identities is so prevalent from Early Christian times onward, however, that Greenough may not have wished to make a distinction between them.

Whether Lucifer or Satan, demon or fallen angel, this male head is not a typical representation of evil. Douglas Hyland calls him, with justification, "diabolically handsome." Indeed, he has the same classically idealized features and blank eyeballs as Christ. His slightly turned head and luxuriant curls are the only aspects of the bust proper that hint at hubris, disobedience, or rebellion. Christ is far more serene in his characterization and recalls the head of the full figure of Christ by Thorvaldsen (original, Church of Our Lady, Copenhagen), which Greenough had admired while it was being carved in Carrara. He knew that he was embarking on a new sculptural adventure when he modeled this bust and wrote to a friend: "I am not aware that any American has, until now, risked placing before his countrymen a representation of our Savior." What he expected

60

his countrymen to think of this unorthodox pairing of the Savior and his chief adversary has not been recorded.

Perhaps the most intriguing aspect of these busts is the presence of the serpents entwined about the socles. The one beneath Lucifer is still alive and potentially dangerous; its head twists to one side with an open mouth, fangs bared and tongue extended. Christ's emblematic serpent is vanquished and perhaps dead, with its head hanging

158

61

limply over the coiled body. Greenough had previously incorporated paired serpents, living and dead, into his iconography. On the right side of the throne of his colossal George Washington is an image of the infant Hercules with two snakes placed in his cradle by Hera; the child-hero has killed one of them and is struggling with the other.

There is a long-standing iconography of serpents associated with Christ and Satan, beginning with the tempter in the Garden of Eden. The vanquished serpent is probably best known from images of the Immaculate Conception, where the Virgin Mary crushes it beneath her feet while standing on the moon. In *Paradise Lost* there is a horrifying image of Satan and all the fallen angels being transformed into serpents (Book 10, lines 504–23), which would be a wholly appropriate reference for Greenough to invoke if his image was meant to be a composite Satan-Lucifer. Between the bust proper and the serpent on both busts are pairs of ornamental heads; for Christ, they are angels, and for Lucifer, devils.

HIRAM POWERS

62.   *Bust of the Greek Slave*

> marble, original model after 1843
>
> height: 24½ inches
>
> width: 16 inches
>
> depth: 7½ inches
>
> Middlebury College Museum of Art. Purchase, with funds provided by The Friends of Art Acquisition Fund and the Salomon-Hutzler Foundation. 1970.6
>
> Signed: H POWERS *sculp* (center back on base support)
>
> Provenance: Michael Hall Fine Arts (New York); purchased in England, 1968

Powers's reputation was initially established as a maker of portrait busts, and he did not model a full-length figure or a nude until after he arrived in Florence. The first in both latter categories was *Eve Tempted* (begun in 1838), followed by the *Greek Slave* and the *Fisherboy* (which were developed simultaneously, 1841–43). Nude statues were common in the European tradition; the greatest masters of antiquity, the Renaissance, and the present had all made them. This was hardly the case in America. These early works by Powers are the first publicly exhibited sculpted nudes made by an American, with the exception of Thomas Crawford's *Orpheus*, which was begun in 1839. As such, they are landmarks in American art and in the growth of sophistication of American artists and their public.

Powers seems to have genuinely believed that the content of this work was chaste and Christian, but he also realized that he would have to convince his puritanical countrymen (and -women) that this was the case. He composed a statement, which is a masterpiece of public relations, to accompany the work during its tour of America (1847–49). In it, he explained that the "event" is from the time of the recent Greek revolution, in the 1820s. This young woman has been abducted from one of the Greek islands by the Turks.

62

Now separated from her family, she is about to be sold in a slave market. "She stands exposed to the people she abhors, and waits her fate with intense anxiety, tempered indeed by the support of her reliance upon the goodness of God. Gather all the afflictions together and add to them the fortitude and resignation of a Christian, and no room will be left for shame. Such are the circumstances under which the *Greek Slave* is supposed to stand."

Nude – but not intentionally undressed – Christian, and as virtuous as the pure white material implies, this statue and its calculated rationale allowed viewers to admire her nudity without guilt. Posters announcing the exhibition (admission: 25 cents) extolled "this World Renowned Statue, Over which Poets have grown sublime, and Orators eloquent." The statue's edifying qualities and just the right hint of titillation were included in the printed promise designed to lure the crowds. The Grecian maiden's plight was made clear; she has been "made captive by the Turks, and exposed for sale in the Bazaar of Constantinople." The morally uplifting qualities, perhaps tempered with a hint of the forbidden, were implied by the fact that "none but ladies and families will be admitted during the afternoon of each day." From the vantage point of the 1990s, we realize that a mastery of manipulating subtexts is at work here. Chains and manacles, the rosary, her powerlessness, and the probability of imminent sexual violation by her captors form an unbeatable synthesis for provoking erotic fantasy, all scripted with a moral imprimatur.

The immense popularity of the *Greek Slave* generated a large demand for busts of it, which became a popular cultural icon during the middle and later years of the nineteenth century. There are references to over one hundred busts, in varying sizes – some with the ornamental pattern at the lower termination of the figure and some without it. Obviously, double accounting must have occurred, and this number is too high. Some that were once recorded as having been made, or in a particular collection, must have been sold or otherwise changed hands; these turned up later without a specific provenance and were recounted.

Powers's command of body language and dramatic characterization was so fully realized in the pose of the *Greek Slave* that the bust communicates much of the dramatic content of the whole statue, even without any of the narrative clues. The averted, downturned gaze, the serenely beautiful profile, the exquisite idealized surfaces, coupled with a large measure of anatomical exactitude, combine to create an aura of innocence and fragility, with a hint of eroticism, even without chains, rosary, or cast-aside drapery.

AUGUSTE RODIN

63. *Head of Balzac*

bronze, original model 1892, or later

height: 10¹⁄₁₆ inches

width: 8 inches

depth: 7½ inches

Williams College Museum of Art. Museum Purchase, with funds given in memory of Karl E. Weston '96. 57.6

Inscription: *A Rodin* (inside back neck in cast)

Provenance: Duveen-Graham (New York)

No other artist experimented more extensively, or more effectively, with the notion of *pars pro toto* – the individual part that embodies the meaning of the whole – than Rodin. This sort of aesthetic synecdoche was already apparent in his work of the later 1870s and continued unabated thereafter. Of course, one of his entire figures could be regarded as a finished work of sculpture, but so too could its head, its head and shoulders, its torso, its limbs, or any combination of these component parts. What is extraordinary and exceptional in Rodin's sculpture is the extent to which his figures – so intrinsically ambiguous and subject to multiple readings – constitute aesthetic wholes which are internally consistent. No comparison could illustrate this point more clearly than a pairing of *Balzac Nude* (cat. no. 24) with the head excerpted from it.

Rodin also made a more conventional bust by isolating the head and shoulders, but the head alone with its massive neck and a V-shaped portion of the upper torso communicates a sense of the whole at least as effectively. The twist of the head from the axis of its implied body conveys the same titanic forcefulness as the entire figure. The inflated corpulence of the face in dialogue with the animated resistance of the skin containing it suggests latent energy which could be released at any moment, just as the surfaces of Balzac's body, arms, and legs do. The arrogant, bemused, sensual expression of the face bespeaks the same gargantuan appetites as the heroic belly of the full figure. Even without a body, this head conveys the sense of both an "athlete of virtue" who creates and an indomitable sensualist who experiences life to its fullest.

64.　*Ceres* [color plate, p. xv]

marble, 1896
height: 26¾ inches
width: 18¾ inches
depth: 16½ inches
Museum of Fine Arts, Boston. Anonymous Gift. 06.1910
Signed: *A. Rodin* (right side, on rough marble)

This sculpture, named for the Earth Goddess and protector of agriculture, is the largest among a group of seven marbles made at approximately the same time. All but one of them are named after goddesses of Greek and Roman antiquity, and all were inspired by the features of the same woman, Mariana Russell. She and her husband, the Australian expatriate painter John P. Russell, resided at a château on Belle-Île, off the coast of Brittany in France. In 1888 Rodin modeled her head in wax, and this beautiful likeness (now at the Stanford University Museum of Art), rather than further sittings, presumably served as inspiration for the later marbles.

63

Ceres is the only one of the seven with a fully carved head of hair, and she lacks all iconographic attributes that might serve to reveal her identity as a Roman goddess. In fact, the drapery that covers her shoulders and upper body evokes fashionable late-nineteenth-century outerwear more than it does a toga. The title thus seems wholly arbitrary, a flattering reference to Mariana Russell's classical beauty rather than an indication that Rodin wished to depict the Earth Goddess.

Ceres is the only Rodin marble included in this exhibition; the other five sculptures by him are bronzes. It is a well-known fact that Rodin was primarily a modeler of clay, rather than a carver of stone. He sometimes finished his marbles, and he exerted tight control over their execution, but they were carved by professional artisans, not by the

64

artist himself. In this respect, Rodin's procedure was the norm rather than an exception to nineteenth-century studio practice. Despite his remoteness from the process of carving, Rodin imposed his vision and personality on the finished marbles. They may vary in quality, but the best ones – among which *Ceres* must be numbered – carry the strongest imprint of his artistic will. Rodin understood that marble, similar to wax but unlike plaster or bronze, has unique optical properties. It absorbs light, as well as reflecting it, and is thus capable of producing the richest possible array of shadows, half-shadows, and reflections. Rodin exploited these effects to their fullest with his emphasis on veiled forms rather than precise ones, and with the contrast between smooth surfaces and roughly chiseled stone.

65.   *Head of Sorrow*

> bronze, original model 1882
> height: 8¾ inches
> width: 9 inches
> depth: 10¾ inches
> Museum of Fine Arts, Boston. Gift of Janet Gregg Schroeder in memory of Dr. Henry A. Schroeder. 1978.397
> Signed: *A. Rodin* (right side)
> Foundry mark: *Alexis Rudier/Fondeur/Paris*
> Provenance: Curt Valentin Estate

Sorrow is a central motif in Rodin's art, and this head, which bears the word as its title, is one of his most expressive. Unlike Bernini's ecstatic female saints depicted with eyes closed and mouth open – which seem to be Rodin's point of departure – *Sorrow* is far more ambiguous and generalized. There is a strong suggestion of erotically tinged pain, as in Bernini, but other emotional states seem to be implied as well. Our inability to pinpoint one mental state at the expense of others is a characteristic response to Rodin's intentionally elusive content. Indeed, the fact that he used this head in a variety of contexts confirms that he attached no single meaning to it.

In its first manifestation, this head belonged to one of Count Ugolino's dying sons from the group Rodin modeled for *The Gates of Hell*. Therefore, it was first conceived as a male head, and the emotion was one that resulted from extreme physical torment, the pain of starvation. On the *Gates*, Rodin reused the head two more times in the context of groups representing the *Inferno*'s condemned lovers, Paolo and Francesca. For the group known as *Fugit Amor*, on the right door, the head was attached to the male figure. On the left door, the lovers' lithe bodies are so similar in structure that it is impossible to say whether this head belongs to Paolo or Francesca, since their grappling poses conceal their sexes. In both cases, however, the facial expression is a response to insatiable physical desire. This head was also used for the *Prodigal Son* (itself a variant on *Fugit Amor*), *Head of Orpheus* (now known as the *Last Sigh*), *Joan of Arc*, and *Head of Eleanora Duse*. A single highly expressive head therefore served a multitude of contexts; the situ-

65

ations range from extreme physical pain to overwhelming emotional torment, and all are tinged with a distinctly erotic undercurrent.

Heads that evoke states of mind are a staple in the repertoire of symbolism, and this pose is characteristic. Closed eyes suggest interiority. The forms themselves are generalized and compact, rather than interacting with their environment. The open mouth implies the most ambiguous of human communications, a sigh. A head extended backward like this one connotes extreme vulnerability, passivity, and absence of control; these all seem appropriate in the context of unfathomable Sorrow that exists independently, without any suggestion of its cause or the identity of the sufferer.

Rodin understood, perhaps better than any other nineteenth-century sculptor, that variations in presentation – even minute ones – can transform a work's apparent meaning. He often altered the orientation of a piece from horizontal to vertical, or vice versa, or changed the angle of its support, creating wholly new and unexpected nuances from its reconfiguration. All of the different contexts and titles cited above maintain the same "extended-backward" pose of the head, except one: the *Eleanora Duse*. For that variant, Rodin changed the orientation to vertical and christened the head with yet another title, *Anxiety*. In this pose, the same head gains authority, and the closed eyes and open mouth recall the great tragedienne dramatically declaiming Dante, as she did when she once visited Rodin.

MEDARDO ROSSO

66.   *Sick Little Boy* [color plate, p. xvi]

> plaster and wax, original model 1893
>
> height: 10½ inches
>
> width: 9⅜ inches
>
> depth: 7 inches
>
> Middlebury College Museum of Art. Purchase, with funds provided by The Christian A. Johnson Memorial Fund. 1979.36
>
> Signed: M ROSSO (bottom right)
>
> Provenance: Ludwig Wittgenstein; Margarethe Stonborough-Wittgenstein, Gräfin Zittau; Shepherd Gallery Associates (New York)

The *Sick Little Boy* is an image of great pathos and communicative power. Rosso did a number of versions of it, each with slight variations, as was his common practice. The exact angle of the inclined head may be adjusted slightly from version to version, but the tilt itself is always present and integral to the work's meaning. It connotes drowsiness or sleep, but the sense of a sagging weight that cannot be sustained by the neck muscles also suggests imminent death. Indeed, the work has been known by different titles that suggest its fundamental ambiguity: *Bimbo* (or *Bambino*) *malato* (*Sick Boy*, or *Sick Little Boy*), *Ragazzo morente* (*Dying Boy*), and *Impression à Laborisière* (a Parisian hospital where Rosso had been a patient in October 1889 and where he may have witnessed a desperately ill child).

The facial features have been modeled with the greatest delicacy, hinting at rather than describing the little boy's physiognomy. As is usual with Rosso, the two sides of the

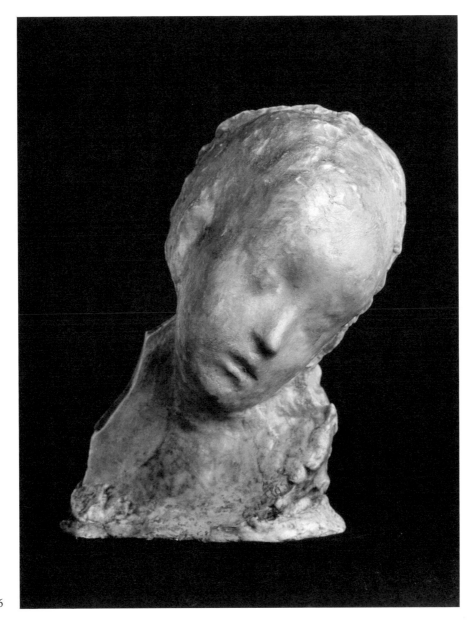

66

face are formed unequally with the suggestion that one is illuminated and the other in shadow. The child seems enveloped in a hazy sfumato; his veiled forms palpably evoke the environment of a sickroom where curtains are drawn, the atmosphere is stale and pervaded with the smell of medications, and an aura of helplessness hovers in the air.

Other artists of the same period also chose to represent sick or dying children. Munch and Carrière come to mind immediately. Zola, who bought Rosso's early *Concierge* in the fall of 1889, had made the death and dying of Claude and Christine Lantier's young son central to the plot of his novel *L'Œuvre* (1886) in the Roujon-Macquart series. Gustave Mahler, who was Rosso's exact contemporary, published his mournful songs, *Kindertotenlieder* (Songs on the death of children) in 1905.

FRANÇOIS RUDE

67.   *Head of a Gaul*

> bronze, original model, reduced size, after 1836
>
> height: 11 inches
>
> width: 8¾ inches
>
> depth: 6¼ inches
>
> Middlebury College Museum of Art. Purchase, with funds provided by The Friends of Art Acquisitions Fund. 1979.20
>
> Signed: *F. RUDE* (edge of left shoulder)
>
> Provenance: Shepherd Gallery Associates (New York)

In his intensely dramatic relief, the *Departure of the Volunteers of 1792* (the *Marseillaise*), for the Arc de Triomphe de l'Étoile, Rude depicted six vigorous male figures who stand on the ground, an array of swords and standards behind them, and an explosive figure of Marianne, the personification of the French Republic – winged, helmeted, and wearing an armored breastplate and voluminous draperies – flying above them. This relief celebrating the effort of 1792 to protect France from the foreign armies massed at her borders shows the protagonists clothed not in historically accurate costume but according to allegorical conventions. Two of the males are nude; all hold classical arms or wear classical armor; three have great, flowing beards that recall Gallic soldiers. Marianne is a fearsome warrior-goddess with her mouth open in a scream of defiance against the enemy, encouraging her troops.

Two of the heads from this rousing, patriotic relief have had a long and extensive afterlife based on bronze editions in various sizes which were cast after the *Departure* was unveiled: that of Marianne herself and that of the bearded Gaul directly beneath her. In the context of the relief this figure plays an intermediary role; with his left arm he embraces the nude young man who is the hope of France's future, and with his right he holds his helmet aloft, gesturing forward and upward in the same direction that Marianne points her sword. When they are displaced from their original context, both heads lose a large measure of their narrative significance and become rather straightforward, animated symbols of patriotic fervor. Both are turned slightly on their axes, so that their

67

primary viewpoint is more frontal than on the relief, and they seem to address the viewer as much as an unseen horde in the vague distance. The *Gaul*, who for some reason is often called the "Old Gaul," is a paragon of vigorous maturity. With his knitted brow, intense and deeply undercut eyes, and hair in wild disarray, he is a model of baroque formal animation and the passionate intensity of a patriot courageously facing a mortal threat to his country.

ARTISTS' BIOGRAPHIES

ANDREONI, Orazio

    active c. 1884–1893
    Italian

Orazio Andreoni remains something of an art-historical enigma. Neither his birth and death dates nor the location of either event has been established, and only the briefest outline of his career is known. Between 1884 and 1892 he exhibited works of sculpture in Turin, Berlin, and Munich. These were historical figures (Ruth, Messalina, a Pharisee) and busts (a Moor and a Moroccan negress), exotic evocations of "otherness," which were much in vogue at the time. He was also a skilled portraitist, and his work especially appealed to British and American collectors.

The largest and most accessible work by Andreoni that can be seen in New England is the marble group *Pereat (Let Him Perish)*, at the Wadsworth Atheneum in Hartford. A gift to the museum in 1910, it is 6½ feet high and signed, dated 1892, and inscribed *Rome*. An extremely unpleasant narrative situation is depicted. Two Roman matrons, their faces contorted with blood lust, are concentrating on a scene we can only imagine – aided by the presence of a bronze gladiator's helmet lying at their feet – as they give the thumbs-down gesture signifying that a felled gladiator should be killed by his opponent. This sort of fanciful artistic re-creation of events from the ancient world can also be found in the work of some of Andreoni's contemporaries, such as Sir Lawrence Alma-Tadema; Frederic, Lord Leighton; and Jean-Léon Gérôme. The Hartford marble hints at the sort of staged drama and narrative predilection which probably characterized other historical figures Andreoni exhibited across Europe at the end of the nineteenth century.

In 1893 Frederick Fairbanks of St. Johnsbury, Vermont, traveled to Rome, accompanied by his granddaughter. There, he commissioned Andreoni to make two bronze lions to stand guard at the entrance of the Fairbanks Museum in St. Johnsbury. These were installed in 1894 and are still in place. At the same time he sat for his portrait bust; this marble likeness is preserved inside the museum.

BARTOLINI, Lorenzo

    1777 (Vernio, Tuscany) – 1850 (Florence)
    Italian

Lorenzo Bartolini was the finest Italian sculptor of the generation after Antonio Canova. He was born in a small Tuscan town and worked mostly in Florence, but in 1797 he went to Paris to study sculpture. His arrival there coincided with that of the young painter Jean-Auguste-Dominique Ingres; they met, became close friends, and eventually would do each other's portraits. Bartolini began his professional career in the French capital in the service of the emperor. Napoleon subsequently sent him back to Italy to direct a school for sculptors in Cararra, where some of the finest and oldest marble quarries in the world are located. After Napoleon's fall, Bartolini established himself as an independent sculptor in Florence, where he worked for a largely foreign clientele, but he also made a number of notable monuments in the city and became a professor of sculpture at the local academy in 1839.

Bartolini's characteristic style blends a high level of naturalism with varying degrees of abstraction. His superb tomb of Countess Zamoyska (1837–44), in a chapel off the north transept of Santa Croce in Florence, evokes the format and hazy, descriptive naturalism of the quattrocento tombs in the same church by Desiderio da Settignano and Bernardo Rossellino, but his uninspired monument to Alberti only a few yards away, in the nave, is emotionally uncommunicative, brittle of form, and ultimately unmemorable. *Trust in God* (1835, Poldi-Pezzoli Museum, Milan) is, to the eyes of a late-twentieth-century viewer, an uneasy blend of idealization and literal rendering of the unclothed body of an adolescent girl who kneels and gazes heavenward, but nineteenth-century patrons were intrigued by the statue and ordered numerous replicas from the artist. Bartolini made many busts of rich and mighty individuals of his day, including Napoleon and members of the French imperial family. One particularly engaging portrait of less-august individuals was the life-size, full-length pairing of the Campbell sisters, rich Scottish travelers who visited Florence during a grand tour of the Continent (1820, National Gallery of Scotland, Edinburgh).

BARYE, Antoine-Louis

1796 (Paris) – 1875 (Paris)
French

Barye was the greatest animalier, or sculptor of animals, of the nineteenth century. At first trained as an engraver and jeweler, he later turned to the fine arts. He studied with the academic sculptor François-Joseph Bosio and the romantic-painter-turned-classicist Baron Gros. His years at the École des Beaux-Arts (1818–23) did not result in the coveted Prix de Rome, and Barye subsequently resumed his career as an artisan, designing for the goldsmith Jacques-Henri Fauconnier. On his own, he studied animals and their anatomy while producing commercial designs to earn a living. The zoo at the Jardin des Plantes in Paris became the training ground where his continuing self-education took place. The Salons of 1831 and 1833 marked a turning point in his career. He exhibited – among other works – the *Tiger Devouring a Gavial of the Ganges* at the former and, at the latter, the *Lion Crushing a Serpent*. These romantic images of violence and savagery in the animal world made a great impression, and there was every indication that Barye would have a stellar career. In 1833 he was inducted into the Légion d'Honneur, at the same time as the sculptor François Rude, whose *Neapolitan Fisherboy* had also been a great success at the same Salon.

Despite the favor of King Louis-Philippe's son, the duc d'Orléans, among whose commissions was a spectacular *surtout de table* with nine groups dedicated to the hunt and animal predators, Barye fell afoul of the official art-world establishment and was excluded from the Salon during the later 1830s and 1840s. He did not lack for commissions during this period of exclusion, however. He executed the monumental lion relief for the column commemorating the Revolution of July 1830 in the place de la Bastille and the atypical marble statue of Sainte Clothilde for the church of the Madeleine. In 1845 he established his own business, which cast and sold bronze editions of his work; he published a catalogue of the works available, their sizes, and prices, a venture unprecedented in the nineteenth century. This commercial enterprise may recall the Florentine workshop of Giovanni da Bologna, which produced bronze editions in the late sixteenth and early seventeenth centuries, but Barye's business was also a response to the new realities of middle-class patronage and the marketing of art, realities that had begun to supersede the old system of state and aristocratic patronage.

The last twenty-five years of Barye's career were very productive; he was widely admired and successful. He designed important sculpture for the exterior decoration of the Louvre; he taught animal drawing at the Musée d'Histoire Naturelle, where the young Rodin was one of his pupils; he was promoted within the Légion d'Honneur and elected to the Institut de France; and he was commissioned to do an equestrian monument of Napoleon I for the city of Ajaccio in Corsica. American collectors were particularly enthusiastic about Barye's work and assembled vast numbers of his bronzes.

CARPEAUX, Jean-Baptiste
1827 (Valenciennes) – 1875 (Courbevoie)
French

Carpeaux's childhood was plagued by poverty; the memory of it haunted him, and he was never free of financial worries. Illness frequently debilitated him, and his difficult temperament led to personal problems and estrangements. Nevertheless, he was exceedingly productive and rose to the heights of his profession. As Dalou and Rodin would later do, he began his artistic career at the free government school, the Petite École, where he studied drawing, modeling, and other practical skills. He subsequently was admitted to the École des Beaux-Arts, studying first with Rude and then with Francisque Duret, who was remarkably successful in negotiating the Prix de Rome for his students. Carpeaux won that prize in 1854 and was the last great sculptor ever to do so.

His reputation was established with the *Ugolino*, which was modeled in Rome, shipped back to Paris in 1861, and exhibited with great success at the Salon of 1863. This multifigure group demonstrated beyond any doubt the extraordinary ambition and facility of the young sculptor. The theme from Dante's *Inferno* was inherently laden with dramatic tension, and Carpeaux presented the theme at fever pitch. The Pisan traitor, imprisoned with his sons to die of starvation, is on the verge of succumbing to cannibalism as his children expire about him. Their hysteria is contained by the all-encompassing pyramidal composition, and the five nude figures are integrated into it with virtuoso skill. Carpeaux meant to attract attention, and his *Ugolino* succeeded brilliantly at doing just that.

Commissions materialized from everywhere. He was entrusted with the architectural sculpture for the Pavilion de Flore of the Louvre, in 1863, and for a major statue to be installed on the facade of the new church of La Trinité. In 1864 he was asked to model a portrait of the heir apparent and produced the engaging *Prince Imperial with His Dog Nero*, which was endlessly reproduced and circulated in various sizes and media. His friend, the ar-

chitect Charles Garnier, arranged for him to make one of the four groups to adorn the facade of the new Opéra; this commission was granted in 1865 and resulted in *La Danse*. In 1867 Carpeaux was commissioned to do the *Four Parts of the World* for a monumental fountain at the Observatoire. There was no official post of court sculptor during the Second Empire, but Carpeaux functioned as if he held that position.

Carpeaux was a superlative portraitist and the master of a great variety of portrait types. Some have the delicacy and fragility of rococo busts (*Amélie de Montfort*, also known as *La Fiancée*, 1869, and *Mlle Eugénie Fiocre*, Salon of 1870); others have the forceful immediacy of "speaking likenesses" (*Charles Garnier*, Salon of 1869, and *Bruno Chérier*, Salon of 1875); while some aristocratic sitters were imbued with the rhetoric of baroque absolutist portraiture (*Princesse Mathilde*, 1862, and *Duchesse de Mouchy*, Salon of 1868).

CARRIER-BELLEUSE, Albert-Ernest
1824 (Anisy-le-Château, Aisne) – 1887 (Sèvres)
French

Like Carpeaux, Dalou, and Rodin, Carrier-Belleuse studied at the Petite École, and, although he was admitted to the École des Beaux-Arts, he remained there for only a brief time. His earliest employment was working for the goldsmiths Fauconnier and Fannière Frères, and he remained closely associated with the commercial art world throughout his career. Between 1850 and 1855 he worked for the Minton China Works in England, and, from 1875 until his death, he was the director of the manufacture of Sèvres porcelain for the French government. His output of designs and models for these two industries, and many others, was prodigious. Carrier-Belleuse also did extensive work in architectural sculpture, and his work adorns many of the fine buildings that were built in Paris during his lifetime. His elaborate torchères (modeled c. 1869) that ornament the grand staircase of Garnier's Opéra number among the finest decorative architectural work of the nineteenth century.

Carrier-Belleuse also made numerous statuettes in bronze and terra cotta, as well as full-scale sculpture. He would rework terra-cotta casts while the clay was still damp so that his multiples would still bear the mark of the artist's touch and thus communicate a sense of freshness and spontaneity. (Dalou would adopt this procedure in the 1870s.) Both artists often aimed to create an intimacy of subject and liveliness of surface, in imitation of their eighteenth-century French predecessors. Like Barye, Carrier-Belleuse sold his work directly to the public, but through the Drouot auction house. After 1867 he received numerous awards and decorations in recognition of his outstanding accomplishments in the fine and decorative arts.

CHANTREY, Francis
  1781 (Norton, Darbyshire) – 1841 (London)
  British

Chantrey came from humble origins and was largely self-taught but nonetheless reached the pinnacle of his profession and died a very wealthy man. His admission to the Royal Academy in 1816, given his lack of formal training, was virtually unprecedented; his candidacy was encouraged by the older and more established sculptor Joseph Nollekens. Only two years later he was raised to the honor of full Academician. He traveled to Italy in 1819 and there met with the two greatest living neoclassical sculptors, the Italian Antonio Canova and the Dane Bertel Thorvaldsen, but Chantrey never subscribed to the abstraction and idealization that characterized their art. He was a superb portraitist and a prolific creator of monuments, both for public spaces and for churches. His equestrian portrait of King George IV (1828) presides over Trafalgar Square in London, and his standing portrait of George Washington (1826) greets visitors when they enter the Massachusetts State House in Boston.

CHARPENTIER, Alexandre
  1856 (Paris)–1909 (Neuilly)
  French

Charpentier had a successful career, primarily as a prolific maker of portrait medals and reliefs. He also made portrait busts, reliefs, and statuettes portraying scenes of modern life, as well as stoneware pieces. His largest and most ambitious work was a wall-size relief made of glazed bricks, celebrating the bakers of Paris (today installed in the square Scipion in the fifth arrondissement, to the southeast of the Jardin des Plantes). Charpentier's training was conventional; he studied at the École des Beaux-Arts and competed unsuccessfully for the Prix de Rome. Later in life he was named to the Légion d'Honneur and won a *grand prix* for his work exhibited at the Exposition Universelle of 1900 in Paris.

CHINARD, Joseph
  1756 (Lyon) – 1813 (Lyon)
  French

Chinard lived through the turbulent events of the French Revolution and participated in them, as both citizen and artist. He received his preliminary training in his native Lyon and subsequently moved to Rome, with the financial support of a local aristocrat, to continue his artistic education (1784–87). On a subsequent trip to Rome in 1791–92, he was jailed on politico-religious charges (his terra cotta, *Apollo Trampling Superstition*, was rightly perceived as antichurch) but was released through the intervention of the influential French painter Jacques-Louis David. Back in Lyon, the authorities jailed Chinard for a time because they found his revolutionary iconography insufficiently zealous. Also in his native city, where he lived and practiced for most of his career, he served as the pageant maker who organized revolutionary fêtes and designed sculptural images to glorify the revolution. Following the revolution, his major artistic accomplishments were portraits, including those of Napoleon, the Empress Josephine, and members of the imperial family.

CLÉSINGER, Jean-Baptiste (called Auguste)
1814 (Besançon) – 1883 (Paris)
French

Clésinger was an artist of considerable talent, overwhelming ambition, and extreme emotions. His father, a professor of sculpture in Besançon, was his first teacher; he took his teen-age son to Rome, where the boy studied briefly with the great Danish sculptor Bertel Thorvaldsen and the architect Salvi. As a sculptor-in-the-making, Clésinger was restless and peripatetic. His travels took him to Switzerland, Florence, and Paris, where he worked for a time in the studio of David d'Angers.

In 1847 Clésinger was catapulted to fame when he exhibited at the Salon a work calculated to attract maximum attention, the *Woman Bitten by a Serpent*. This marble depicts an adult female nude, voluptuous and unidealized, lying on her back in a spiraling pose in a bower of flowers. Her agony could be explained (or justified, if the viewer felt the need) by the supposed bite of the small snake curled about one of her legs, but hardly anyone was fooled into thinking this was anything other than the most explicit depiction of erotic abandon ever seen at the Salon. Even more deliciously scandalous was the common knowledge that the model for it had been the great courtesan Madame Sabatier, former mistress of both Baudelaire and Clésinger, and that the statue had been commissioned by her current lover, the financier Alfred Mosselman. Most critics – and the public – were delighted. The prudish Chopin, however, was one of those who thought it "more than indecent." At the same time, Clésinger was working on a seated, draped statue of George Sand for the Théâtre-Français; he married Sand's daughter in 1847, but their tempestuous marriage lasted only five years.

Clésinger produced a vast body of sculpture. He did other erotic pieces featuring horizontal female nudes, plus monuments, busts, patriotic and religious pieces, and equestrians. When a plaster of his state commission for a colossal equestrian Francis I was temporarily installed in the Louvre courtyard in 1856, scathing criticism was leveled against it by his enemy, the sculptor Auguste Préault. In response Clésinger chose to withdraw from Paris and the Parisian art world altogether; he moved to Rome for an eight-year, self-imposed exile. There he nursed his wounds, with his confidence unshaken and arrogance intact; in a letter to his sister, he wrote: "I have seen all the sculpture ateliers in Rome; no one has half my talent."

Clésinger went back to Paris in 1864 and spent the rest of his life and career there. On his return he was made an officer of the Légion d'Honneur and received a number of major commissions. His colossal seated image of the Republic greeted visitors to the Exposition Universelle of 1878, which was held in Paris. He continued to do equestrians and before his death managed to complete three of the four which the government had commissioned him to make for the École Militaire.

DALOU, Jules
1838 (Paris) – 1902 (Paris)
French

Dalou never won the Prix de Rome as his mentor-hero Carpeaux had done. Neither did he complete his full course of study at the École des Beaux-Arts. Instead, he went to work in the art industry and achieved distinction by the late 1860s as a designer for the goldsmiths Fannière Frères and the ornamental sculpture firm Lefèvre. He also sent works of sculpture to the Salon and eventually scored a genuine success there in 1870 with a life-size figure of a contemporary young woman embroidering. The Franco-Prussian War and Commune disrupted his life and burgeoning career. For his role in the Commune, as one of the revolutionary curators of the Louvre, he was forced into exile and spent the years 1871–80 in London. He thrived there, producing superlative portraits and genre subjects of great seriousness and quality, especially mothers and their children.

By 1879 Dalou's ambition and self-image had expanded considerably. Although he continued to make portraits until the end of his life, he abandoned genre subjects and focused his considerable energies on the making of monuments, which he regarded as the sculptor's highest calling. When he returned to Paris after the amnesty proceedings of 1879–80, he already held the largest and most important commission of his life: the colossal *Triumph of the Republic*, which would eventually be erected in bronze in the place de la Nation, in the eastern part of Paris, where the eleventh and twelfth arrondissements meet. His monuments are prominent throughout the French capital (for example, *Delacroix Monument*, Luxembourg Gardens; *Levassor Monument*, Porte Maillot; tombs of Blanqui and Victor Noir, Père-Lachaise Cemetery). Some, like the *Triumph of the Republic*, were commissioned by the city of Paris; others were commissioned either by the French government or by independent committees of citizens.

Dalou and his wife had a single child, a retarded daughter named Georgette. Before Madame Dalou's death in 1900, she and her husband had arranged for Georgette's care after their deaths. She would enter an orphanage (the Orphélinat des Arts, for the children of artists) as an "older sister" and live among the youngsters; she would be provided with the supervision and care she would require for the rest of her life. In return, the Orphélinat became the beneficiary of Dalou's estate, which included the entire contents of his studio, over three hundred pieces of sculpture. This was sold to the city of Paris in 1905 by Dalou's executors and installed in the Musée du Petit Palais, but the Orphélinat retained reproduction rights. During Dalou's lifetime, he had allowed some of his sculptures to be edited: a few in bronze and others in stoneware or Sèvres porcelain, but in general he resisted dissemination of his work in this manner. In 1899, however, with Madame Dalou ill, his own health precarious, and considerable financial anxieties, he entered into an agreement with the bronze foundry Susse Frères to edit a number of his works. They cast a reduc-

tion of his *Lavoisier* (the original is a three-meter-high stone colossus in the amphitheater of the New Sorbonne), and Dalou was pleased with its quality. Using this previous agreement with Susse as their moral justification, the executors decided to edit most of the work found in Dalou's studio for the benefit of the Orphélinat. Just as Degas's heirs would do in 1918, they chose in 1907 the firm of A.-A. Hébrard to cast the earliest posthumous editions of Dalou's work in *cire perdue*. Some casting of Dalou's work remained the province of Susse Frères and continues to be to this day. There also exist casts by other firms active during the late nineteenth and early twentieth centuries, such as Thiébaut, Valsuani, and Lehmann.

DEGAS, Edgar
1834 (Paris) – 1917 (Paris)
French

During the nineteenth century there emerged what might be called an alternative history of sculpture. Relatively few works and artists belong in this category, but their historical and qualitative importance far outweighs their numbers. Degas is the foremost sculptor in this group, which also includes such luminaries as Daumier, Gauguin, and Géricault. They share a lack of systematic, professional training in sculpture. They made sculpture from their perspective as painters who, for reasons that were personal and never articulated, wished to expand their formal and expressive range by making art in three dimensions.

We know that artists from the Renaissance through the nineteenth century sometimes fashioned three-dimensional figures to establish or clarify the pose of a figure for a painting; it has been argued by John Rewald and others that Degas modeled figures for this same reason, but this is no longer generally believed. The accomplishment of Degas and his nineteenth-century counterparts is something more akin to that of universal artists of the past – such as Michelangelo and Bernini – who produced architecture, painting, and sculpture of comparable importance; it also anticipates the brilliance of Picasso as a sculptor on days (or hours) when he was not painting, drawing, or making prints.

The practice and teaching of sculpture in the nineteenth century were, if possible, even more rigidly codified than was true for painting. Technical procedures and compositional formulas became so ingrained that they were employed as automatic responses, the artistic equivalent of spoken language used in the daily routine of living. The human form, fully comprehended as a functioning mechanism even when its surface appearance was idealized, was the alpha and omega of the nineteenth century's professionally trained sculptors. The concept of *ponderation* occurs repeatedly in contemporary discussions of sculpture; it dictated that the human form always be depicted proportionally and interacting rationally with gravitational forces. Every pose of the figure conformed to this dictate, and every armature was constructed with this rule in mind. Even the best of the professionally trained sculptors – artists of the caliber of Dalou or Saint-Gaudens – could never unlearn, even if they had wanted to, what had been so forcefully and effectively inculcated in them during their artistic educations. Degas had no such training to constrain him, nothing to unlearn. He came to sculpture as a fully formed two-dimensional artist with a penchant for experimenting and expanding parameters. He used his freedom to produce an extraordinary body of sculpture that broke the rules and achieved dramatic, unanticipated results.

In almost every aspect, Degas's sculpture was unconventional. His internal and external armatures were experimental and often flexible, unlike the solidly constructed ones used by his contemporaries who were professionals. The poses taken by his figures were very often not about *ponderation* at all, but about precariousness and flux. He preferred wax to clay when modeling; he incorporated found objects (as we refer to them in the era after Picasso and surrealism) and cloth freely with his modeled forms and crude supports. Degas had

a handful of his sculptures cast in plaster by professionals but never saw one of them translated into bronze or stone during his lifetime.

Although we know that Degas made sculptures over a period of decades, we can date only one of them (which may well be his first) with precision: *Little Fourteen-Year-Old Dancer* (cat. no. 5). This is the single sculpture that Degas exhibited publicly during his lifetime, at the "impressionist" exhibition of 1881. Scholars have attempted to date Degas's other sculptures by comparing them with paintings or drawings that share the same subject matter and that can be dated with certainty, or with at-best ambiguous references that appear in his letters. To date, however, no real consensus has been established, beyond the fact that after exhibiting the one piece in 1881 Degas continued to make sculpture well into the twentieth century.

Those who visited Degas's home saw pieces of his sculpture placed in vitrines, and many were scattered about his studio, but no systematic record of them was made until after his death. The dealer Durand-Ruel recorded that about 150 pieces were found; over half were in an advanced state of decomposition. Degas's heirs decided that those which were salvageable should be cast in bronze editions, and seventy-three of them were. (One additional model was cast separately, at a later date.) The sculptor Paul Bartholomé, a friend of Degas, repaired some of the damage to salvageable pieces, and the renowned bronze-casting firm Hébrard did the casting in *cire perdue*. A master craftsman, Albino Palazzolo, was placed in charge. Sixty-nine of the wax originals survived the procedure in which negative molds were made from them, the first step of the casting process.

As was also true in large part for the sculptor Dalou, Degas's sculpture is best known – and for a long time was *only* known – from the posthumous bronze casts. Hébrard made twenty-two casts of each of seventy-two sculptures: a master set, the models from which all subsequent casts were made (this complete set is now in the Norton Simon Museum, Pasadena), a set for the heirs, and twenty for the market. Additional casts of the *Lit-*

tle Fourteen-Year-Old Dancer were made; twenty-seven are currently known to exist, but there could be others. After the bronze casting enterprise, which lasted from 1920 until perhaps as late as 1932, it was erroneously believed that the wax originals had all been destroyed. Then, in 1955, they reappeared, after having been hidden away in the Hébrard storage rooms, and were publicly exhibited. From November 9 through December 3, 1955, they were shown at M. Knoedler & Company in New York and subsequently entered the collection of Mr. and Mrs. Paul Mellon. Four were given to the Louvre and can now be seen at the Musée d'Orsay in Paris. Several are currently on view at the National Gallery of Art in Washington, D.C., and the rest are still in the Mellon collection.

DUBOIS, Paul
1829 (Nogent-sur-Seine) – 1905 (Paris)
French

W. C. Brownell, an astute American critic, thought that Dubois was "probably the strongest of the academic group of French sculptors of the day," and his assessment still seems accurate. Although Dubois trained at the École des Beaux-Arts, he did not long remain a student in that august institution to which he would one day return as its director (1878–1905). His family was well-to-do and supported his wish to become a sculptor. They financed his lengthy period of independent study in Italy, where, between 1859 and 1863, he absorbed the lessons of Renaissance masters from firsthand observation. At the Salon of 1863, his two standing plaster figures, a young Saint John the Baptist and a bathing Narcissus, provided him with his first public acclaim and inaugurated the neo-Florentine trend, which would be an important category of French sculpture during the 1860s and 1870s.

From this first success onward, Dubois produced many distinguished, conservative sculptures, which look to the past for inspiration. Rarely does one of his sculptures seem to derive from life itself, as is the case with his somewhat younger French contemporaries, Dalou and Rodin; they evoke instead sensations of life that have been distilled and transformed by art. Among Dubois's works are the *Florentine Singer* (first shown at the Salon of 1865 and destined to become one of the best-known and widely reproduced sculptures of the nineteenth century), a Virgin and Child for the new Parisian church of La Trinité (1864), the tomb of Général de Lamoricière (Medal of Honor at the Exposition Universelle of 1878), and an equestrian Joan of Arc (Salon of 1889; bronze casts later installed at Reims, beside the cathedral, and in front of St.-Augustin, Paris).

EAKINS, Thomas
1844 (Philadelphia) – 1916 (Philadelphia)
American

Although Eakins is generally recognized as one of the greatest American painters, his accomplishment as a sculptor is much less well known. His artistic training in Paris had included study in the atelier of the sculptor Augustin Dumont, as well as the study of painting in the ateliers of Gérôme and Bonnat. When he taught at the Pennsylvania Academy of the Fine Arts, he included the study of sculpture along with drawing and painting. His own activity in three dimensions was limited to relief sculpture, some sketches used to clarify figures and poses for his paintings, and one life mask, which is closely related to a known, painted portrait. During the early 1880s he produced the serenely beautiful reliefs *Knitting* and *Spinning*, as well as the bucolic *Arcadia* – all of which are closely related to his photography and other work in two dimensions. In 1892–93 Eakins also executed two commissions for public sculpture: the horses for the equestrian reliefs of General Grant and President Lincoln (the human protagonists were modeled by William O'Donovan) located under the triumphal arch on Grand Army Plaza, adjacent to Prospect Park in Brooklyn, and two historical reliefs for the Trenton Battle Monument.

FALGUIÈRE, Alexandre
1831 (Toulouse) – 1900 (Paris)
French

In his youth Falguière went to Paris from his native Toulouse, trained at the École des Beaux-Arts, and won the Prix de Rome; he established a thriving atelier in Paris on his return from Rome, became a professor at the École, and was awarded all the highest honors the art world could bestow. Two early works were received enthusiastically at the Salon and established his reputation: the *Winner of the Cockfight* in 1864 and *Tarcisius* in 1867 (both now in the Musée d'Orsay, Paris). The first represented a nude youth, shown in midstride as he runs joyfully, while cradling a victorious pet rooster in his arm. This work demonstrated Falguière's compositional skills when arranging a figure's complex forms balanced effortlessly on the tip of one foot – a learned reference to Giovanni da Bologna's *Mercury*, a masterpiece of Italian Renaissance sculpture. The second statue depicted a clothed, adolescent male figure reclining on his side. Falguière chose for his subject a narrative moment that demonstrated his mastery of static composition and pathetic content. Tarcisius was a character in Cardinal Weisman's *Fabiola*, a popular novel of the 1850s. An early Christian martyr, he secretly carried the viaticum (consecrated bread of the Eucharist) to condemned fellow Christians. When his mission of mercy was discovered, he was stoned to death by Roman pagans. Falguière's Tarcisius, a frail youth, is on the verge of expiring, the viaticum clutched to his breast and the stones of his martyrdom lying at his side. Critics and the public loved the sentimental piece, and Falguière won that year's Medal of Honor.

Falguière never lacked commissions for portraits, monuments, and independent pieces for collectors. While Paris was under siege by the Prussians in December 1870, he made a great impression by modeling a colossal snow sculpture, *Resistance*, on the city ramparts, with hopes – one suspects – that his contemporaries would recall the story of Michelangelo's building a snow sculp-

ture for Piero de' Medici in the courtyard of his family's Florentine palace.

Falguière's female nudes were received with special enthusiasm because of their intense realism, which he cleverly rendered acceptable with the barest pretense that they were mythological subjects. From 1881 until 1886, his colossal plaster maquette of a quadriga with allegorical figures, the *Triumph of the Revolution*, was installed atop the Arc de Triomphe de l'Étoile, but it was never translated into permanent materials. When the Société des Gens de Lettres refused to accept Rodin's *Monument to Balzac* after the legendary fiasco of 1898, the commission was transferred to Falguière. His alternative, "house-broken" version shows the author seated on a bench with his legs crossed and his coarse features idealized; it was shown at the Salon of 1899 and installed on avenue Friedland in Paris after Falguière's death. In a public display of mutual support meant to dispel any suspicion of enmity between them, Rodin and Falguière each modeled a portrait bust of the other.

FRÉMIET, Emmanuel
1824 (Paris) – 1910 (Paris)
French

Frémiet trained at the Petite École and with François Rude, who was his uncle by marriage, but he never attended the École des Beaux-Arts. Nevertheless, he became a highly respected artist, who was elected to the French Academy, received numerous state commissions, and earned all three degrees of the Légion d'Honneur. He was a superb animalier, or sculptor of animals, but his work is different in kind and temperament from that of Barye, whose position as teacher of animal drawing Frémiet assumed at the Musée d'Histoire Naturelle after Barye's death in 1875. Frémiet's animals do not kill other animals or devour their prey; they are very often domesticated, and quite anthropomorphic in character.

Domestic animals were central to Frémiet's career, but he did not limit himself to the depiction of lovable pets. Between 1855 and 1860 he made for the emperor fifty-five small soldiers, dressed in all the uniforms of the French army. Some of these were exhibited at the Exposition Universelle of 1855, and others at the Salon of 1859. This remarkable and famed miniature army perished when the Palais des Tuileries burned in 1871. Frémiet also did a number of equestrian statues; the gilded bronze *Joan of Arc*, unveiled in 1874 in the place des Pyramides – off the rue de Rivoli – is by far the best-known and finest of his works in this genre (the present statue on that site is an improved, revised version, which Frémiet installed at his own expense in 1899). His colossal bronze *Ferdinand de Lesseps* (Salon of 1899) was erected at the entrance to the Suez Canal.

Frémiet introduced a category of three-dimensional images in which animals and humans are adversaries. Unlike the hunting groups designed by Barye, in which the human hunter always prevails, Frémiet's combats are heavily weighted in favor of the anthropomorphic beasts. The Salon jury of 1859 rejected his *Gorilla Carrying off a Woman* for its violence and, no doubt, for its intimation of sexual violation of the woman by the gorilla. Frémiet reworked the group and exhibited a life-size version of it at the Salon of 1887; this time the public was delighted, and he was awarded the Medal of Honor. In the gardens of the Jardin des Plantes in Paris there is a cast of the *Bear and Man of the Stone Age*, which was shown at the Salon of 1885. The human hunter has killed a bear cub, whose carcass is tied to his belt. The bear's mother has attacked, and although the hunter has planted a knife in her throat, she holds him in a deadly embrace as she rips his flesh. Inside the foyer of the Musée d'Histoire Naturelle, a short distance away within the Jardin, is Frémiet's formidable marble relief showing an orangutan strangling a native of Borneo (Salon of 1895), where once again an animal mother avenges the death of her offspring.

FRENCH, Daniel Chester

1850 (Exeter, New Hampshire) – 1931 (Stockbridge, Massachusetts)

American

Unlike most American sculptors, who came from modest circumstances and began their careers as artisans, French came from a privileged and sophisticated family, who encouraged his natural talent for modeling; he regarded himself as a professional sculptor by the time he had reached his early twenties. He studied briefly with three notable American artists: anatomy with William Rimmer; drawing with William Morris Hunt; and sculpture with John Quincy Adams Ward. When the town of Concord, Massachusetts – where he had grown up – commissioned him to create his first public monument, he modeled the renowned *Minute Man* (1873–74) and proved that he was the master of full-length, clothed figures, as well as sophisticated iconographic conceits. Like a contemporary Cincinnatus, the *Minute Man* rests one hand on his plow and holds a rifle in the other. His pose is a variant on that of the Apollo Belvedere, a plaster cast of which French had borrowed from the Boston Athenaeum while working on this monument.

It was only after the *Minute Man* had been completed that French went abroad to study; Florence was his destination. There for two years he lived with the family of Hiram Powers's son, Preston, and worked in the studio of the American sculptor Thomas Ball. After his return, he executed many portrait busts, did the impressive seated *John Harvard* (1884) which was placed in Harvard Yard, and undertook his first large-scale sculptures for architectural contexts. In 1886 French traveled to Paris and honed his modeling skills in the studio of Antonin Mercié.

In 1888 he established himself in New York, where Augustus Saint-Gaudens and numerous other artists lived and worked during the winter season. He received many commissions for public sculpture. One of his finest and most moving works is the *Angel of Death and the Sculptor* (1891–

92), designed for the tomb of his friend, the sculptor Martin Milmore (1844–1883, Forest Hills Cemetery, Boston). French portrayed Milmore working on one of his own statues, when the angel of death comes and places a hand between his chisel and the work in progress. At the World's Columbian Exposition of 1893 in Chicago, French's colossal *Republic* dominated the reflecting pool of the great White City. The demand for his services thereafter exceeded his ability to produce. In 1893 he bought a farm in the Berkshires (Stockbridge, Mass.) that would be his summer retreat and workplace for the rest of his life. Chesterwood was the analogue to Saint-Gaudens's summer home in Cornish, New Hampshire; both are now museums where the two sculptors' works can be seen in the ambience where many of them were originally created.

Whereas earlier statues erected at American expense in foreign capitals had been casts or reductions of works by Europeans (Bartoldi's *Liberty Enlightening the World*, on the pont de Grenelle in Paris, immediately comes to mind), French designed the equestrian *George Washington*, erected in the place d'Iéna in Paris, in collaboration with Edward Potter (inaugurated July 3, 1900). His monument to Richard Morris Hunt (1898), across Fifth Avenue from the Frick Collection in New York, is one of the most dignified sculptural commemorations of an individual erected in the United States during the nineteenth century. His seated *Lincoln* (1915–18), for the Lincoln Memorial in Washington, D.C., is probably the best known of all French's works.

GEMITO, Vincenzo
1852 (Naples) – 1929 (?)
Italian

Gemito was a gifted sculptor whose life and career do not fit neatly into preconceptions about nineteenth-century artists. He was born into straitened circumstances in Naples and abandoned as a foundling; he received his only training from two local artists, Emmanuele Caggiano and Stanislao Lista. He left the studio of the latter in annoyance and began his life as a professional sculptor; instinctive talent and force of personality sufficed in forging a career. In 1873, when he was only twenty-one, Gemito modeled a portrait bust of the great composer Giuseppe Verdi, whose opera *Aïda* had recently been given its triumphant world premier. The original terra cotta of this bust adorns the composer's home, Villa Verdi in Busseto, and a bronze cast of it has been placed in the foyer of the Metropolitan Opera House in New York.

Gemito derived inspiration from his impoverished childhood and from the streets of his native city. In 1877 he sent a life-size *Neapolitan Fisherboy* to the Salon in Paris. In subject matter, this statue recalled earlier successes by Rude, Duret, and Carpeaux, but with Gemito's insistence on the urchin's ungainly pose, scrawny body, and unidealized features, he espoused a hyperrealism in sculpture that exceeded the normal expectations of Parisians. The work attracted considerable attention, and a cast of it was purchased by the academic genre painter Ernest Meissonier. A cast of the *Fisherboy* can also be found in the internal courtyard of the Bargello, the national sculpture museum in Florence. Gemito did other sculptures of Neapolitan genre subjects, such as the *Water Seller* (after 1881), which was commissioned by Francesco II, the former king of Naples. Between 1883 and 1886 Gemito operated his own bronze foundry in Naples and cast his own works.

Gemito had been precocious, and his career flourished during the 1870s and 1880s in his native Italy and in Paris, but he was subject to debilitating depression, which effectively ended his career. In 1887 he became dysfunctional and hid away from the world for twenty years. Even though he became active again after 1909, his career never resuscitated.

GIBSON, John

1791 (Gyffin, England) – 1866 (Rome)

British

Gibson was apprenticed to wood- and stone-carvers in Liverpool, where his family had moved when he was a child. His extraordinary facility attracted attention, most importantly that of the historian William Roscoe, who commissioned a chimney piece and was so pleased with the results that he took charge of the talented boy's education and introduced him to other influential residents of Liverpool. Gibson traveled to London in 1817 but stayed only briefly; by the end of the year he was in Rome, where he would live and work for the rest of his life.

Antonio Canova was still active in Rome at that time, and he took the aspiring young Englishman into his studio for five years. Since Gibson's previous experience was minimal, he was able to learn mechanical procedures, like the construction of armatures, from firsthand experience. After Canova's death in 1822, Gibson studied with the expatriate Dane Bertel Thorvaldsen. Gibson's credentials as a neoclassicist were therefore impeccable; he had the imprimatur of its two principal practitioners in sculpture. He developed an international reputation, but almost all his patrons were British. In 1833 he was received into the Royal Academy and became a full Academician in 1838. Queen Victoria commissioned her portrait on more than one occasion (1844, Buckingham Palace, and 1849, Osborne House).

Gibson's finest works are highly personal variants within an idiom characterized by aspirations toward impersonality and idealization. His poses and groupings are always imaginative. His cool surfaces intimate quelled passions which might erupt at any moment. The group *Hylas and the Water Nymphs* (1826) has long stood in front of the Tate Gallery in London. His Royal Academy reception piece, *Narcissus* (1838), is a superlative treatment of the adolescent male nude. From the 1840s onward, Gibson experimented with applied polychromy; by 1846 he could write, "I cannot bear to see a statue without colour." He had incorporated it into his 1844 portrait of the queen and achieved his most spectacular coloristic effects with his *Tinted Venus* (1851–56, Walker Art Gallery, Liverpool).

Gibson bequeathed his fortune, his plaster models, and the contents of his studio to the Royal Academy. His own masters, Canova and Thorvaldsen, had also wanted their life's work maintained as a unit that could be studied by future generations and had thus made similar bequests to their hometowns, where museums were established for that very purpose: Possagno for the former and Copenhagen for the latter.

GOTT, Joseph

1785 (Calverley, near Leeds) – 1860 (Rome)

British

Gott's career is chronologically parallel to Gibson's, but he is a lesser light in the history of British sculpture. He first worked in the studio of the eminent sculptor John Flaxman and was later a pupil in the Royal Academy schools, where he repeatedly won prizes and medals. In 1824 Gott moved to Rome, which would be his primary residence for the rest of his career, even though most of his patrons were English and he traveled frequently to his native land. His first journey to the Eternal City was made possible by a wealthy resident of Leeds, Benjamin Gott (not a relative), who regularly commissioned from the sculptor pieces for his estate, Armley House, and his own tomb monument. Although Gott's work spanned the range of nineteenth-century sculpture – classical figures, portrait busts, and monuments – he nevertheless became a specialist in marble groups depicting animals; one of his contemporaries described him as "the Landseer of marble," comparing him to Queen Victoria's favorite painter, who also specialized in animal subjects.

GOULD, Thomas
1818 (Boston) – 1881 (Florence)
American

Thomas Ridgeway Gould came to a career in sculpture circuitously. He was an amateur who had studied drawing and modeling while working as a dry-goods merchant in his native Boston. The failure of his business during the early 1860s allowed him to pursue sculpture full-time, first in Boston and then abroad. In 1868 he moved to Italy and settled in Florence, following the example of his fellow Bostonian – Horatio Greenough – who had done the same forty years earlier. There Gould worked as a sculptor for the rest of his life. On only two occasions, in 1878 and 1881, did he return to America.

Gould was a maker of idealized statues, portrait busts, and full-length portrait sculptures. Examples of this latter category can still be found in public spaces near Boston – in Lexington, Hingham, and Cambridge. His stunning portrait of the Hawaiian king, Kamehameha I, once installed in Kapua, Hawaii, now resides in the Statuary Hall of the United States Capitol. His *West Wind*, modeled the first year after his move to Florence and inspired by Canova, portrays a running young woman, nude to the waist, with agitated draperies covering her lower body. After having been exhibited at the Centennial Exhibition of 1876 in Philadelphia, a number of marble replicas were commissioned. During the 1870s, Gould did several reliefs and busts based on Shakespearean subjects, which number among his best works. He had a strong affinity for Shakespeare, which manifested itself in his parallel pursuits as scholar, drama critic, author, and friend to actors, as well as sculptor.

GREENOUGH, Horatio
1805 (Boston) – 1852 (Somerville,
    Massachusetts)
American

Greenough's career was a turning point in the history of American sculpture. He was the first to journey abroad to study and absorb the European sculptural tradition, past and present. On a personal level, he was eminently capable of fitting into the learned and cultured circles of European artists; he had a classical education, a degree from Harvard, and uncommon linguistic facility. He was America's first true sculptor, rather than an artisan who came to make sculpture after working as a wood- or stonecarver. His countrymen warmly encouraged him in his pursuits. The great romantic painter Washington Allston took an intense interest in his career; the eminent collector, Robert Gilmor, Jr., became an early patron; and President John Quincy Adams sat for a portrait bust when the young sculptor was still relatively unknown.

Greenough was naturally predisposed toward a vocation in sculpture. His father, a successful Boston dealer in real estate, had placed a copy of a classical statue in the garden of their home, and the young Horatio was much impressed by it. He studied with local carvers and was given free access to the plaster casts after famous antique works that had already been installed in the Boston Athenaeum. When he traveled abroad for the first time, in the summer of 1825, his goal was Rome. On that first trip, he met and was encouraged by two of the greatest living sculptors, Lorenzo Bartolini, in Florence, and the expatriate Dane, Bertel Thorvaldsen, in Rome. When he returned to Italy in 1828, he established himself in Florence, where he became Bartolini's pupil. He was not only the first American to become a professional sculptor but also the first of many to live and practice his art in the city that had given birth to the Renaissance. American painters who already lived there and helped pave his way included Samuel F. B. Morse and Thomas Cole. James Fenimore Cooper, who also lived in Florence, became one of his patrons.

Greenough's stature was confirmed in 1832 when Congress commissioned him – rather than a European master – to make a colossal image of George Washington for the center of the rotunda of the United States Capitol. Earlier, the state of Virginia had imported the great French sculptor Jean-Antoine Houdon; the Massachusetts legislature had turned to an Englishman, Francis Chantrey; and the Carolina legislature had chosen the Italian Antonio Canova, when they commissioned marble images of the first president. Greenough conceived the work with the most noble aspirations and learned references to the past. He depicted Washington enthroned with his lower body draped in a classical toga and his arms and torso heroically nude; conception and pose were borrowed ultimately from Phidias's statue of Zeus at Olympia. Greenough had formulated this conception after studying Ingres's colossal painting *Jupiter and Thetis*, also based on Phidias, in the artist's Parisian studio. When Greenough's marble was established in the Capitol, it provoked one of the recurring outrages that has plagued American response to new art from the beginning, and continues to this day. After being removed from the rotunda, his *Washington* has lived in ignominious exile: first on the Capitol lawn, then in a corner of Renwick's Smithsonian, and now in the lobby of the National Museum of American History.

Toward the end of his short life, Greenough directed considerable energy to recording his biography (*The Travels, Observations, and Experience of a Yankee Stonecutter*, published in 1852) and theorizing about art. His essay, "Form and Function," has frequently been invoked during the twentieth century as a prophesy of modern architecture and truth to materials, usually at the expense of a serious consideration of his sculpture.

GRIFFIN, Walter

1861 (Portland, Maine) – 1935 (Portland, Maine)

American

With the sole exception of a bust of his father, Walter Griffin is known to the history of art as a painter of competent, but minor, impressionist landscapes, made from the late 1880s until his death, and as a respected teacher. After working in his father's wood-carving shop in Portland, Maine, and sketching with his father and other local amateurs, Griffin moved to Boston in 1878 at the age of seventeen to attend the newly inaugurated School of the Museum of Fine Arts as a scholarship student. At the same time, he worked nights in the studio of the sculptor Truman Bartlett. In 1882 he moved to New York and entered the National Academy of Design, where he came to know such prominent artists as William Merritt Chase, Childe Hassam, and Augustus Saint-Gaudens. While at the National Academy he was awarded the Bronze Medal for the best life drawing in 1885 and would be decorated frequently throughout his career, including the Medal of Honor at the Panama-Pacific International Exhibition in San Francisco in 1915. In 1887 he left for a period of study in Paris and subsequently spent protracted periods of time working in Europe.

In a highly laudatory essay of 1917, L. Merrick elaborated on Griffin's association with the art of sculpture: "As a wood carver he worked during his boyhood, under his father's direction. Later he was drawn to sculpture, which mode of expression occupied him for a considerable length of time. When he had mastered form in the moulding of figures, decorative design, bas-reliefs, etc., his ambition carried him into the fields of colour." This information was apparently provided by the artist himself. It suggests that, for Griffin, sculpture was only an aspect of his artistic training and that he regarded painting as his true calling. Understandably, the bust of his father was made at the end of his Boston period, which included the study of sculpture. It may have been intended as both a tribute to his father and a valedictory to sculpture.

HOSMER, Harriet Goodhue
1830 (Watertown, Massachusetts) – 1908 (Watertown, Massachusetts)
American

Hosmer's decision to become a sculptor was made while she attended finishing school in the Berkshires. Her father encouraged her independence, built her a studio, and supported her studies. Wayman Crow, a wealthy St. Louis businessman and the father of one of her school friends, arranged for her to study anatomy independently with a St. Louis physician in 1850. When she returned to Watertown, she began her first ideal bust, *Hesper, the Evening Star*. This brought her to the attention of the celebrated actress Charlotte Cushman, who encouraged her to pursue her career in Rome. Arriving in Rome in late 1852, Hosmer persuaded the English neoclassical sculptor John Gibson to take her as a pupil; she remained under his tutelage for seven years.

Crow commissioned a piece from her without specifying a subject. She produced her first full-length figure, *Oenone* (c. 1855), the woman spurned by Paris after he won Helen as a reward for pronouncing his famous judgment. This seated figure, nude to the hips with her lower body draped (Washington University, St. Louis), indicates how thoroughly and effectively she had mastered the neoclassical idiom under Gibson. Hosmer specialized in female figures. Some, like *Beatrice Cenci* (1857, Mercantile Library, St. Louis) and *Oenone*, are overcome by external circumstances, but others, like *Zenobia* and *Queen Isabella*, demonstrate great personal resolve. Her most impressive single figure was a colossal bronze statue of Thomas Hart Benton, another St. Louis commission (1862–68).

Hosmer became a celebrity and a fixture in Roman society. She was fiercely independent in her life as well as in her profession. At a time when women did not become sculptors, she learned the indelicate mechanics of carving marble and supervised a large atelier. Hosmer never married, and she very pointedly referred to her sculptures as her "children." She was the first American sculptor to receive a commission for a work to be placed in a Roman church. Her funerary monument to Judith Falconnet (1857–58) was installed in the second chapel to the right in the nave of Sant' Andrea delle Fratte, only a few yards away from two late masterpieces by Bernini, angels intended for the Ponte Sant' Angelo. Other American women sculptors gravitated to her circle in Rome: Emma Stebbins, Margaret Foley, Edmonia Lewis, and Anne Whitney. Henry James dubbed this group of artists, rather condescendingly, "the white, marmorean flock." Virtually every important English-speaking visitor to Rome met Hosmer and visited her studio.

IVES, Chauncey
1810 (Hamden, Connecticut) – 1894 (Rome)
American

Ives was one of many nineteenth-century American artisan-carvers who transformed themselves into sculptors. As a youngster he was apprenticed to a wood-carver in New Haven, Connecticut, for about a decade. When he moved to Boston in about 1837, he began making portrait busts, and his first piece was a Sir Walter Scott, based on the plaster by Chantrey in the Boston Athenaeum (cat. no. 38). Between then and 1844, Ives worked in New England and New York. With the financial assistance of patrons, he set sail for Italy in 1844. After seven years of working and studying in Florence, he moved to Rome in 1851 and spent the rest of his life there among his fellow expatriate American sculptors.

Ives continued to make portraits, some of them excellent, and monuments, but his most characteristic pieces are figures borrowed from mythology and literature. These satisfied the taste of the era for marble sculpture that alluded to demonstrable literary sources and was appropriate for display in parlors and libraries. One of the most dazzling of these is *Undine Receiving Her Soul* (c. 1855), a voluptuous water sprite who raises her arms above her head, creating a cascade of form-revealing drapery folds. This virtuoso demonstration of marble carving was enthusiastically greeted by many patrons, who ordered at least ten replicas.

KLINGER, Max
1857 (Leipzig) – 1920 (Nuremberg)
German

Klinger's formal artistic training was limited to drawing, painting, and graphics. He attended the academies of Karlsruhe and Berlin and traveled extensively. At one time or another between 1879 and 1893, he lived in Brussels, Munich, Berlin, Paris, and Rome. His desire to make sculpture was triggered, by his own admission, after he had seen a male nude by the contemporary sculptor Adolf Hildebrand. We know that in 1884 Klinger saw an exhibition of Hildebrand's sculpture during a visit to Berlin. The following year, in Paris, he began a large mixed-media work, a painting of the Judgment of Paris with a frame that included three bas-reliefs of painted plaster – his first attempt in three dimensions. While in Paris (1885–86), he also produced the first version of his *Beethoven* in gilded and painted plaster. Paris was, of course, the world capital for modern sculpture when Klinger lived there. The extent of his awareness of French sculpture is not clear, but he did know and admire Rodin's work.

Between 1888 and 1893 he lived in Rome. It was there that he assembled his first sculpture of various tinted marbles and amber, *The New Salome*, after a colored plaster model of 1887 (Museum der Bildenden Künste, Leipzig). This morbidly fascinating piece portrays Salome as a hieratically frontal and impassive femme fatale with her grisly trophy – a decapitated male head – propped against her body. The *Beethoven Monument* (1897–1902; also Leipzig Museum), unveiled at the Vienna Secession exhibition of 1902, was Klinger's most ambitious and extravagant achievement in sculpture, the evolutionary climax of the model he had first conceived in 1885. On a high bronze throne inlaid with mother-of-pearl and semi-precious stones sits an Olympian Zeus with the features of Beethoven, made from various colored marbles and alabaster. These tinted and multi-media pieces are similar to sculptures made by Jean-Léon Gérôme and Louis-Ernest Barrias during the late 1890s and recall precedents created by Cordier and Gibson earlier in the century.

LEWIS, Edmonia
c. 1844 (upstate New York?) – after 1909
American

Lewis, one of the more fascinating sculptors of the later nineteenth century, is shrouded in mystery. It is known, however, that her mother was a Chippewa and that her father was black, and that she may have been born in upstate New York in 1843 or 1844. But this is not certain, since it has also been claimed authoritatively that she was born in Greenhigh, Ohio. A group identifying itself as The Committee to Historify the Legend of American Neoclassic Sculptress Edmonia Lewis convinced New York State to declare July 14, 1980, Edmonia Lewis Day. In the official declaration made by Governor Carey it was stated as fact that she had been born "near Albany, New York, July 14, 1843." But there are no concrete facts, and the end of her life is equally obscure. She seems, quite simply, to have disappeared.

We do know that she was educated at Oberlin College. She subsequently traveled to Boston, met the abolitionist William Lloyd Garrison who became a mentor, and through him met the sculptor Edward Brackett, who recognized her instinctive talent. Before long she had modeled a head of the Civil War hero Colonel Robert Gould Shaw. (She often chose her subjects because of the affinity she felt for them. Shaw was the white Bostonian who led a regiment of black soldiers and who died in battle.) This sculpture was the turning point in her career. She was able to sell about one hundred plaster casts of it and to earn enough money to finance a journey to Rome. Arriving in 1865 or somewhat later, she joined the circle of Charlotte Cushman and Harriet Hosmer and worked in Rome until the early 1870s. Apparently, she was not adept at financial affairs, ordered materials she could not pay for, and had to be bailed out by friends. Contrary to common practice, she did not hire Italian stonecutters to assist her in carving her marbles.

A number of her sculptures are based on themes of black or native American experience or on literary sources that deal with them. *Forever Free* features a slave whose chains have been broken. The *Old Indian Arrow Maker* depicts the craftsman of the title with his daughter or granddaughter seated beside him. She did several works that have as their subjects the hero and heroine of Longfellow's "Song of Hiawatha." A high point in her career came with the exhibition of the *Death of Cleopatra* at the Philadelphia Centennial Exhibition of 1876.

MacMONNIES, Frederick
1863 (Brooklyn) – 1937 (New York)
American

MacMonnies was a spontaneous modeler, but – being the child of struggling immigrant parents – he needed to find lucrative work at an early age. One of his first jobs was that of a "boy Friday" in the studio of Augustus Saint-Gaudens, begun when he was seventeen. By chance, Saint-Gaudens discovered the young man's talent and made him an assistant in sculpture. At the same time, MacMonnies began studying drawing at the Art Students' League and the National Academy of Design. By 1884 he was ready for study in Paris, following the pattern set by his mentor. Saint-Gaudens had studied under François Jouffroy at the École des Beaux-Arts; MacMonnies entered the studio of Jouffroy's most acclaimed student, Alexandre Falguière. MacMonnies was a great suc-

cess there, winning the highest honors available to a foreigner and eventually becoming Falguière's assistant. In 1889 he exhibited a full figure, a nude *Diana*, at the Salon and attracted considerable attention. The following year he was commissioned to make his first public sculptures: *Nathan Hale* for City Hall Park in Manhattan (very close to the site of Hale's execution) and *James Stranahan* for Prospect Park in Brooklyn. Both are animated, full-length figures, in historically accurate costumes, Hale's of the eighteenth century and Stranahan's of the 1890s.

At the World's Columbian Exposition of 1893 in Chicago, MacMonnies shared the spotlight of public attention with Daniel Chester French. Both did colossal, temporary sculptures for the Court of Honor. French's gilded *Republic* stood at the head of the great reflecting pool, and MacMonnies's *Barge of State* dominated the opposite end. This enormous ship, with a full complement of oars and exuberant allegories, seemed to be afloat in the pool itself. Probably equal in terms of publicity was his over-life-size *Bacchante*, modeled in 1893, cast in 1894, and banished from the courtyard of the new Boston Public Library in 1896 (see Butler essay).

MacMonnies was deluged with commissions for the rest of his life. His work could be uneven, but his finest sculpture demonstrates full mastery of the academic idiom he learned from Saint-Gaudens and Falguière, coupled with individuality and passion. His superb *Horse Tamers* (1899–1900) dominate the southeastern entrance to Prospect Park in Brooklyn. Each pair is made up of two wild horses and a nude male who rides one of them. Their wild abandon is only barely contained by the riders' rational will and the sculptor's rhythmic control.

MATISSE, Henri
1869 (Cateau-Cambrésis, Nord) – 1954 (Nice)
French

Like Degas, Matisse was an artist who worked primarily in two dimensions but who also made brilliant sculpture. He himself admitted, "I sculpted as a painter. I did not sculpt like a sculptor." Indeed, he was basically self-taught as a three-dimensional artist. He made drawings after sculpture in the Louvre. He modeled two conservative portrait medallions in 1894 and a free adaptation of Barye's *Jaguar Devouring a Hare* (1899–1901), which captured the dynamism of the whole but did not attempt to match the surfaces or the details. Before 1900 he purchased a cast of Rodin's *Bust of Rochefort* from the dealer Ambroise Vollard, at the same time that he acquired one of Cézanne's small *Bathers* in oil. Although he took some of his drawings to Rodin for criticism, he was not greeted warmly or encouragingly. For a short time, Matisse regularly visited the studio of Antoine Bourdelle – a former Rodin student and assistant – for advice and perhaps instruction, while he learned to sculpt. In a famous photograph of 1909 we see Matisse modeling clay in the presence of a male nude model and a group of students.

MÈNE, Pierre-Jules
1810 (Paris) – 1879 (Paris)
French

Mène is the third Parisian animalier included in this exhibition. A more modest man and artist than either Barye or Frémiet, he limited himself to small-scale production of individual animals, animal groups, or hunt scenes; he also did still lifes of dead game, three-dimensional variants on a popular tradition in French painting. There are no monuments, architectural sculptures, or government commissions among his works.

Mène came from a very modest background and was trained as an artisan who produced mod-

els for porcelains and commercial sculpture. He had a natural inclination for modeling animals, studied sculpture informally, and spent whole days in the Jardin des Plantes, studying animal anatomy and drawing and modeling from the live animals kept there in captivity. His work was very popular among his contemporaries. He exhibited regularly at the Salons and the international expositions. He was admitted to the Légion d'Honneur in 1861, and one of his works, a *Mounted Kennel Master Leading His Pack*, was purchased by the state in 1869.

MEUNIER, Constantin
1831 (Etterbeek, Belgium) – 1905 (Ixelles, Belgium)
Belgian

Meunier was trained at the Brussels academy by the painter François Navez – who had been a pupil of the great neoclassicist Jacques-Louis David – and the sculptor Charles-Auguste Fraikin. Although Meunier began his career as a painter, exhibiting successfully in Paris as well as his native Belgium, he started modeling in wax and clay sometime after 1880, and sculpture became his primary medium. He was drawn by temperament to religious subjects (such as his deeply moving *Ecce Homo*, 1890–92) and issues of social justice; like Vincent van Gogh, he spent time among the miners in the Borinage and gained firsthand knowledge about their lives that he would later use in his work. His earliest three-dimensional figures were puddlers and other workers from the steel industry, stevedores, and miners, and he made variants of them throughout his career. A life-size cast of his resting *Stevedore* erected in the port of Antwerp has become the visual symbol of that city. His group *Firedamp: Woman Finding Her Son among the Dead* (1888–90) is a stunning invention, a pietà set in a mining community after one of the inevitable underground explosions. It recalls a comparable scene in Zola's novel *Germinal* (1885), when Maheude discovers the body of her eldest son amid the corpses that have been retrieved from the mine.

Meunier's images of the working class have such a strong feeling of timelessness and idealization that they were widely admired despite their content, which could have been perceived as dangerous, or even socialist. He was honored in his own country and in France, where his workers were shown at the Paris Salon and won awards in 1886, 1889, and 1900. He accepted a professorship at the Academy of Louvain in 1887, and later one in Brussels. The French government honored him with the Légion d'Honneur in 1889. At the end of his life, he expended great effort on his project for a monument to labor, which had been a concern of his ever since the 1880s.

MINNE, George

1866 (Ghent, Belgium) – 1941 (Laethem-Saint-Martin, Belgium)
Belgian

George Minne was one of the luminaries of fin-de-siècle symbolism. His mournful, often fragile figures seem weighed down with the cares of the world and are so withdrawn that their isolation can never be breached. They constitute a virtual definition of symbolist sculpture. Minne had been trained as an architect and worked for his architect father, but he also came into close contact with the new generation of Belgian symbolists, both artists and writers. He was a prolific book illustrator, and his illustrations often accompanied the published work of his literary friends. As a sculptor, he was largely self-taught.

Minne's career as an artist was long, but the quality of his output was not consistent. From the late 1880s until shortly after 1900, he produced a body of superlative sculptures, but his inspiration withered and his later years were spent in obscurity. During his most creative years, he exhibited his work regularly with other young and progressive Belgian artists – first with the group Les Vingt, and then with La Libre Esthétique, which super-

seded it. His sculptural ensemble of 1898, the *Fountain of Kneeling Youths* (Folkwang Museum, Hagen, Germany), is his most extraordinary creation. The figure of an emaciated, kneeling nude male adolescent – who wraps his arms around his torso with self-absorption as he gazes downward – was repeated five times in a circle that enclosed a fountain. This melancholy crystallization of narcissicism and self-absorption was exhibited with great success at the exhibition of the Vienna Secession in 1900.

Minne's output was not prolific during his best years, and his work is not often encountered in North American collections. The Museum of Modern Art (New York), the Cleveland Museum of Art, Oberlin College, and the Tanenbaum collection of Toronto all include at least one work by Minne from the 1890s. Middlebury's plaster included in this exhibition is apparently the only sculpture by Minne in a New England collection.

POWERS, Hiram

1805 (Woodstock, Vermont) – 1873 (Florence)
American

The unfolding of Powers's early career as an artist has a familiar ring to it; it mirrors that of many other nineteenth-century American sculptors. Born into modest circumstances in Woodstock, Vermont, and living as a teenager in Cincinnati, he showed precocious artistic and mechanical talent. He took advantage of the provincial art training that was available to him and discovered that he had a talent for modeling highly realistic likenesses in wax. A wealthy Cincinnati businessman took an interest, encouraged him to become a sculptor, and provided financial support. Making numerous portraits of friends, the young Powers transformed himself into a masterful portraitist. Traveling east, he made a number of portrait busts of distinguished Americans, especially in Washington and New York. Just as John Quincy Adams had posed for the young and little-known Horatio Greenough, President Andrew Jackson posed for Powers in 1835.

When he arrived in Florence in 1837, he was welcomed and assisted by Greenough, who was already established there. By 1841 Powers held a professorship in sculpture at the Florentine academy. His *Greek Slave* (1841–43) was the work that established his international fame. Her nudity, her pose that derives from the famous Medici Venus, and the topical references contained in her narrative predicament (the recent Greek war of independence and the current antislavery movement in the United States) combined to make the statue a stunning success. Powers sent it on a triumphant public tour of America (1847–49), which turned out to be highly profitable. He also exhibited it at the Crystal Palace Exhibition of 1851 in London. Powers and his workshop carved six replicas of the figure, with minor variations, and dozens of copies of the bust alone; the *Greek Slave* was one of the most widely disseminated three-dimensional images of the nineteenth century. Powers also made many Ideal figures, continued to be a prolific portraitist, and designed public sculpture, such as the bronze *Daniel Webster* (1858, Massachusetts State House, Boston).

RIMMER, William

> 1816 (Liverpool, England) – 1879 (South
> Milford, Massachusetts)
> American

Rimmer was an artist of brilliance, who constructed a career without formal training, by assimilating past and present sources with great originality. Manually dexterous, he – like his father – cobbled shoes when necessary to earn money and did other semiskilled work with his hands. When he followed a course in anatomy that included dissection at Massachusetts Medical College in the early 1840s, he gained further mastery in his already impressive knowledge of the human body's appearance and structure; he subsequently practiced a rudimentary brand of medicine, along with his art and cobbling. Later in life he preferred to be addressed as "Dr. Rimmer," recalling his ear-

lier practice of medicine. As imaginative and astonishing as his art was, it never brought the artist financial security or fame. His contemporaries admired him as a teacher of "artistic anatomy" and as a public lecturer on the same topic, but not as a sculptor. Among his pupils in anatomical study were the highly successful Daniel Chester French and Anne Whitney.

By the time he was fifteen, Rimmer had learned how to carve soft stones with great facility. He began carving portraits in granite when he was about forty; amazingly, these were done directly in the stone, without preliminary models. The wealthy art patron Stephen H. Perkins, of Milton, Massachusetts, became aware of Rimmer's work, championed his cause, and encouraged him to become a full-time artist; he also purchased Rimmer's anguished *Head of St. Stephen* in granite (1860, The Art Institute of Chicago) and underwrote the expense of the *Falling Gladiator* (1861) which he promoted abroad; this moving work, which shows a mortally wounded gladiator as he falls to the ground, appeared in the notorious Salon des Refusés held in Paris in 1863, but attracted no notice.

In 1865 Rimmer's first public monument was unveiled on Commonwealth Avenue in Boston, the *Alexander Hamilton*. This granite effigy is a work of great dignity and reserve, but it was not well received. His one other public commission, an image of Faith for the Pilgrims' Monument in Plymouth, Massachusetts, was so altered in the carving process that it does not reflect Rimmer's intentions or count as his work. Between 1866 and 1870 he served with distinction as the director of the School of Design for Women at Cooper Union in New York City. His first book, *Elements of Design*, was published in 1864, and the second, *Art Anatomy*, appeared in 1877. He was much in demand as a lecturer and delivered his addresses on "artistic anatomy" at Harvard, Yale, the Boston Museum of Fine Arts, and throughout New England.

During Rimmer's final decade, he produced three of his finest works: *Dying Centaur* (1869),

Fighting Lions (1870–71), and *Torso* (1877). The centaur is notable for its great pathos as the man-beast makes one last futile gesture upward and for its unprecedented truncations. Both arms have been purposely severed: the right just above the nonexistent elbow and the left just below the shoulder. Such arbitrary truncations became frequent in the later work of Rodin and would be taken up by younger sculptors, such as Matisse with *The Serf* (cat. no. 21), but no other sculptor in the Western world made such a boldly expressive gesture as early as 1869. The two male lions are locked in mortal combat, and their ferocity exceeds that encountered in even the most violent works by Barye and Frémiet. The torso (cat. no. 23) appears so aggressively modern to us today that it comes as a shock to realize that an artist made it in 1877 while living in Boston.

RODIN, Auguste

1840 (Paris) – 1917 (Meudon)
French

Rodin was for the nineteenth century what Donatello, Michelangelo, and Bernini had been for their respective time periods: the greatest contemporary sculptor whose achievements eclipse those of all other sculptors. Revisionism in taste and scholarship have expanded our awareness of the richness and complexity of nineteenth-century sculpture seen in toto, but they have not undermined Rodin's centrality to it. Taken as a whole, Rodin's work not only reached the pinnacle of achievement, but it also posed so many fundamental questions and offered so many unorthodox solutions that it redefined what sculpture was and could be in the future.

Rodin's career began unpromisingly. Like Dalou, he studied drawing, modeling, and the fundamentals of decorative art at the Petite École, where he too encountered and was inspired by Carpeaux. Unlike Carpeaux and Dalou, however, Rodin was never admitted to the École des Beaux-Arts, never competed for academic honors, and never learned how to think according to standard compositional formulas. He was never a student in an academician's atelier, but he studied modeling with Barye at the Musée d'Histoire Naturelle in the Jardin des Plantes and worked as a designer in Carrier-Belleuse's studio. His experience as a professional sculptor was extensive, but he learned in a hands-on atmosphere while working independently or as a subordinate in a studio where he followed instructions or executed predetermined tasks. His lack of traditional training was in fact salutary; it gave him a conceptual and procedural freedom analogous to Degas's.

During the 1860s and 1870s, Rodin simultaneously made independent sculpture and worked in the art industry to earn a living for himself, his companion Rose Beuret, and their son, Auguste. Rodin made many busts in the early years of his aspiring career, including the *Man with a Broken Nose.* This unconventional, masklike head was the only piece he submitted to the Salon jury during the 1860s, and it was rejected. After the Franco-Prussian War and before the Commune, Rodin left Paris for Belgium, where he found employment first with Carrier-Belleuse and later with Antoine-Joseph van Rasbourg. These stints of employment entailed a variety of responsibilities: models made "for the trade" (inexpensive popular bronzes), architectural embellishments, and collaboration on monumental work.

After a revelatory trip to Italy in 1875, where he absorbed firsthand the lessons of Michelangelo and other masters of the Renaissance, Rodin completed one life-size male nude begun before the trip and modeled another. With these two plaster figures, he established a reputation and gained the attention of critics, potential patrons, and the public. Both of them grew out of the neo-Florentine climate of taste established by Paul Dubois over a decade earlier, but they were far more animated, particularized, and dramatic than Dubois's idealized figures. Whereas Dubois chose to evoke the cool classicism of Michelozzo or Andrea Sansovino, Rodin preferred the intense realism and expressiveness of Donatello or Rustici. The

Age of Bronze, exhibited in Brussels and at the Paris Salon of 1877, and *Saint John Preaching*, shown at the Salon of 1878, were both purchased by the French government, commissioned as bronze casts, and installed in the Luxembourg Gardens. Rodin, then in his late thirties, had finally achieved a foothold in the hierarchy of the official art world, despite his lack of traditional preparation for a career in sculpture.

In 1880 Rodin received what turned out to be his greatest commission: a monumental portal based on the *Divine Comedy* of Dante. This portal was intended to adorn a building that did not yet exist, a museum for decorative arts, planned for the site of the old Cour des Comptes, which had been destroyed during the Commune. (This site is across the Seine to the southwest of the Louvre, where a great train station was built instead – the present Musée d'Orsay.) Edmond Turquet, the undersecretary for the Ministry of Fine Arts who was responsible, had faith in Rodin's potential that exceeded any evidence available to him when he engineered this commission. Rodin had never before done large-scale, multifigure compositions. For twenty years, he struggled with the herculean task, but he never saw the work transferred to a permanent material and died without knowing its ultimate fate.

Rodin's reputation and public stature grew steadily during the 1880s, as his work became familiar to French audiences and was exhibited in other European capitals. Commissions for portraits came his way, as did one for *The Burghers of Calais* in 1885 for the coastal city of the same name. In 1889 he received the commission to design the much-coveted *Monument to Victor Hugo* for the Panthéon. When he and Monet held a joint exhibition at the Georges Petit Gallery in 1889, at the time of the Exposition Universelle, his fame was confirmed, and he became a hero to the emerging generation of symbolist writers and artists. The commission for the *Monument to Balzac*, awarded by the Société des Gens de Lettres in 1891, resulted in Rodin's greatest single statue but also provoked the greatest fiasco of his professional life. Reviled by his detractors and greeted ecstatically by supporters when it appeared at the Salon of 1898, the *Balzac* was subsequently rejected by the society that had commissioned it. In the press reports, the vehemence of the Balzac Affair sometimes overshadowed the Dreyfus Affair, which was exactly contemporary.

The year 1900 nonetheless brought something approaching apotheosis. In conjunction with that year's Exposition Universelle, Rodin held a private exhibition outside the fairgrounds on the place de l'Alma, the same site where Courbet had held his alternative exhibitions in 1855 and 1867, and Manet his in 1867. Thereafter, Rodin may have had his detractors, but he was also widely regarded as an old master reincarnated, a living monument, and the greatest contemporary artist. Portrait commissions and orders for replicas or reductions of his most famous pieces made him a very rich man. In 1908 he bought a superb property in Paris consisting of the eighteenth-century Hôtel Biron, its walled gardens, and an abandoned chapel, within the shadow of the Invalides. It served as one of his several studios and ultimately became – according to Rodin's bequest to the state – the Musée Rodin. This institution also includes the Villa des Brilliants in the suburb of Meudon, where Rodin and Rose Beuret lived until their deaths in 1917. Divided between these two locations is virtually all of Rodin's lifework: casts of his major monuments, marbles, numerous studies and plasters, drawings, and works of other artists owned by Rodin. The museum was also entrusted by the terms of Rodin's bequest with the responsibility of overseeing the dispersal and sale of limited editions of authorized casts of his work.

Rodin was deeply concerned about posterity's awareness of his art. He envisioned not only an institution that would conserve it as a whole but – through provision for authorized casts to be made (and the practice continues to this day, until the stipulated maximum number of twelve casts of any one sculpture have been made) – for dissemination of those works and for financial resources to maintain the institution itself. Rodin also arranged for an extensive archive documenting his work and its reception. Letters he received, numerous copies of letters he sent, evidence relating to commissions, records of payments to workmen, and the result of decades of subscribing to clipping services, which perused the world press for mention of Rodin's name, have all been preserved in dossiers organized by his various secretaries.

ROGERS, Randolph
1825 (Waterloo, New York) – 1892 (Rome)
American

Rogers was a prominent member of the American expatriate colony of sculptors who lived and practiced in Rome, in the vicinity of Palazzo Barberini, after midcentury. His life prior to becoming a sculptor bore no relation to his later success. In Ann Arbor, Michigan, and in New York City, he worked for a bakery and for a dry-goods business. His New York employers apparently took his innate talent very seriously and offered to finance his study in Italy. Between 1848 and 1850 he was Bartolini's pupil in Florence. After the master's death, Rogers moved to Rome and began independent work in earnest. Among his early sculptures are subjects drawn from the Old Testament and recent literature, such as *Ruth Gleaning* (1853) and *Atala and Chactas* (1854), from Chateaubriand's romantic novel set in the New World. The turning point in his career came with *Nydia, the Blind Girl of Pompeii*, which he modeled in 1855–56. This became one of the most popular and most frequently replicated works of the nineteenth century.

In addition to such works, made for the market and reproduced according to demand, Rogers was eager for public commissions and received many of them. The *Columbus Doors* for the main entrance to the United States Capitol constitute a truly impressive accomplishment, meant to evoke the *Gates of Paradise* which Ghiberti had made in the fifteenth century for the Baptistry of the Florence cathedral. Rogers had no false modesty about his achievement. In a letter of August 20, 1856, addressed to the superintendent of the Capitol Extension, he wrote: "I think both you and Mr. Walter [the architect of the Capitol] will agree that my design is not inferior to that of Ghiberti." He completed Thomas Crawford's ambitious *Washington Monument* in Richmond, Virginia, and designed war memorials which were erected in Providence, Worcester, Detroit, and Cincinnati. Mrs. Samuel Colt commissioned him to do a memorial to her husband in Hartford, which resulted in the *Angel of the Resurrection* atop a large freestanding column (1863–64). His *William Seward Monument* (1873–75) faces the crossing of Fifth Avenue and Broadway from New York's Madison Square, and his *Genius of Connecticut* (1877–78) once crowned the dome of the State House in Hartford, before being melted down for its materials during World War II. Later in life he was elected to membership in Rome's Accademia di San Luca – the first American ever so honored – and was knighted by the king of Italy.

ROSSO, Medardo
1858 (Turin) – 1928 (Paris)
Italian

Rosso created boldly original work, but he never learned how to negotiate the intricacies of the international art world and its politics; he ended his days as a bitter and unproductive has-been. From the beginning of his career, he enthusiastically embraced the modern world and disparaged the great Italian tradition, which was his birthright. The Brera Academy in Milan expelled him in 1883 for unruly behavior that grew out of a dispute over the use of models in classes. In self-conscious gestures of aesthetic heresy, he ridiculed Michelangelo and expressed contempt for Florence as the cradle of the Renaissance. Whether or not he was aware of the historical parallel, he was behaving in much the same manner as his troublesome countryman, Michelangelo Merisi da Caravaggio, who – exactly three centuries earlier – had also received his artistic training in Milan.

By the time he was twenty-four and still a student, Rosso had produced an impressive group of sculptures based on an intensely visual perception of modern life (among them were the *Unemployed Singer* and *Kiss under the Lamppost*). These works bear some resemblance to sculptures by his Italian contemporaries, Vincenzo Gemito and Giuseppe Grandi. During the following year, 1883, Rosso developed his signature handling of form and materials, which is based on fleeting visual sensations rather than sculptural solidity. Although he sought to capture unstable visual perceptions and successfully did so even when working in traditional materials such as plaster or bronze (for example, the *Sacristan* in the Hirshhorn Museum and Sculpture Garden, Washington, D.C.), his most original accomplishment was the invention of a material correlative to visual flux: plaster covered with wax (the *Concierge*, now in the Museum of Modern Art, New York, is one of his first masterpieces utilizing this mixture of media). One or more plaster casts of a work would be dipped in wax, and then pliant wax of varying densities could be added and modeled; each version that was completed would have the characteristic form of the original invention because of the plaster cast but would also be a unique variation on it because of Rosso's manipulation of the wax.

These works did not aspire to become absolute, integral entities – as sculpture had traditionally done – but appear as forms interacting with their environment. Solid form is regarded as only one component in a whole fabric of sensations that includes shadows and reflections, air and atmosphere. There is no one-to-one correlation between the solid human form that was Rosso's original motif and the surfaces of his sculpture. He did not regard any contour or profile as absolute. There are constant breaks, gouges, and protrusions in the surfaces which form the equivalents of visual interactions between a solid form and its surroundings. The wax absorbs and reflects varying amounts of light according to its thickness and texture; the plaster serves as the neutral base on which wax and light interact. There always seems to be a single viewpoint from which Rosso calculated the most satisfactory visual impression. His use of materials to capture the range of visual sensations forms a sculptural analogue to impressionism, which had already been invented and developed in two dimensions.

In 1884 Rosso left for Paris, the capital of the art world. His experiences there on this first trip have not been clearly established, but he did work for a time as an assistant in Dalou's studio and also met Rodin. After this visit, he returned to Milan. When he went back to Paris in 1889, Rosso enjoyed a consistently productive period for several years, with enthusiastic patronage and high levels of inspiration. After 1894, however, his creative energies diminished; he became bitter and paranoid, and aged prematurely. Rosso was obsessed with the idea that Rodin had plagiarized his ideas for the final version of the *Monument to Balzac* (1897–98). He worked less and less, became ill, and spent his remaining energies trying to shore up his reputation after creative inspiration had left him altogether.

RUDE, François
1784 (Dijon) – 1855 (Paris)
French

Rude was a brilliant sculptor who had been conventionally trained in the French academic system but found himself on the political and aesthetic periphery for much of his professional life. Born in Dijon, he learned what he could in that provincial Burgundian city before leaving for Paris to continue his studies. He was accepted in the École des Beaux-Arts and won the highest official honor and the goal of all art students – the Prix de Rome – in 1812. The government's lack of funds in a time of war and its aftermath, however, prevented his going to Rome at government expense for extended study, which was the normal procedure for Prix de Rome winners; he never made the journey to the Eternal City.

After Napoleon's final defeat in 1815, Rude

joined the expatriate Bonapartists in Brussels, where he worked as a sculptor for twelve years. Not until after his return to Paris in 1827 did his work hint at the greatness that was to come. His earlier sculptures were competent, but bland, achievements in the contemporary neoclassical idiom. Beginning with the over-life-size *Mercury Attaching His Wings* (Louvre) at the Salon of 1828, however, Rude proved that he was a great sculptor with a highly individual artistic personality. His next successes came at the Salons of 1831 and 1833, at which he exhibited his ingratiating genre piece, the *Neapolitan Fisherboy*, first as a plaster and then as a marble (latter, Louvre). His reputation had been made, official honors came his way, and he received the commission that would assure him a place in the pantheon of French sculpture, the *Departure of the Volunteers of 1792* (the *Marseillaise*), to adorn the Arc de Triomphe de l'Étoile in Paris, facing the Champs de l'Élysées. After its unveiling in 1836, this colossal relief (over forty feet high) became one of the icons of French art and patriotism.

After this great success, Rude should have been able to find a niche in the official hierarchy of the French art world, including a professorship at the École des Beaux-Arts, but this did not occur. Instead, he experienced a second twelve-year exile, this time in Paris, at the center of the world from which he was excluded. He rarely showed at the Salon, and his students were discriminated against in the official exhibitions as well. During the time of his difficulties under the July Monarchy, Rude nevertheless produced some of his finest sculpture. The Crucifixion group for the new church of St.-Vincent-de-Paul in the tenth arrondissement is one of the finest sculptures made for an ecclesiastical environment during the nineteenth century. Between 1845 and 1847 he made two superlative monuments out of private conviction and for no remuneration: the shrouded *gisant* figure of Godefroy Cavaignac for that republican hero's tomb in the Montmartre Cemetery and *Napoleon Awakening to Immortality* for a private site in Fixin

– outside Dijon – owned by his friend and fellow Bonapartist, Claude Noisot.

Rude's great public monument in Paris – other than the *Marseillaise* – is *Maréchal Ney*, which adorns the Observatoire, very near the site where this military hero from the era of Napoleon was executed after the Bourbon Restoration. Although commissioned earlier, it was modeled only in 1852–53. A dramatic piece, like the baroque predecessors it emulates, it suggests figures and actions that cannot be seen, only imagined: Ney holds his sword aloft and turns back to the troops he commands in battle. During his final years Rude withdrew, surprisingly, into a more ideal and pristine aesthetic world while making two large marble sculptures for his native Dijon.

SAINT-GAUDENS, Augustus
    1848 (Dublin, Ireland) – 1907 (Cornish,
        New Hampshire)
    American

Saint-Gaudens was the greatest American sculptor of the nineteenth century. Born into modest circumstances and trained as a cameo cutter in New York City, he nevertheless aspired to a career based on the highest international standards. With that goal in mind, he moved to Paris at age nineteen, gained admission to the École des Beaux-Arts (the first American sculptor to do so), and studied under François Jouffroy, an extremely successful teacher of academic sculpture during the 1860s. The Franco-Prussian War ended Saint-Gaudens's studies and forced his departure from France; he moved to Rome and established himself among the community of American expatriate sculptors in the vicinity of Palazzo Barberini. In 1870–71 he modeled his first major work there: a life-size *Hiawatha*, based on Longfellow's "Song of Hiawatha" (marble now in the Metropolitan Museum of Art, New York). This work fused two aspects that would remain central to Saint-Gaudens's career for the rest of his professional life: subject matter based on the cultural and historical traditions of his own country and a wholly European sophistication in the process of making his work in three dimensions.

Saint-Gaudens returned to the United States for a short time in 1872 and would spend extended periods working and teaching here, but he was in fact a citizen of the world who also lived, worked, and exhibited in Europe, especially in Rome and Paris. His patrons were cultured Americans, who were fully aware that their nation was experiencing an artistic Renaissance. He frequently worked in creative collaboration with the finest American designers and architects of his day, especially John La Farge, Charles F. McKim, and Stanford White.

Like his fifteenth-century Florentine predecessor, Donatello – with whom his contemporaries sometimes compared him – Saint-Gaudens was a master of three distinctly different aspects of his chosen art form: sculpture in the round, sculpture designed for architectural settings, and relief sculpture. He excelled in the conception and execution of public monuments, as well as in the more intimate realm of portraiture. He invented a new formula for portraits in relief, with his sitters usually shown in profile; these reliefs were sometimes irregularly shaped, with elegantly crafted inscriptions integrated into the overall design.

From the time of the unveiling of his *Farragut Monument* in New York's Madison Square in 1881, Saint-Gaudens was acknowledged as a master monument-maker, and he would never lack for commissions during the rest of his life. For the *Farragut*, he had collaborated with Stanford White, as he would many times in the future. Among their many joint endeavors were the standing *Lincoln*, for Lincoln Park, Chicago (1885–87); the *Adams Memorial*, installed in Rock Creek Cemetery, Washington, D.C., in 1891; and the two *Dianas* for the tower of White's Madison Square Garden (1891 and 1893). His collaborations with White's architectural partner, McKim, resulted in the *Shaw Memorial*, unveiled in 1897 on the Boston Common facing the Massachusetts State

House, and *Sherman Led by Victory* (1897–1900), installed on the southeast extremity of Central Park, between the Plaza Hotel and the Metropolitan Club, in 1903. This last monument is the only "great man on a horse" in modern times that can hold its own against equestrian statues of the past by such masters as Donatello, Andrea del Verrocchio, Giovanni da Bologna, and Francesco Mochi.

The works by Saint-Gaudens included in this exhibition are all relief sculptures, which demonstrate the richness of his achievement in a single aspect of the sculptor's art. His reliefs were unusual for the nineteenth century because they tended to be very shallow and to depend almost exclusively on nuances of modeling – for both figures and backgrounds. The result is an extremely visual relief style that evokes sensations more frequently encountered in painting. Once again, there is a close historical antecedent in fifteenth-century Florentine sculpture, the flattened relief (*relievo schiacciato*) invented by Donatello.

In 1885 Saint-Gaudens bought a farm in Cornish, New Hampshire, where he established a studio and spent his summers. Although he – unlike Canova, Vela, and Rodin – did not arrange for a museum to be established there, such a commemoration has nonetheless taken place, almost six decades after his death. Today the Saint-Gaudens Historical Site is the single greatest repository of his works, presented for the public's contemplation at the very location where many of them were created.

SARGENT, John Singer
  1856 (Florence) – 1925 (London)
  American

Sargent is known almost exclusively as a painter and, as such, occupies a secure place as one of the finest American artists of the late nineteenth century. Although he did many landscapes, figurative compositions, and superlative Venetian scenes, his reputation rests primarily on his prolific portraiture. At his best, these portraits have the technical brilliance of his seventeenth-century predecessor, Anthony van Dyck, as well as the psychological urgency and disquiet of late-nineteenth-century symbolism (for example, *The Daughters of Edward Darley Boit*, 1882, Museum of Fine Arts, Boston).

A commission of 1890 – for a mural cycle to adorn a large barrel-vaulted space in the new Boston Public Library – gave Sargent the opportunity to create something wholly atypical, including sculpture as a component part. He chose no less a theme than the development of religious thought from paganism through Judaism to Christianity. These murals were created over a long period and put in place piecemeal. The initial installation took place in 1895; the second – which included his three-dimensional *Crucifix* – occurred in 1903. When he completed the cycle in 1916, Sargent personally undertook the work of gilding, molding ornament, repainting the whole to bring it into harmony, and even adding corduroy fabric to the surfaces to modify the effect of light on the images.

VELA, Vincenzo

    1820 (Ligornetto, Switzerland) – 1891
      (Ligornetto, Switzerland)
    Swiss-Italian

Although Vela was from the Ticino – the Italian-speaking canton of Switzerland – his training and career were for the large part based in Italy. He received his artistic education at the Brera Academy in Milan and for fourteen prime years of his career was the leading sculptor, and professor of sculpture, in Turin. His reputation was international in scope, and he was showered with honors and awards in many countries later in life. The piece that established his reputation was *Spartacus*, 1846–47, which caused a sensation when it was exhibited at the Brera in 1851 and at the Exposition Universelle of 1855 in Paris. A highly theatrical piece, it shows Spartacus excitedly rushing down a flight of stairs after his chains of servitude have

been broken. (A decade after *Spartacus* was modeled, Randolph Rogers also scored a major success with a narrative, neo-baroque statue in agitated movement, *Nydia, the Blind Girl of Pompeii*, cat. no. 8). Audiences inflamed by the ardor of the Italian risorgimento saw their own historical situation reflected in Vela's work. The crucial role this statue played in Vela's career can be surmised by the fact that he named his only son Spartaco.

Two of Vela's most memorable and successful pieces were done without a patron or commission. The *Last Days of Napoleon*, 1866, attracted a vast amount of attention when Vela sent it to Paris for the Exposition Universelle of 1867. The Emperor Napoleon III and Empress Eugénie personally intervened before the exhibition opened to make sure that the seated effigy of the emperor's famous uncle would receive the most favorable presentation possible; they subsequently purchased the work and had it installed at the Château of Versailles. In 1883 there was to be a Swiss national Exhibition of Fine Arts held in Zurich. For this event, and in commemoration of the recently completed San Gottardo tunnel, which had been burrowed through the Alps in his native Ticino at a great cost in human life, Vela designed what is probably his most deeply moving work, the over-life-size relief known as the *Victims of Labor*. Three anonymous workmen are carrying the corpse of one of their comrades while a fourth lights the way in their underground chamber. Vela wanted this relief cast in bronze and installed at the southern entry to the tunnel; although this has subsequently been done, it was not achieved until long after his death.

Before his death in 1822, Canova arranged for a museum to be established in his native Possagno where his works would be exhibited in perpetuity. This is the origin of the concept of the personal museum-memorial. Vela's museum was accordingly established in his hometown of Ligornetto and is still maintained there. It is an important historical link between Canova's *gipsoteca* at Possagno and the Musée Rodin in Paris.

VON STUCK, Franz
  1863 (Tettenweis, Bavaria) – 1928 (Tetschen, Germany)
  German

Stuck was trained, and is best known, as a painter and a draftsman. He belongs to that select group of nineteenth-century artists whose artistic accomplishments raised them from very modest circumstances to great heights. In Stuck's case, the rise was stellar, culminating in his being elevated to the nobility in 1906 and henceforth called "von Stuck." He won numerous awards, both in Germany and abroad. A founding member of the progressive artists' group known as the Munich Secession in 1893, he also became a professor of fine arts at the Munich academy in 1895, where his students included the future luminaries Wassily Kandinsky and Paul Klee. In 1890 he first turned his energy to sculpture and later built a lavish villa in Munich where he fused his abilities as architect, designer, and artist to create a *Gesamtkunstwerk*, an aesthetic whole composed of various media in accordance with the latest artistic thinking of the turn of the century.

WHITNEY, Anne
  1821 (Watertown, Massachusetts) – 1915 (Boston)
  American

Anne Whitney was almost exclusively self-taught, although she did study drawing and anatomy, including lessons in the latter with William Rimmer during the early 1860s. The story of her discovering a natural inclination for sculpture when she began to model on the spot a pot of clay that overturned in a friend's greenhouse is the stuff of legends, but might just be true. She came to the art of sculpture rather late in life, when she was in her mid-thirties and had already published examples of her poetry, but she pursued her vocation with single-mindedness and determination and was very successful at it.

Whitney was a formidable individual, who was firm in her beliefs about abolition and social reform, and her work frequently reflected her convictions. Although the Civil War prevented her from going abroad as early as she would have liked, in 1867 she traveled to Italy and established herself in Rome for three years. There, she and a group of talented women – Harriet Hosmer, Emma Stebbins, Margaret Foley, and Edmonia Lewis – practiced the art of sculpture alongside their expatriate male counterparts. She made three extended visits to Europe, all filled with professional activity.

Whitney's career included a number of major commissions. The Commonwealth of Massachusetts in 1873 commissioned her to sculpt a marble Samuel Adams for the Statuary Hall of the United States Capitol. The result so pleased her fellow Massachusettensians that they ordered a bronze replica, which was erected in front of Faneuil Hall in Boston. She also made portraits of the abolitionist reformer William Lloyd Garrison, the explorer Leif Ericsson, and the Massachusetts senator and abolitionist Charles Sumner. The latter project became a personal crusade for Whitney. Although she had won the commission in 1875 with an anonymous submission, when it was discovered that its author was a woman, she was granted a prize of five hundred dollars but lost the commission itself to Thomas Ball. Late in life, she returned to the Sumner portrait with great perseverance, working on the statue until she was eighty years old. In 1902 it was installed on Cambridge Common near the Harvard Law School.

SELECTED BIBLIOGRAPHY

General Sources

Emmanuel Bénézit, *Dictionnaire critique et documentaire des peintres, sculpteurs, dessinateurs et graveurs*, 10 vols. (Paris, 1976).

Horst W. Janson, *Nineteenth-Century Sculpture* (New York, 1985).

Stanislas Lami, *Dictionnaire des sculpteurs de l'école française au dix-neuvième siècle*, 4 vols. (1914–21; Paris, 1970).

Ulrich Thieme and Felix Becker, *Allgemeines Lexikon der bildenden Künstler von der Antike bis zur Gegenwart*, 37 vols. (Leipzig, 1907–50).

Short References

Craven 1968

Wayne Craven, *Sculpture in America* (New York, 1968).

Gerdts 1973

William H. Gerdts, *American Neo-Classic Sculpture: The Marble Resurrection* (New York, 1973).

Greenthal 1986

Kathryn Greenthal, *American Figure Sculpture in the Boston Museum of Fine Arts* (Boston, 1986).

Los Angeles 1980

Peter Fusco and Horst W. Janson, *The Romantics to Rodin*, exh. cat., Los Angeles County Museum of Art (Los Angeles, 1980).

Louisville 1971

Ruth Mirolli (Ruth Butler) and Jane van Nimmen, *Nineteenth-Century French Sculpture: Monuments for the Middle Class*, exh. cat., J. B. Speed Art Museum (Louisville, 1971).

New York 1973

Robert Kashey and Martin L. H. Reymert, *Western European Bronzes of the Nineteenth Century*, exh. cat., Shepherd Gallery (New York, 1973).

New York 1985

Robert Kashey and Martin L. H. Reymert, *Nineteenth-Century French and Western European Sculpture in Bronze and Other Media*, exh. cat., Shepherd Gallery (New York, 1985).

By Artist

Andreoni

C. D. Johnson, *"I See by the Paper": An Informal History of St. Johnsbury* (St. Johnsbury, Vt., 1987).

Dorothy Reed Mendenhall, excerpts from typewritten "Autobiography," Smith College Museum of Art Archive, Northampton, Mass.

Thomas Mendenhall, letter of October 22, 1980, Smith College Museum of Art Archive, Northampton, Mass.

Edmund Wilson, *Upstate* (New York, 1971).

Bartolini

Jonathan P. Harding, *The Boston Athenaeum Collection: Pre-Twentieth-Century European and American Painting and Sculpture* (Boston, 1984), p. 73.

Douglas Hyland, *Lorenzo Bartolini and Italian Influences on American Sculptors in Florence, 1825–1850* (New York and London, 1985).

Walter Muir Whitehall, "Portrait Busts in the Library of the Boston Athenaeum," *The Magazine Antiques* (June 1973): 1141–56.

Barye

Glenn F. Benge, *Antoine-Louis Barye: Sculptor of Romantic Realism* (University Park, Pa., 1984).

James A. MacKay, *The Animaliers: Animal Sculptors of the Nineteenth and Twentieth Centuries* (New York, 1973).

New York 1973.

Stuart Pivar, *The Barye Bronzes* (Woodbridge, Suffolk, 1974).

Carpeaux

Los Angeles 1980, pp. 144–59.

Louisville 1971, pp. 61–84.

Jennifer G. Lovett, *A Romance with Realism: The Art of Jean-Baptiste Carpeaux*, exh. cat., Sterling and Francine Clark Art Institute (Williamstown, Mass., 1989).

Anne Wagner, *Jean-Baptiste Carpeaux: Sculptor of the Second Empire* (New Haven, 1986).

Carrier-Belleuse

Catalogue des marbres, terres cuites, bronzes, maquettes, esquisses, modèles: Œuvres originales de A. Carrier-Belleuse, dont la vente avec droits de reproduction aura lieu par suite de décès, sale cat., Hôtel Drouot (Paris, March 20–23, 1893).

June E. Hargrove, *The Life and Work of Albert Carrier-Belleuse* (London and New York, 1977).

Los Angeles 1980, pp. 160–72, cat. no. 50.

Chantrey

Sir Francis Chantrey, 1781–1841: Sculptor of the Great, exh. cat., National Portrait Gallery (London, 1981).

Jonathan P. Harding, *The Boston Athenaeum Collection: Pre-Twentieth-Century European and American Painting and Sculpture* (Boston, 1984), p. 78.

Margaret Whinney, *Sculpture in Britain, 1530–1830* (Baltimore, 1964).

Chinard

The Age of Neo-Classicism, exh cat., Arts Council of Great Britain (London, 1972), pp. 222–26, cat. no. 346.

Madeleine Rocher-Jaunequ, "Joseph Chinard et les bustes de Madame Récamier," *Bulletin des musées et monuments lyonnais* (1978): 133–45.

Daniel Rosenfeld, ed., *European Painting and Sculpture, ca. 1770–1937, in the Museum of Art, Rhode Island School of Design* (Providence, 1991), pp. 47–49.

Clésinger

Luc Benoist, "Le sculpteur Clésinger, 1814–1883," *Gazette des Beaux-Arts* (1928).

Louisville 1971, pp. 97–99.

New York 1985, pp. 100–105.

Dalou

Jean d'Albis, "Some Unpublished Ceramics of Dalou," *Connoisseur* (July 1971): 175–81.

Henriette Caillaux, *Aimé-Jules Dalou, 1838–1902* (Paris, 1935).

De Carpeaux à Matisse: La sculpture française de 1850 à 1914 dans les musées et les collections publiques du Nord de la France, exh. cat., Musée des Beaux-Arts, Lille (Lille, 1982), pp. 179–84.

Andrew S. Ciechanowiecki, *Sculptures by Jules Dalou*, exh. cat., Mallett at Bourdon House (London, 1964).

Jules Dalou, 1838–1902, exh. cat., Galerie Delestre (Paris, 1976).

Dalou inédit, exh. cat., Galerie Delestre (Paris, 1978).

Maurice Dreyfous, *Dalou: Sa vie et son œuvre* (Paris, 1902).

John Hunisak, *The Sculptor Jules Dalou: Studies in His Style and Imagery* (New York and London, 1977).

Christian A. Johnson Memorial Gallery (Middlebury College) Annual Report (1982).

Christian A. Johnson Memorial Gallery (Middlebury College) Annual Report (1987).

Los Angeles 1980, pp. 185–200.

Louisville 1971, pp. 105–17.

Ulysse Parent, *Acquisition d'une groupe allégorique de Jules Dalou, dont l'esquisse a figuré à l'exposition du concours pour l'érection d'une statue monumentale de la République* (Paris, 1880).

Daniel Rosenfeld, ed., *European Painting and Sculpture, ca. 1770–1937, in the Museum of Art, Rhode Island School of Design* (Providence, 1991), pp. 137–42.

Succession de feu M. Jules Dalou, sale cat., Hôtel Drouot (Paris, December 23, 1906).

Degas

Edgar Degas, 1834–1917: Original Wax Sculptures, exh. cat., M. Knoedler & Co. (New York, 1955).

Degas, exh. cat., National Gallery of Canada and The Metropolitan Museum of Art (Ottawa and New York, 1988), pp. 342–46, 349–53, 455–56, and 462–63.

Patricia Failing, "Cast in Bronze: The Degas Dilemma," *Art News* (January 1988): 136–41.

Los Angeles 1980, pp. 228–32.

Louisville 1971, pp. 155–59.

Charles Millard, *The Sculpture of Edgar Degas* (Princeton, 1976).

Theodore Reff, *Degas: The Artist's Mind* (New York, 1976), pp. 239–69.

——, *Degas in the Metropolitan* (New York, 1977).

——, "Edgar Degas' *Little Ballet Dancer of Fourteen Years,*" *Arts* (September 1976): 66–69.

Lois Relin, "La *Danseuse de Quatorze Ans* de Degas, son tutu et sa perruque," *Gazette des Beaux-Arts* (November 1984): 173–74.

John Rewald, *The Complete Sculpture of Degas* (London, 1977).

——, *Degas: Works in Sculpture* (New York, 1944).

——, *Degas Sculpture: The Complete Works* (New York, 1957).

——, *Studies in Post-Impressionism* (New York, 1986), pp. 117–56.

Dubois

William C. Brownell, *French Art: Classic and Contemporary Painting and Sculpture* (New York, 1920).

J. M. Delahaye, "Paul Dubois, statuaire," thesis (École du Louvre, 1973).

Christian A. Johnson Memorial Gallery (Middlebury College) Annual Report (1984).

Los Angeles 1980, pp. 242–47.

Louisville 1971, pp. 161–64.

New York 1973.

New York 1985, pp. 140–44.

Eakins

American Art at Amherst: A Summary Catalogue of the Collection at the Mead Art Gallery (Middletown, Conn., 1978), pp. 74–75.

Carolyn K. Carr, "A Friendship and a Photograph: Sophia Williams, Talcott Williams, and Walt Whitman," *American Art Journal* 21, no. 1 (1989): 2–12.

Gordon Hendricks, *The Photographs of Thomas Eakins* (New York, 1972).

Phyllis D. Rosenzweig, *The Thomas Eakins Collection of the Hirshhorn Museum and Sculpture Garden* (Washington, D.C., 1977).

Sylvan Schendler, *Eakins* (Boston, 1967), pp. 96, 111–16.

Falguière

"Acquisitions 1977," *Yale University Art Gallery Bulletin* (Fall 1978): 36, 57.

Léonce Bénédite, *Alexandre Falguière, suivi d'un catalogue des œuvres de Falguière exposées à l'École Nationale des Beaux-Arts du 8 février au 8 mars 1902* (Paris, 1902).

La Gloire de Victor Hugo, exh. cat., Grand Palais (Paris, 1985), pp. 270–82.

June Hargrove, *The Statues of Paris: An Open-Air Pantheon* (Antwerp, 1989), pp. 166–68.

Horst W. Janson, *Nineteenth-Century Sculpture* (New York, 1985), p. 189.

Los Angeles 1980, pp. 255–65.

Louisville 1971, pp. 169–74, cat. no. 65.

Mead Art Museum, *Masterworks of European Sculpture* (Amherst, Mass, 1983), pp. 27–28.

Frémiet

Los Angeles 1980, pp. 272–80.

Louisville 1971, pp. 175–83.

James A. MacKay, *The Animaliers: Animal Sculptors of the Nineteenth and Twentieth Centuries* (New York, 1973).

French

Craven 1968, pp. 392–406.

Michael Richman, *Daniel Chester French: An American Sculptor*, exh. cat., The Metropolitan Museum of Art (New York, 1976).

—, "The Early Career of Daniel Chester French, 1869–91," Ph.D. diss. (University of Delaware, 1974), pp. 156–66.

Gemito

Peter Fusco, "Medusa as a Muse for Vincenzo Gemito," *The J. Paul Getty Museum Journal* 16 (1988): 127–32.

New York 1973.

New York 1985, pp. 164–66.

Gibson

New York 1985, pp. 42–43.

Benedict Read, *Victorian Sculpture* (New Haven and London, 1982).

Gott

Joseph Gott, 1786–1860: Sculptor, exh. cat., Stable Court, Temple Newsam, and Walker Art Gallery (Leeds and Liverpool, 1972).

Gould

Boston Athenaeum, *A Climate for Art* (Boston, 1980), pp. 34–35.

Craven 1968, pp. 204–5.

Gerdts 1973, pp. 74–75 and 116.

Greenthal 1986, pp. 87–88.

Jonathan P. Harding, *The Boston Athenaeum Collection: Pre-Twentieth Century European and American Painting and Sculpture* (Boston, 1984), p. 33.

The Second Fifty Years: American Art, exh. cat., Worcester Art Museum (Worcester, 1976), cat. no. 49.

Leon Shulman, "White Marble Idealism: Four American Neo-Classical Sculptors," *Worcester Art Museum Bulletin* (November 1972): 3–4.

Worcester Art Museum Bulletin (January 1920): repr. p. 81.

Greenough

Craven 1968, pp. 100–111.

Gerdts 1973, pp. 74–75.

Greenthal 1986, pp. 4–8.

Douglas Hyland, *Lorenzo Bartolini and Italian Influences on American Sculptors in Florence, 1825–1850* (New York and London, 1985).

Horace G. Wadlin, *The Public Library of the City of Boston: A History* (Boston, 1911).

Griffin

L. Merrick, "Walter Griffin, Artiste," *International Studio Magazine* (August 1917): xlviii.

Obituary notice, *Portland Evening Express*, May 20, 1935.

Hosmer

Nicolai Cikovsky et al., *"The White, Marmorean Flock": Nineteenth-Century American Women Neoclassical Sculptors*, exh. cat., Vassar College Art Gallery (Poughkeepsie, N.Y., 1972).

Craven 1968, pp. 325–32.

Gerdts 1973, pp. 62–63 and 136–37.

Greenthal 1986, pp. 159–62.

Joy Kasson, *Marble Queens and Captives: Women in Nineteenth-Century American Sculpture* (New Haven and London, 1990), pp. 142–46 and 155–61.

Dolly Sherwood, *Harriet Hosmer, American Sculptor, 1830–1908* (Columbia, Mo., and London, 1991).

Ives

Craven 1968, pp. 325–32.

Gerdts 1973, pp. 54–55.

Greenthal 1986, pp. 159–62.

Joy Kasson, *Marble Queens and Captives: Women in Nineteenth-Century American Sculpture* (New Haven and London, 1990), pp. 190–202.

Klinger

Mead Art Museum, *Masterworks of European Sculpture* (Amherst, Mass., 1983), p. 25.

New York 1973, cat. no. 88A.

New York 1985, pp. 184–86.

Lewis

Craven 1968, pp. 333–35.

Gerdts 1973, pp. 132–33.

Phebe Hanaford, *Daughters of America, or Women of the Century* (Augusta, Maine, 1883), p. 298.

Lynda Hartigan, *Sharing Traditions: Five Black Artists in Nineteenth-Century America* (Washington, D.C., 1985).

Dolly Sherwood, *Harriet Hosmer, American Sculptor, 1830–1908* (Columbia, Mo., and London, 1991).

Theodore E. Stebbins, Jr., et al., *The Lure of Italy: American Artists and the Italian Experience, 1760–1914*, exh. cat., Museum of Fine Arts (Boston, 1992), pp. 241–42.

Eleanor Tufts, "Edmonia Lewis: Afro-Indian Neo-Classicist," *Art in America* (July–August 1974): 71–72.

MacMonnies

Craven 1968, pp. 420–28.

Greenthal 1986, pp. 295–98.

Matisse

Alfred Barr, *Matisse: His Art and His Public* (New York, 1951), pp. 48–52.

John Elderfield, *Henri Matisse: A Retrospective*, exh. cat., The Museum of Modern Art (New York, 1992), pp. 45–48, cat. no. 25.

——, *Matisse in the Collection of the Museum of Modern Art* (New York, 1978), pp. 28–34.

Albert E. Elsen, *Origins of Modern Sculpture* (New York, 1974), pp. 79–80.

——, *The Sculpture of Henri Matisse* (New York, 1971), pp. 25–48.

Henry Geldzahler, "Two Early Matisse Drawings," *Gazette des Beaux-Arts* (November 1962): 497–99.

Caroline Jones, *Modern Art at Harvard: The Formation of the Nineteenth- and Twentieth-Century Collections of the Harvard University Art Museum* (New York and Cambridge, Mass., 1985).

Isabel Monod-Fontaine, *The Sculpture of Henri Matisse* (London, 1984).

Mène

Louisville 1971, pp. 193–95.

Meunier

S. Lane Faison, *Handbook of the Collection*, Williams College Museum of Art (Williamstown, Mass., 1979), cat. no. 38.

M. Hanotelle, *Paris/Bruxelles: Rodin et Meunier: Relations des sculpteurs français et belges à la fin du XIXe siècle* (Paris, 1982).

New York 1985, pp. 192–95.

Jacques van Lennep, *Catalogue de la sculpture: Artistes nés entre 1750 et 1882*, Musées Royaux des Beaux-Arts de Belgique (Brussels, 1992).

Minne

Horst W. Janson, *Nineteenth-Century Sculpture* (New York, 1985), pp. 233–35.

Christian A. Johnson Memorial Gallery (Middlebury College) Annual Report (1990).

Elizabeth Kashey and Robert Kashey, *European Nineteenth-Century Watercolors, Drawings, Paintings, and Sculpture*, exh. cat., Shepherd Gallery (New York, 1989), cat. no. 46.

George Minne and Art around 1900, exh. cat., Museum voor Schone Kunsten (Ghent, 1982).

Jacques van Lennep, *Catalogue de la sculpture: Artistes nés entre 1750 et 1882*, Musées Royaux des Beaux-Arts de Belgique (Brussels, 1992).

Powers

American Art at Harvard (Cambridge, Mass., 1972), no. 57.

Craven 1968, pp. 111–27.

Gerdts 1973, pp. 52–53.

Greenthal 1986, pp. 27–31.

Christian A. Johnson Memorial Gallery (Middlebury College) Annual Report (1970).

Joy Kasson, *Marble Queens and Captives: Women in Nineteenth-Century American Sculpture* (New Haven and London, 1990), pp. 69–72.

Donald Reynolds, *Hiram Powers and His Ideal Sculpture* (New York and London, 1975).

Richard Wunder, *Hiram Powers: Vermont Sculptor, 1805–1873*, 2 vols. (Newark, Del., 1991).

Rimmer

American Paintings, Drawings, and Sculpture, sale cat., Sotheby's (New York, December 1, 1988), lot no. 85.

Craven 1968, pp. 346–59.

Greenthal 1986, pp. 67–79.

Christian A. Johnson Memorial Gallery (Middlebury College) Annual Report (1988).

William Rimmer: A Yankee Michelangelo, exh. cat., Brockton Art Museum (Hanover and London, 1985), cat. nos. 1, 2, and 8.

Jeffrey Weidman, "William Rimmer: Critical Catalogue Raisonné," Ph.D. diss. (Indiana University, 1981), pp. 140–43.

Rodin

Ruth Butler, *Rodin: The Shape of Genius* (New Haven, 1993), chap. 15.

——, *Rodin in Perspective* (Englewood Cliffs, N.J., 1980).

Jacques de Caso and Patricia Sanders, *Rodin's Sculpture: A Critical Study of the Spreckels Collection, California Palace of the Legion of Honor* (Rutland, Vt., and Tokyo, 1977).

Albert E. Elsen, *Rodin* (New York, 1963).

——, *Rodin and Balzac* (Beverly Hills, Calif., 1973).

Albert E. Elsen et al., *Rodin Rediscovered*, exh. cat., National Gallery of Art (Washington, D.C., 1981).

S. Lane Faison, *Handbook of the Collection*, Williams College Museum of Art (Williamstown, Mass., 1979), cat. no. 37.

Marion Hare, "Rodin and His English Sitters," *Burlington Magazine* (June 1987): 372–80.

Mead Art Museum, *Masterworks of European Sculpture* (Amherst, Mass., 1983), pp. 19–21.

Auguste Rodin, exh. cat., Curt Valentin Gallery (New York, 1954).

Daniel Rosenfeld, ed., *European Painting and Sculpture, ca. 1770–1937, in the Museum of Art, Rhode Island School of Design* (Providence, 1991), pp. 169–72, cat. no. 67.

John Tancock, *The Sculpture of Auguste Rodin: The Collection of the Rodin Museum, Philadelphia* (Philadelphia, 1976).

K. Williamston, *Life of Henley* (London, 1930), p. 136.

Rogers

Edward Bulwer-Lytton, *The Last Days of Pompeii* (1834; New York, 1946).

Craven 1968, pp. 312–20.

Gerdts 1973, pp. 120–21.

Joy Kasson, *Marble Queens and Captives: Women in Nineteenth-Century American Sculpture* (New Haven and London, 1990), pp. 23–28.

Millard F. Rogers, Jr., "Nydia: Popular Victorian Image," *The Magazine Antiques* 97 (March 1970): 374–77.

——, *Randolph Rogers: American Sculptor in Rome* (Amherst, Mass., 1971).

Rosso

Margaret Scolari Barr, *Medardo Rosso* (1963; New York, 1972).

Christian A. Johnson Memorial Gallery (Middlebury College) Annual Report (1979).

Nineteenth-Century European Drawings, Paintings, and Sculpture, exh. cat., Shepherd Gallery (New York, 1979), cat. no. 88.

Rude

Christian A. Johnson Memorial Gallery (Middlebury College) Annual Report (1979).

Louisville 1971, pp. 233–39.

New York 1973, cat. no. 8.

Saint-Gaudens

Craven 1968, pp. 373–92.

John H. Dryfhout, *The Works of Augustus Saint-Gaudens* (Hanover, N.H., and London, 1982), pp. 105, 131–33, 171, and 234–35.

——, *Augustus Saint-Gaudens: The Portrait Reliefs*, exh. cat., National Portrait Gallery (Washington, D.C., 1969), cat. nos. 17 and 35.

Greenthal 1986, pp. 214–17.

Kathryn Greenthal, *Augustus Saint-Gaudens: Master Sculptor* (New York, 1985).

Lois Marcus, "Augustus Saint-Gaudens: The Sculptor of the American Renaissance," *Arts* (November 1979): 144–48.

Sargent

William Home Downes, *John S. Sargent: His Life and His Work* (Boston, 1925), pp. 37–39 and 52.

Martha Kingsbury, "Sargent's Murals in the Boston Public Library," *Winterthur Portfolio* 11 (1976): 153–72.

Sally M. Promey, "Triumphant Religion in Public Places: John Singer Sargent and the Boston Public Library Murals," in *New Dimensions in American Religious History: Essays in Honor of Martin E. Marty*, ed. J. P. Dolan and J. P. Wind (Grand Rapids, Mich., 1993).

von Stuck

Mead Art Museum, *Masterworks of European Sculpture* (Amherst, Mass., 1983), p. 26.

New York 1973, cat. no. 90.

Whitney

Nicolai Cikovsky et al., *"The White, Marmorean Flock": Nineteenth-Century American Women Neoclassical Sculptors*, exh. cat., Vassar College Art Gallery (Poughkeepsie, N.Y., 1972).

Craven 1968, pp. 228–32.

Greenthal 1986, pp. 131–34.

Elizabeth R. Payne, "Anne Whitney: Art and Social Justice," *Massachusetts Review* (Spring 1971): 245–60.

——, "Ann Whitney, Sculptor," *Art Quarterly* (Autumn 1962): 244–61.

INDEX OF ARTISTS

Printed and bound by The Stinehour Press, Lunenburg, Vermont.
Book design and typography by Christopher Kuntze.